Framing of the Witch

Crypt Witch cozy paranormal mystery series - book 6

K.E. O'Connor

K.E. O'Connor Books

FRAMING OF THE WITCH

Copyright © 2022 by K.E. O'Connor

ISBN: 978-1-915378-04-0

Written by: K.E. O'Connor

Chapter 1

"Tempest, if you want to take off for the evening, we've got a handle on things here." Merrie Noble nudged me with her hip as she leaned against the bar.

"No, I'm good. Why do you ask?" I looked up from the notes I'd been studying.

She grinned. "That customer's been trying to get your attention for five minutes." Merrie nodded to the warlock standing at the bar with an empty glass in front of him.

I sighed. My head wasn't in the game tonight. I tapped my finger on the notes. For the past month, I'd become obsessed with finding out Toby Matlock's dark secret. Everything else had been put on the backburner, serving thirsty customers at Cloven Hoof included.

"And, I don't want to make you mad, but you look pale. Maybe you should take the night off if you're not feeling well," Merrie said.

I wasn't feeling all that lively. I'd been exhausted and grouchy for days. I also had a headache. "I'm fine." I made a move toward the customer, but Merrie stopped me.

"Don't worry. I've got this." She dashed over and swiftly served the customer, dazzling him with her easy charm and excellent bartender skills.

My gaze traveled around the bar. It was the usual midweek crowd in this evening. Everyone was here to kick back and enjoy themselves after work. It was only Merrie, Izzie, and me on tonight. I didn't want to leave them shorthanded, but I had two more piles of notes I needed to plow through before bed.

Whenever I had a spare moment, I'd been hassling the angels about information on Toby. Dazielle had stuck to her word and had given me access to the stacks of papers relating to the investigation they'd been running on him. They'd been trying to pin something on Toby for five years.

I'd initially scoffed at their incompetence, but having read through the files, the angels had tried just about everything to get him. As I was well aware, Toby was wily and excelled in covering his tracks. Although there were plenty of rumors about him and his underhanded dealings, there was no evidence to link him to any crime.

I turned my head as somebody cleared their throat.

Axel Shadowsoul stood by the bar, a sly smile on his face. Gone were the days of his slick, too tanned appearance. Axel came with a sharper edge, messed up dark hair, and a gleam in his eyes that suggested all his thoughts were impure.

"What will it be?" I shoved the papers under the bar.

"Are you studying for an exam?"

"My studying days are long gone." I placed an empty glass on the bar.

Axel's gaze went to the papers. "So, what are you up to?"

"Bringing down a problem," I said. "Although, it's taking longer than I thought it would."

Axel leaned his elbows on the bar, intrigue lighting his gaze. "What's the problem?"

I hadn't shared what I've been doing with many people. Granny Dottie knew, as did Mom, but that was about it. If word got back to Toby that I was investigating him, he might try more of his mind manipulation on me. The last time that had happened, I ended up wearing a lemon-yellow bridesmaid's dress, declaring him to be my closest friend, and hugging him. I'd felt grubby for days after that experience.

"Have you ever had dealings with Toby Matlock?" I asked.

Axel's eyebrows rose slowly. "I can't say I have. Of course, I know about him. He's probably wealthier than I am, but his magic creeps me out. All that messing with people's minds. You need to play fair when you use magic."

"You're telling me you always play fair?"

He grinned. "I bend the rules a little. Why are you interested in Toby?"

"Because he's soon to become my brother-in-law, and I'm not keen on that prospect."

"Oh, sure, he's getting hitched to Aurora." Axel shook his head. "I never saw that one coming. Does she have a thing for older guys?"

"So she says. It's hard to know what's going on in Aurora's head these days." We hadn't spoken in weeks.

"I noticed that Heaven's Door has been closed for a while," Axel said. "Is Aurora giving up the business when she's married?"

"Definitely not." I ground my teeth. Toby had been slowly taking over every aspect of Aurora's life. She'd given up her apartment, not opened her store for weeks, and taken to wearing ridiculous flouncy dresses and high heels that weren't her style. It was all Toby's doing; it had to be. My little sister could be ditzy, but she knew her own mind and had never let herself get manipulated by a guy before.

"When's the big day?" Axel asked.

"If I have anything to do with it, never," I said.

Axel's gaze went back to the pile of papers. "Oh! I get it. You're digging for dirt on Toby."

I tilted my head from side to side, trying to work out the kinks that had been lodged in my neck for days. "There's something about him that sets my teeth on edge. The angels know he's dodgy, but they can't get evidence to take him out of circulation."

"What do they think he's done?"

"He's defrauded money from former girlfriends."

"Why do that?" Axel asked. "The guy's crazy wealthy. He doesn't need more money."

"Maybe he does it because he can. Toby could get a thrill from taking whatever he wants from other people. He's done that with my sister. The problem is, there's no proof. He's always insisted that these girlfriends gifted the money to him."

"What do the former girlfriends have to say?"

"They came forward with the same story originally but then changed it." My lips pursed. "Anyone would think their minds had been manipulated."

Axel smirked. "I'd place money on the likelihood of that happening. Have you talked to these women? Maybe their stories will be different now Toby's out of their lives."

"I'm having trouble getting hold of them. The first complaint was submitted by Marianne O'Hanrahan. She reported that Toby had taken over a million from her private account."

Axel whistled out a breath. "Surely that's enough to charge Toby."

"The angels were building a case, but Marianne suddenly withdrew her complaint. She said there'd been a mix-up and Toby hadn't taken anything. I've got contact details for her, but she's responded to none of my messages."

"What about the other women?"

"There's also Ava Capaldi. She had double the amount taken by Toby, but exactly the same thing happened. She complained and then withdrew her statement. Olivia Dearhart's the same."

"None of them have gotten back to you?"

"Nope. Much like the angels, I can't locate them."

"Are they hiding? Maybe they've experienced Toby's oily charm one too many times and want to keep out of his way."

"I wondered about that. Either they've gone to ground, or Toby's done something to them." I rubbed the back of my neck. The ache behind my eyes felt almost unbearable. It had been building all day. If I wasn't careful, I'd give myself a migraine.

Axel touched the back of my hand. "Is everything okay with you?"

I hadn't realized I'd closed my eyes until he touched me. I pulled my hand away and nodded. "Nothing that won't be solved once Toby's behind bars, but I could do with some fresh air."

"Merrie can look after me while you're gone." Axel looked over at Merrie and winked.

"About that," I said. "I hope you're treating her well."

"I treat all my women well."

"That's what bothers me. You've never been a one-woman kind of half-demon. Don't mess around with Merrie."

Axel's eyes narrowed a fraction. "I have no plans to mess her around. Merrie's great. She's cool and fun. We understand each other."

"This place would be nothing without her. If you go fooling around with Merrie and break her heart, she might not stay. You prop up this bar most nights, and she won't want to see your smug face here if you do anything wrong."

Axel raised his hands before placing one over his heart. "Merrie is safe with me."

"She's anything but that." I jabbed a finger at him. "I'm watching you."

"What a treat." Axel chuckled. "You have nothing to worry about. I like Merrie."

"Just so long as she knows the situation. You're known for overpromising and under delivering when it comes to relationships." Axel was something of a playboy. I'd never seen him stick with anyone for more than a couple of months. Maybe things could be different with Merrie. Just in case they weren't, I'd keep an eye on their relationship. If Axel messed up, he'd be in a world of pain. No one upset my bar staff.

After giving him one final stern look, I headed out from behind the bar.

Wiggles had been doing his usual social rounds all evening, chatting up the customers in the hope of getting a free snack.

He trotted over when he saw me walking to the door. "Are we going somewhere?"

"Do you fancy a midnight stroll?"

"Any time."

I waved at Merrie and gestured to the door to let her know I was leaving.

She waved back to show she'd seen me before turning back to Axel.

I sucked in a welcome breath of icy air as we got outside. My head instantly felt better as the music faded and the door swung shut behind us. I normally loved being in my bar, but not tonight. My eyes felt puffy, and my head was tender. Maybe I was getting sick.

"I saw you chatting to Mr. Smooth," Wiggles said as we strolled under the moonlight.

"Axel's not so bad. He seems sweet on Merrie."

"He's mildly less of a creep these days. Whatever his father did to him when he was out of Willow Tree Falls, it improved Axel."

Axel's father was Kroni, a powerful demon. After Axel had almost been killed, he'd recuperated with his dad for a couple of days and had returned a changed half-demon. It was a darker version of the half-demon I knew, which was another reason I was keeping an eye on him. My sideline was hunting rogue demons. I hoped Axel would never become one of those. I considered him an ally.

"Hey, look! It's your mom." Wiggles picked up the pace as he spotted Mom heading toward the cemetery.

She stopped when she saw Wiggles and bent to pet him. Mom stood as I got near.

"Hi, Mom. Have you got the midnight shift?"

She kissed my cheek. "That's right. I'm meeting your Granny Dottie there. How's everything with you? You look tired. Aren't you sleeping?"

"I'm good. The bar's quiet, so we're just taking a stroll," I said.

She tilted her head. "Have you heard from your sister?"

I frowned. "She's not been in touch."

"Have you been in touch with her?"

"I don't dare go near Toby's house after the last time," I said. My visit to Toby's had involved an unpleasant experience with mind manipulation, almost tearing Toby's head off when he'd revealed his true colors, and Wiggles facing off with Toby's terrifyingly large butler.

"I wish you two would make up," Mom said. "There are only three weeks until the wedding."

"Which I'm no longer invited to." I tried to pretend it didn't hurt that Aurora had sent me a letter telling me I was no longer welcome at the celebration. Before that, I was to be her only bridesmaid. Not anymore. I wasn't even allowed to go to the reception. There would be no wedding cake and buffet for me.

"I keep asking her to change her mind, but Aurora has dug her heels in." Mom patted my arm.

"I've been watching her store, hoping she'll stop by," I said. "It's neutral territory, so I planned to go in and speak with her."

"If it's about what happened to the dress, Aurora will understand if you apologize." Mom knew all about me ruining my bridesmaid's dress. It hadn't been deliberate, but I wasn't sad that I'd no longer have to prance around looking like a giant ear of corn in lemon-yellow.

"It's so much more than the dress." I kicked my foot through the dirt. "This wedding can't happen."

Mom clasped her hands together. "None of us are thrilled about what's going on, but it's Aurora's decision. And so far, you haven't found anything against Toby. There's nothing to prove that his intentions are dark."

"Mom! You have to admit Aurora's not herself."

Mom sighed. "I agree, but I can't get her to talk about it. Every time I mention that she seems different, she tells me it's wedding jitters. She's so busy planning everything and making sure their big day is perfect. Maybe she's right. A bride-to-be gets nervous about her big day."

"Aurora's not letting anyone help," I said. "She's keeping us away for a reason. I understand why she kicked me out of the wedding, but none of you have done anything wrong. You hardly see her."

"Which I don't enjoy, but I do understand. I have managed to corner Toby on two occasions and see if he's up to anything dubious. Nothing he tells me sets off alarms. He always has Aurora's best interests at heart."

I shook my head. "It's not in her best interest to abandon Heaven's Door. And it can't be good for her to live with Toby."

"We just have to accept that we're adding Toby Matlock to our family."

"I can't accept that," I said. "If I can speak to the three women he's already messed with, I'm sure this will be resolved. Maybe they'll speak to Aurora and tell her what Toby's really like. She'd have to believe them."

Mom hugged me. "Keep looking, but I'm trying to fortify myself that this wedding will happen. You have to be prepared for that, too."

"I won't be." I pulled back from the hug. "We could always kidnap Aurora. If we can get her away from Toby, we can break his hold on her."

"Kidnap your sister!" Mom chuckled and shook her head. "She'd never forgive us."

"I'm willing to do it. She already hates me, so it can't get any worse. She's not walking down that aisle with Toby."

"Aurora doesn't hate you," Mom said. "It would be so good if you reunite before the wedding."

"Aurora won't let me anywhere near the wedding. She knows that, if I'm there, I'll do everything I can to stop it."

"Tempest! Don't do anything rash. Think about this. Your sister's happiness is at stake."

"It's all I've been thinking about." Toby had become an unhealthy obsession. Nothing else mattered. I had to get people to see the real Toby Matlock and get Aurora away from him.

"I'd better go," Mom said. "Granny Dottie's all alone in the cemetery. You know what she's like when she gets bored."

I grimaced. Granny Dottie was worse than an unsupervised school child on a sugar high.

"I'll see you later." I walked away with Wiggles, not going in any particular direction. I just needed quiet time to think about this wedding.

"We could sabotage it," Wiggles said. "I could get some buddies together. We could sneak in and eat the food."

"How is that sabotaging the wedding?"

"Everyone will be miserable because there's no nice food."

"Aurora and Toby will still be married."

"There's no food at the actual wedding ceremony, is there?"

"I don't think so."

"There's no point in me being there then. Eating is what I'm best at."

I sighed, not able to work up the energy to warn Wiggles away from the wedding buffet. Every bone in my body ached like I'd had a wrestling match with a giant demon.

He nudged me with his nose as we continued to walk. "I get it. It sucks being excluded. I love Aurora, too. She's making a huge mistake, but she can't see it."

I nodded. "It's a good job we can. If being excluded from Aurora's life is what it takes to stop Toby Matlock from marrying her, then that's what I'm prepared to do."

"I still vote for the buffet sabotage."

"You focus on the buffet. I'll figure out how to get Aurora away from Toby."

Whatever it took, this wedding wasn't happening.

Chapter 2

"Bleurgh. I'm dying." My head throbbed, my eyes felt swollen, and my mouth was Sahara dry.

I hadn't moved from my bed since I'd collapsed into it last night.

My skin was sticky with sweat, and I longed for a shower, but I couldn't face moving from under the warm duvet.

Wiggles' head appeared over the edge of the bed. "We're out of dog biscuits."

I groaned. "I can't go to the store. You'll have to order in."

"Pizza?"

I made a horrible gurgling sound. "Whatever you like. I can't face eating." I'd figured that yesterday's headache had been because of too much work, but it must have been the start of this flu or whatever it was I had. I didn't have the time to be unwell, but I could barely move.

Wiggles trotted out of the room and returned a couple of minutes later. "Pizza's on its way. I also ordered garlic bread. That's supposed to be good for illness, isn't it?"

I flopped onto my back and stared at the ceiling. "I hope so."

"And I called in reinforcements." Wiggles trotted away again. "Granny Dottie's on her way."

I wanted to protest, but I was glad someone was coming to see me. I felt miserable, sorry for myself, and lonely.

Fifteen minutes later, a knock sounded on the apartment door, rousing me from my doze.

I didn't move. Or rather, I couldn't move. My limbs were leaden, and my head pounded.

The knock came again.

"Wiggles! Get the door."

"I have paws," Wiggles said. "They don't do doorknobs."

With a Herculean effort, I rolled out of bed, wrapped myself in the duvet, and shuffled to open the door.

Tate Rathmore stood outside, a grin spreading across his face as he saw me. "Blimey, Tempest. You don't look so hot."

I scowled at him and growled. He did. Tate was his usual gorgeous, muscled self and smelt faintly of pizza dough and herbs.

"Pizza for two," Tate said.

I glared at Wiggles. "You ordered two pizzas for yourself?"

"And garlic bread," Wiggles said. "I thought that, once you smelt the pizza, you might want some. I didn't want you to miss out."

"Sure, you didn't." I shuffled backward and let Tate into the apartment.

He set the pizza boxes on the kitchen counter and looked around. "How long have you been sick?"

"Since last night," I said. "It started with a headache and got worse. There must be a bug going around the village."

Tate shook his head. "Nothing that I've heard of. Maybe you're the start of it." He pinched his nose and covered his mouth with a hand. "I don't want to catch anything."

Wiggles hopped onto a stool by the counter and nudged open the pizza box. "Tempest is too sick to be useful. Dish up this food for me, Tate."

Tate arched an eyebrow. "What's in it for me?"

"A free slice of pizza?"

"A free slice of pizza that I made for you, brought over here, and you've paid me for?"

"Sure. Whatever works for you."

Tate shook his head as he pulled out two slices of pepperoni pizza and gave them to Wiggles.

He glanced at me, and his nose wrinkled. "Go back to bed, Tempest. If you go downstairs looking like that, you'll scare off your customers."

"I don't look that bad," I grumbled.

Tate walked back to the door. "Get better soon." As he headed down the stairs, I heard him stop. "Hey, Dottie. Looking lovely as always. How's everything going?"

"I can't complain. I'm here to see my sick granddaughter. Wiggles messaged me to say she's dying."

"Erm, jeez! I hope it's not terminal. She does look a bit green."

"It's not terminal. Get out of here, Tate." The delicious smell of homemade soup drifted up the stairs. It was soon followed by Granny Dottie.

She blinked at me as she reached the top step. "My goodness! What have you been up to?"

"Getting sick." I hunched under the duvet, feeling sweaty and gross. "I feel lousy."

"Get back to bed right away. I brought you my magic soup. That cures everything."

I didn't protest as I shuffled to the bedroom and dropped onto the bed. It wasn't just my head that ached. My vision was blurry, and my tongue felt like it was covered in a film of toxic fur.

My eyes snapped open as Granny Dottie walked into the bedroom. I must have dozed off again.

"This will do the trick." She set a tray by the side of the bed. There was a bowl of soup for me, two slices of pizza for her, two mugs of tea, and a cream horn.

"I'm not sure I can eat," I said.

"This will make you feel better. There are healing spells in here, an elixir of health, and a pinch of dried vampire blood. That always puts a spring in your step."

I shuffled up the bed, using the pillows to prop myself up. I took the soup and had a taste. It was good. No hint of vampire blood could be detected.

Granny Dottie tucked into her first slice of pizza. "What's brought this on? It's not like you to get unwell."

"I blame stress. No, I blame Toby." I slurped more soup.

Granny Dottie's eyes glittered. "I hope you're being careful around him."

"As careful as I can be. I haven't seen him for weeks."

"And you've still not found anything that will change your sister's mind?" Granny Dottie bit through the pizza crust. "I'm no fan of Toby Matlock. Men with goatee beards always look like villains."

I recapped the information I had on Toby so far. "He's clever. Great at covering his tracks, and even though he's not supposed to, he's using his mind manipulation magic on anyone who crosses him. I'm certain that the three women he defrauded were manipulated into keeping their mouths shut."

"But what does he want with Aurora?" Granny Dottie asked. "She's a beautiful young woman, but she's not wealthy. Perhaps Toby has simply fallen in love."

I poked my tongue out.

"Tempest! Put that away. It looks like you've licked the floor of a dragon's den." She pressed a hand to my forehead. "You are running hot."

I had a few more sips of soup and passed the bowl to her. "That's enough." I settled against my pillows. "Toby's plans are bigger than Aurora."

"Bigger how?"

I stared at her and swallowed. I had no proof to back up my concerns. Was there any point in worrying the family with my theory about the demon prison?

Granny Dottie's expression became shrewd. "What aren't you telling me, girl?"

I sucked in a breath slowly. I didn't want to frighten anybody until my theory was proven. "I think that Toby's interest in Aurora has to do with the demon prison."

She snorted. "Toby's after our prison? What does he want with a bunch of unruly demons?"

"Maybe he doesn't want anything," I said. "Someone else could. Someone could be desperate to bust their friend out. They pay Toby enough, and he uses Aurora to get a foot in the door at the prison. If he's manipulating her, she might give away our secrets. That will make the prison vulnerable."

Granny Dottie shook her head. "The prison's too well-guarded. We'd know if anyone was trying to get in or break anybody out. And Toby would need Aurora's blood to get it open. Only Crypt witch blood opens the doors. She'd never give him her blood."

"She would if he convinced her using his mind tricks."

"Aurora's a strong witch and has her magic eraser pendant. She'd snap any hold Toby has over her if that's what he's up to."

"We still need to be careful," I said.

"I don't think Toby's ever visited the cemetery. He's never paid any attention to the demons beneath it. Why now?"

"Because he has an opportunity and received an offer that's too good to turn down," I said.

Granny Dottie finished her pizza and wiped her fingers on a napkin. "Hmm, it's possible, but unlikely. Have more soup. You need to be well if you're going to deal with Toby."

"You don't believe me." I sipped more of the soup, even though my stomach protested. It didn't seem to be having any effect.

She patted the back of my hand. "I have every confidence that the demon prison is secure. There's always at least one of us there, usually two."

"We should get extra patrols," I said, "and more protective magic."

"I'll speak to your mom and see what she thinks," Granny Dottie said. "As for patrols, we're doing everything we can. Aurora keeps missing her duties, and you're currently too ill to patrol, so we are spread thin."

"We need reinforcements," I said. "How about we get Raine and Azura here early? They must be coming to Aurora and Toby's wedding."

"That's a good idea," Granny Dottie said. "They're busy girls, though. I'll see if they can come a few days early. It will be lovely to have them here."

"Get them here as soon as possible." My cousins were awesomely powerful witches. They'd whip Toby's butt if he crossed the line. I managed a few more mouthfuls of the soup before I couldn't stomach anymore.

Granny Dottie tutted and shook her head. "You won't get better if you don't eat."

"I just need more sleep," I said. "I'll be fine tomorrow."

"Do you want to share my cream horn?" Granny Dottie lifted the huge, cream-filled pastry.

I grimaced as I slumped back into the bed. "It's all yours." I closed my eyes and tried to shut out the sound of Granny Dottie slurping cream from the end of her horn. I had to get better. I had no time to spare, but all I could think about was snuggling under my duvet and getting rid of this pounding headache.

My breathing slowed, and I slipped into a welcome sleep.

The light was so dazzling that I had to blink and shield my eyes. Where was I?

I turned and took a step back. Rows of chairs were filled with friends and family, all of them dressed in their finery. Mom sat in the front row with Aurora, Granny Dottie, and the rest of my family. She smiled when I caught her eye.

I turned back, feeling disoriented. I raised my clasped hands to discover I held a huge bouquet of lilies. Their scent was overpowering, and my stomach churned.

My eyes widened as I saw my outfit. I wore an ivory gown and matching ivory shoes that pinched my toes.

I must be having this wedding dream because of Aurora and Toby. In my fevered state, I imagined my own wedding, but who was I getting hitched to?

"Is everybody ready?"

I jumped at the sound of the deep male voice and turned to see a Druid high priest in front of me, wearing a long gold robe.

His gaze went to me, and he raised his eyebrows. "Tempest? Are you ready?"

I glanced back at Mom and saw her nod. "I guess so."

"Then we shall begin." The Druid priest gestured to the side.

A strangled cry fell from my lips. Toby Matlock appeared, dressed in a white tuxedo. I was wrong. This wasn't a dream; this was a nightmare.

Shaking my head, I backed away. Even if this was a dream, I wasn't marrying Toby.

He held his hand out, a smug smile on his face. "There's no need to be nervous, my dear. You've been waiting for this day for a long time."

"You've got the wrong person," I stammered. "We aren't getting married."

"If we don't get married, I can't give you my gift."

I held up a hand. "That's fine. You keep your gift. You can get a refund if you kept the receipt."

Toby lunged at me, knocking the bouquet out of my hands. The flowers writhed on the floor as if they had a life of their own. Two huge black snakes uncoiled from the flowers and slid away on their bellies.

"Was that your gift?" I struggled in Toby's strong grip.

"That was just for starters." Toby bared his teeth. "I warned you what would happen if you kept interfering in my life."

I glowered at him. "And I warned you that I was never letting you marry my sister."

"And as you can see, you got your wish. I'm to wed you instead."

"Only in my nightmares."

"This is more real than you realize." His nails dug into my palms, breaking the skin. "You brought this on yourself. This is my gift to you." He dropped one of my hands and gestured at the people watching us.

My mouth fell open as I turned to look at them. Everyone was dead. They still sat in the chairs wearing their finest clothes, but their eyes were glazed. They saw nothing. Their skin was gray and lifeless.

I kicked out at Toby. He stepped out of my way, releasing his hold on me. I raced to my mom and grabbed her shoulders. She was ice cold.

"Mom! What's going on?" This couldn't be happening, but I could feel everything. I smelt the white roses, felt the hot sun on the back of my neck, and heard the buzz of insects in the nearby flower meadow. It made my panic worse. Toby wouldn't do this. He wouldn't harm my whole family because I didn't let him have Aurora.

"This will be a wedding day you'll never forget," Toby whispered in my ear.

I spun and raised my hands. Although sparks of magic flickered on my fingers, nothing happened.

I tried again. My panic muddled my focus. "Frank, I need you." I rarely called upon my incumbent demon unless it was a real crisis, but this was serious. Toby Matlock had to die.

Toby chuckled and crossed his arms over his chest. "Is something the matter, my dear? You seem a little out of sorts."

"You're the one who'll be out of sorts. Frank! Get out here, now!" Nothing happened. I couldn't feel

Frank. It was the first time in almost two decades there was no movement from the demon who lived inside me. What had Toby done to me?

"This will be a day you'll never forget," Toby said. "You messed with me. Now, live with the consequences."

My eyes jerked open, and I gasped in a ragged breath. The room was pitch black, and it felt like it was spinning.

"Granny Dottie?" My words scraped out. The last thing I remembered, it had been the middle of the day and Granny Dottie was sitting by my bed sucking on a cream horn.

My stomach roiled, and I closed my eyes and pressed my lips together to get control.

As I breathed in, I smelled something salty and metallic. I moved my arms slowly. They slid through something sticky and warm. Whatever I lay on, it didn't feel like my bed.

My stomach threatened to do something dramatic as I moved again, so I stopped shifting around.

I cast a simple light spell. Magic flickered out of my fingers but died. I tried again. There were a few seconds of dim light before it faded.

I must be sicker than I'd realized. Illness often drained magic, but I'd never been so weak that I couldn't create a simple light spell. Maybe this flu was something more serious.

"Wiggles?" There was no sound. It often took him a minute to wake if he was in a deep sleep, but he usually slept on my bed. He could be in the lounge. Wiggles wasn't a big fan of sick people.

I tried again. "Wiggles. I don't feel so good. Get in here."

He didn't respond.

"Lazy hellhound." With another groan, I slowly eased myself upright. Maybe in my fevered state I'd sleepwalked. But where had I walked to? I was inside and warm, but that was all I could figure out. No light crept into the room.

Grumbling under my breath, I rolled onto my hands and knees and landed in more of the sticky stuff. I waited for the room to stop tilting before I staggered to my feet. There must be a light around here somewhere. I raised my hands, the strange metallic smell coming with me as I walked slowly through the darkness.

I hissed in a breath as my bare foot made contact with the side of a chair. I rubbed my toe until the pain subsided. After walking around for a few seconds, I collided with a wall. I spread my fingers across it and began my search for a light switch.

"Come on, come on," I muttered. I bashed into several more pieces of furniture before I found what I was looking for. I let out a sigh of relief as I found the light switch and flicked it on.

It was so bright that I squeezed my eyes shut for a few seconds as I slowly turned.

I shuffled forward, blinking as I tried to figure out where I was. My foot bashed something warm and soft. I looked down and sucked in a breath.

Wiggles lay on his side, his eyes closed. I ducked and touched him. "Hey, wake up."

He didn't stir.

I kept my hand on his side as I looked around the room. My throat tightened, and I stopped breathing as I saw footprints of red sliding across the carpet. The carpet that was in Toby Matlock's study!

How had I gotten here? What shocked me even more was that my footprints led from a bare foot that stuck out from behind the couch.

I lifted my hand from Wiggles' side and saw I'd left a bloody handprint on his fur. "Wiggles! Please, I need you."

He still didn't move, but he was breathing and didn't look injured. I stood slowly. I had to see who the foot belonged to.

Horror crept up my spine as I inched closer. I looked down to see I was still in my pajamas. They were coated in blood. It wasn't mine. I wasn't injured. That meant it belonged to the person behind the couch.

I struggled to keep my panic in check as I crept toward the couch. "Are you okay back there?"

What kind of idiot question was that? This person wasn't okay. The blood had to be theirs, and you don't lose that amount of blood and be okay.

I rounded the couch and froze. Toby lay face down, his head twisted to the side. His mouth hung open, and his eyes were glazed.

I swallowed against the tightness in my throat. This was bad. This was a nightmare. This was also something I'd dreamed about happening. Toby dead. Toby out of Aurora's life forever. I shook my head.

"Toby, it's Tempest. Can you hear me?" I edged around the blood on the carpet and knelt to feel for a pulse. Although he was still warm, there was none. Toby Matlock was dead.

I withdrew my hand. I still felt stunned and dizzy. What was I doing in Toby's study? How had I gotten here? Who had killed Toby?

His body was a mess of jagged slashes. This wasn't a natural death.

As I stood and looked over at the still unconscious Wiggles, a knock sounded on the front door.

Chapter 3

Despite not being able to see outside, it felt like the dead of night. No one would be stopping by Toby's house for a social call. Whoever was knocking on the front door was a problem, especially with a dead body at my feet.

I blew out a breath when the knocking stopped. I ran my hands through my hair, and they came away sticky.

My stomach flipped. Nothing good would come out of this situation. I was standing in the middle of a murder scene and had no memory of how I got here.

The thudding on the door started again. I shook myself into action. I checked Toby one last time to convince myself this was happening. There was still no pulse.

I hurried back to Wiggles. He was snoring gently, but I couldn't wake him. I placed a hand on his head and stared at my knuckles in horror. The skin was split, and I could see bruising. It looked like I'd gone ten rounds with a demon prize fighter.

I tensed and spun toward the door. Maybe we weren't alone. Whoever had done this could still be in the house, ready to pounce.

My heart clenched. What about Aurora? She must be here. Had she been injured, too?

I gently shook Wiggles, but he still didn't stir. I left him for a moment and hurried to the study door.

As I pulled it open, a wave of dark, fetid feeling magic pulsed over me. I staggered back, my lungs protesting as I breathed in the rank smelling air.

Something twisted had gone down here, and it still lingered. Whatever had done this could be lurking in one of the dense pockets of darkness in the hallway.

I peered into the corridor. Nothing stirred, but it felt like I'd just missed whoever was involved in this messy incident.

I tested my magic again. It felt like I had beginner grade magic. Although I felt a tingle of power cross my skin, no spell formed. I tried a light spell and a reveal spell to see if anyone was lurking in the dark, but neither worked.

Whoever was waiting outside the house pounded against the door again. "Toby! It's Dazielle. What's going on in there?"

Every muscle in my body tensed. Angel Force was outside! How could I talk my way out of being here covered in Toby's blood and his body in the study?

I ducked back into the room and shut off the overhead light. I needed time to think. I had to figure out what had happened before the angels burst in and came to the conclusion everyone else would when they saw the scene.

Shaking my head, I inched back into the hallway and hurried toward the staircase. "Aurora?" I whispered into the darkness. "Are you up there?"

No one replied.

As I took the first few steps, I realized my headache had gone. The flu I'd been suffering from had vanished. There was no ache behind my eyes, and no sickness in my stomach. Other than the bruises and the rank smell of Toby's blood on my pajamas, I felt fine. Confused as anything, but physically, I was well. Flu didn't come and go that quickly.

I continued up the stairs. I had to check on Aurora. She might be hiding somewhere, panicked and terrified after she'd discovered an attacker in the house.

My fingers tightened around the banister. I still didn't know how I'd gotten here. How had I left my apartment, walked here in my pajamas, and woken on the floor of Toby's study with his rapidly cooling body beside me?

I didn't have time to figure these questions out. "Aurora! Where are you?"

The sound of splintering wood had me spinning on the staircase. The angels were breaking down the front door.

I raced back down the stairs and hurried into the dark study. I concealed myself behind a bookcase in the corner of the room. I was just in time. A few seconds later, Dazielle strode into the study, a ball of light hovering above her hand.

"Someone find the main lights," she ordered.

There was the sound of fumbling before the overhead lights came on.

I risked a glance from behind the bookcase. Dazielle was there, along with Dominic and Jophiel. The three of them stood in the doorway, surveying the scene.

"That's Tempest's dog, Wiggles," Dominic said. "Is he okay?"

"Don't worry about the hellhound," Dazielle said. "Worry about the trail of blood and that person's foot sticking out from behind the couch."

Dominic inhaled sharply. I ducked my head back behind the bookcase. If I stayed still, they might not see me. That was my grand plan. All I could think about was hiding.

There was evidence of me everywhere in this room. I'd walked bloody footprints across the floor, and I was certain there'd be bloody fingerprints all over the wall as I'd fumbled to find the light. And, of course, there was Wiggles.

"It's Toby Matlock." Dazielle stood behind the couch staring down at Toby.

"Is he okay?" Dominic was peering at Wiggles.

"If you looked like this, would you be okay?" Dazielle shook her head. "Get Cassiel. She needs to deal with the body."

"I'm on it." Dominic hurried away while Dazielle remained by Toby. Jophiel remained in the doorway.

"This is recent," Dazielle said. "The killer could still be here. Jophiel, search the upstairs rooms. Be careful. Whoever did this is dangerous."

Jophiel nodded and left the room.

I held my breath as Dazielle's gaze shifted around the study. If she saw me hiding, that was it. She'd arrest me and charge me on the spot. I'd do the same. I looked guilty. But I'd panicked. I couldn't think of anything else to do but hide.

Dazielle looked down at Toby one more time before striding out of the room. "Dominic, stand guard of this room. Only angels come in and out."

"Yes, boss," Dominic said. "Cassiel's on her way."

"Good. I'm going to check the ground-floor rooms and make sure whoever did this isn't still on the premises."

My breath came out shaky as I heard the angels hurry around, looking for signs of an intruder. Maybe they'd find evidence of who got in and did this. A broken window or an unlocked door or maybe signs of a fight in another room. Something that would show them that I had nothing to do with this mess.

A worrying thought slid into my head. What if it had been me? Could my flu, or whatever I'd had, have made me delirious and carry out something I'd longed to do? I'd wanted Toby out of Aurora's life for a long time and had been feeling increasingly desperate because I couldn't figure out a way to get rid of him. What if, in my sickened state, I'd transported myself here and killed Toby? The problem would be solved. With Toby dead, Aurora couldn't marry him.

Whatever had happened and however deeply I was involved in this, I couldn't be discovered. I had to get out. I needed time and space to think about this. I had neither of those while wedged against a book case at the scene of the crime. The crime it looked like I'd committed.

I ducked my head around the bookcase. Other than the unconscious Wiggles and the dead Toby, the room was empty. I stepped out and inched closer to the door.

Dominic had his back to me, his wings spread, and his legs splayed.

My bare feet made no sound as I tiptoed across the carpet. I couldn't get out through the front door, not without Dominic seeing me. And with my magic malfunctioning, there was no way I could stand up to an angel. But there was someone who could. I didn't dare say anything, but I thought about Frank. I needed backup, and he was the only one I could turn to in this moment.

I waited for him to stir, make some smart comment about saving me from the angels, and try to bargain with me over what he'd get out of it. All I got was silence.

I tried again, my gaze not leaving Dominic's back. He could turn at any second.

My stomach clenched. There was nothing. It felt like Frank wasn't even there. He was always there, lurking in the background, waiting for a chance to grab Aurora.

Typical demon. They could never be relied upon. All I had left was my luck. I had to hope it would hold out.

I tiptoed to the nearest window and eased it open. Once it was wide enough, I crept back and hoisted Wiggles into my arms. I couldn't leave him. It was bad enough that the angels had spotted him; we went everywhere together. It wouldn't take them long to come looking for me to find out what Wiggles had been doing at a crime scene.

With Wiggles clasped in my arms, getting out of the window wasn't easy. I had one leg out and the other still inside the room when Dominic turned.

He stared at me, shock clear on his face. He blinked, and his wings fluttered. "Tempest? What are you doing?"

I grimaced as I threw my other leg out the window.

"Wait! Stop! You can't leave." Dominic hurried toward the window.

I waited until he was close enough, aimed my hand at his chest, and conjured a blast spell.

The magic misfired, the spell sparking out in a jagged mess. It missed Dominic's chest, and red sparks flew into his face. It was a second-rate spell, but it got the result I needed. Dominic staggered back, his hands flying to his face.

I felt lousy for hitting him in the face. But the magic wouldn't leave any permanent damage. I had to use what little advantage I had.

Glancing around the garden to make sure we were alone, I hurried along the path. I peeked into the windows as I passed them, expecting Dazielle to look out. I was in so much trouble now I'd been spotted. As soon as Dominic recovered, he'd report seeing me.

I needed a cover story. I could say that I'd arrived to collect Wiggles, but then I'd have to explain what he was doing here in the first place. And how did I even know that Wiggles needed me?

I groaned as I hurried along, my feet stinging from the sharp stones under my bare feet. What kind of idiot kills someone in their bare feet?

Maybe when I got back to my apartment, there'd be some clue as to why I left and how this had happened. I had to piece this together before the angels came for me.

I broke into a jog, trying to ignore the pain in my feet as I ran.

I rounded the corner, and my eyes widened. A solid wall of white feathers was in front of me.

I was going too fast to stop and slammed into the angel's wing, my head bouncing off it. I staggered backward, trying to keep hold of Wiggles.

My grip failed, and as my head hit the ground, everything went black.

Chapter 4

The groan that came out of my lips sounded more animal than human. My forehead throbbed, not from a headache, but from what felt like an enormous bruise. I moved my hand slowly and touched my forehead, wincing as I did so.

I remembered now, the escape from Toby's, being spotted by Dominic, and then running headfirst into an angel's wing and being knocked out.

My eyes opened, and I peered blearily at the ceiling. I was inside and lying flat on my back. I shifted and saw the bars of a cell and let out a sigh. I'd failed. The angels had caught me.

Dazielle was sitting outside the bars. Her eyes narrowed as she saw me wake. "Is there something you'd like to tell me?" She shifted closer to the bars, bringing her chair with her.

I licked my dry lips and eased my head up. The throbbing increased. "Before I say anything else, you have to know I'm innocent."

"What crime do you think you're innocent of?"

I sat up slowly on the single bed. "Unless I've just had the worst nightmare of my life, I guess I'm innocent of Toby Matlock's murder." I looked at my hands to see they'd been cleaned. My clothes were also different. Gone were the pajamas. I now wore loose white pants and a white tunic.

"Your clothes were taken as evidence," Dazielle said. "And there is quite a lot of it on them. If you're innocent of this crime, why were you covered in Toby's blood?"

I rubbed my forehead gingerly. "Is there any chance of a mug of tea?" I needed a minute to compose myself. Being smacked in the face with an angel's wing was never an enjoyable experience. It only added to the mind-numbing confusion I felt.

Dazielle nodded. She disappeared from the room and returned a moment later, sitting back in the seat. "It's on its way. Now talk."

I looked around the cell. There was no point in trying to use magic. The angels used protective spells to stop magic users from breaking out. Besides, the state my magic was in, it would be pointless trying.

"Where's Wiggles? The last thing I remember, he was unconscious. What happened to him?"

"We brought him back here when we found you at Toby's house," Dazielle said. "There didn't seem anything wrong with him. We took him to your mom's."

"Does she know I'm here?"

"Your entire family knows. They've been demanding to see you and shouting about your innocence."

I smiled. Of course, my family would be trying to get me out of this mess. "Can I see them?"

"Not yet. You've got questions to answer."

"Is Wiggles awake?"

Dazielle sighed. "According to your mom, he's awake and has eaten three bowls of food."

I smiled despite my dire situation. "That's good. I couldn't wake him when we were at Toby's."

"So, you admit to being there?"

I nodded as I slumped against the wall. "You know I was there. Dominic saw me leaving."

Dazielle clasped her hands together and rested her elbows on her knees. "Tell me what happened."

I closed my eyes and blew out a breath. "I wish I knew. I'll tell you everything I remember. Yesterday, I was feeling sick. I thought it was the flu. I was in bed. Granny Dottie came over with some soup and stayed until I fell asleep. The next thing, I'm having a nightmare about getting married to Toby Matlock. He was being super creepy. Oh, and everyone attending the wedding was dead."

"I'm not interested in your nightmare, Tempest," Dazielle said. "I want to know what you did when you got to Toby's house."

"That's what I'm telling you. I had this nightmare and then woke up. It took me a few minutes to figure out where I was. Somehow, I'd gotten from my apartment, across the village wearing nothing but my pajamas, and woke in Toby's study. I was on the floor, on my back, and it was dark. When I finally got the lights on, I found Wiggles unconscious and Toby dead. That's when you knocked at the door."

"What did you do next?"

"When you smashed down the door, I was looking for Aurora. I was worried about her. She's been staying with Toby, and I thought she might be in the house. Did you find her?"

"You're answering my questions, not the other way around. What happened next?"

I scowled at Dazielle. "I panicked. I realized how bad it would be if you found me in Toby's house covered in his blood. So, I hid from you."

"Why hide if you're innocent? Doesn't that suggest you're guilty?"

"No. Yes, but I didn't know what else to do. I knew what you'd think if you found me in that situation. When I was hiding behind the bookcase in the study—"

"You were hiding in the study? When we were there?"

"I couldn't find anywhere else. I only had seconds when you broke the door down." I rolled my shoulders. "I admit it doesn't look good."

"It looks terrible. You hid at the scene of the crime. The crime it looks like you committed."

"I didn't. I have no memory of harming Toby. I have no memory of how I got to his house or what happened to him. The first thing I remember is waking up and discovering his body. I didn't kill him."

"You blasted Dominic in the face with magic. You were running from the house. Why run if you're innocent?"

I felt my anger stir but kept it under control. If I was in Dazielle's position, I'd be thinking the exact same thing. I'd done it. "There must be a reason that I ended up in Toby's house. Somebody's framing me."

Dazielle's bright blue eyes studied me for several seconds. "You were covered in blood, none of it yours, all of it Toby's. You have significant bruising on your hands and several other parts of your body."

I lifted a finger. "Just a small complaint. It's not cool to strip someone and look at them when they're unconscious."

"Agreed, but your mom was present the whole time. We needed to make sure you didn't have any serious injuries. Everything was done by the book."

I grudgingly nodded. Mom would have made sure the angels played by the rules.

"Not only that, but you were seen fleeing the crime scene. And, you've made no bones about hating the fact Toby's marrying your sister. You've been here most days getting information about him. You don't trust him. You don't like him, and you were determined that he wouldn't marry your sister. Now that he's dead, it can't happen. You've gotten what you wanted."

I hated to admit it, but I'd had the exact same thought. "I didn't kill him."

"You look guilty."

"It isn't the first time you've thought that." Panic flared inside me as my jumbled thoughts knitted together. I couldn't see a way out. It was my word against the insurmountable evidence stacked against me. Everyone would think I was guilty. My family probably thought I was guilty. Would they abandon me? What about Aurora? If she thought I'd killed her fiancé, she'd be devastated. I couldn't lose Aurora.

There was a knock on the door. Dominic opened it, holding a plastic mug of tea. "Can Tempest have a visitor?"

"Who is it?" Dazielle asked.

"Kenny." Dominic passed me the tea.

I nodded. "Yes, let me speak to Uncle Kenny. He'll figure this out." Uncle Kenny was the calmest, most logical person in the family. If anyone could sort out this puzzle, it would be him. He'd know what to do. He'd know how to get me out of this mess.

"He can come in," Dazielle said.

Dominic's brow furrowed. "He's got Wiggles with him."

She sighed. "Very well. They can both come in."

I grabbed the cell bars as Uncle Kenny and Wiggles walked through the doorway. I ignored the sting of magic as I reached through to pet Wiggles. "How are you doing?"

"I'm still recovering from being blasted off my paws by my owner." Wiggles glared up at me. "What were you playing at?"

I looked at Dazielle. "I can't answer that. Doesn't this prove to you that something weird happened? I'd never hurt Wiggles."

Dazielle shrugged. "It proves nothing. If Wiggles was my hellhound, I'd be tempted to blast him with magic most days."

"No self-respecting hellhound would ever slum it with an angel." Wiggles turned his back on Dazielle.

"May we have some time alone?" Uncle Kenny spoke softly.

"Five minutes," Dazielle said. She nodded at Uncle Kenny before leaving us alone.

Uncle Kenny was a quiet man, never one to jump to conclusions. He was the leveler to Auntie Queenie's craziness. I could see the tension in his face as he settled in the chair Dazielle had vacated.

"Uncle Kenny, I didn't do this."

He nodded, his dark brown eyes intense. "We all know that. We'll fix this."

"I don't know how that can happen," I said. "I'm stuck here."

"The angels seem confident that they have everything they need to hold you for as long as they like."

I sat on the floor and continued to pet Wiggles through the bars. The protection magic stung my skin, but I ignored it. Usually, it was much stronger, but it wasn't having much of an effect on me. "I know that. Dazielle's run through the overwhelmingly horrible evidence they have."

"Do you remember anything about last night?"

"It's a blank. As I told the angels, I fell asleep in my apartment and woke up in Toby's house. The bit in between has gone. It's like my memory's been erased."

"I can fill you in," Wiggles said.

"Of course!" I thumped my head against the bars. I wasn't thinking clearly. Wiggles would have seen it all. "What happened? What did I do?"

Wiggles sat on the floor and made himself comfortable. "We were in your apartment. Granny Dottie stayed for a while, but you'd fallen asleep. She left to let you rest. You were in bed, but you were restless and muttering to yourself in your sleep. I tried to get on the bed, but you kicked me off."

"Ah, I don't remember that. Sorry. And then what?"

"Suddenly, you were in the lounge. You freaked me out. You stood there, your eyes wide, not really staring at anything. I asked if anything was wrong, but you ignored me. Then you left."

"I don't remember that either. I didn't give you any hint as to what I was doing?"

"Not a thing. It was as if you couldn't see me," Wiggles said. "I followed, thinking you were going down for a late-night snack. Instead, you went out the main door of Cloven Hoof. I walked with you and kept asking you what was going on, but all you kept saying was I must see him. I must see him. You wouldn't even tell me who he was. It wasn't until we turned onto Toby's lane that I figured that's where we were going."

"Did you try to stop Tempest?" Uncle Kenny asked.

"Several times. I stood in front of you and grabbed the leg of your pajamas. I even tried breathing fire. None of it slowed you. All it did was irritate you. You told me to go away."

"You know I didn't mean that."

Wiggles huffed softly. "By then, I'd figured out that something was wrong with you. We got to Toby's house, and you walked right in."

"The front door was open?"

"It was unlocked," Wiggles said. "I thought the zombie butler, Feodor, would come after you, but he let you walk right on in. The whole place was quiet. You went into Toby's study and launched yourself at him."

My heart clenched. I had attacked Toby. "I killed him?"

"I missed that bit."

"Why? What happened to you?" I asked. "When I woke in Toby's study, you were out cold."

"You happened to me." Wiggles' eyes glowed. "You turned, blasted a spell at me, and that was it. I came around to find myself in your mom's house."

"Have you told the angels this?" Uncle Kenny asked.

"All of it. They said I'm an unreliable witness because I'm so close to Tempest and possibly an accomplice. They also said some nonsense about hellhounds being untrustworthy. They've been hanging with the wrong hellhounds if they believe that."

"Someone else must have seen us last night," I said. "We'd have to walk past all the stores to get to Toby's. Have the angels checked?"

"They're working on it," Uncle Kenny said. "So far, they have no witnesses. They're trying to find people who saw you and Wiggles, but it was late when you left Cloven Hoof. Most people would have been in bed."

"Somebody must have seen something," I said. "Me wandering around in my pajamas with bare feet. That's odd."

"The whole thing is odd," Uncle Kenny said.

Worry pinched inside me. The angels wouldn't look for anybody else now I was in custody. I had to get out. "How long can they hold me?"

"There's no talk of letting you go anytime soon," Uncle Kenny said. "They might never let you go."

"I can't do anything from here. You know what the angels are like. I'm the only one they're interested in, so they'll stop investigating properly."

"We won't let them do that," Uncle Kenny said. "Everyone is asking around and finding out what they can. You're right. There must be witnesses, and this behavior is out of character."

I nodded. "Absolutely. It doesn't add up."

"And why would Toby let you attack him?" Uncle Kenny asked. "He had power. He would have stopped you."

"Exactly!" I was warming up to the idea that I was innocent. "It's too obvious. The way he died was messy. If I'd killed Toby with magic, it would have been easy to conceal. Instead, I wake up at the crime scene covered in his blood."

"You think someone set you up?"

"They must have." I rubbed my forehead. "I have no idea what the cause of death was. Toby didn't look good when I saw him, but I didn't have time to investigate. I'd only been awake a couple of minutes before the angels arrived. What killed him?"

"Someone sliced him up real good," Wiggles said.

"We haven't seen him," Uncle Kenny said. "From what the angels said, it looked like he was slashed with claws."

"I don't have those." I held up my bruised hands.

"It could have been a claw-shaped weapon. A garden trowel would do it," Wiggles said.

"Did you see a garden trowel in the study?"

"I did not."

"It makes no sense to me," I said. "You're right, Uncle Kenny. Toby had magic. He'd used it on me before. He could manipulate me. If I'd come at him with some kind of claw-shaped weapon, he'd have simply stopped me."

"The angels said there were defensive wounds on his arm suggesting he did resist. There's no suggestion you overpowered him with magic."

I groaned and dropped my face into my hands, my enthusiasm waning. "I'm going down for this, aren't I?"

"Don't think like that," Uncle Kenny said. "When we're not here asking about you, the whole family is out asking questions. We'll find out who set you up."

I raised my head. "Everyone knows I don't like Toby. No one would be surprised to hear I killed him."

"Some of us would be," Uncle Kenny said. "Tempest, I know you're not a murderer."

"Thanks, Uncle Kenny. But to prove my innocence, I have to get out of here."

He reached over for my hand. The magic buzzed a warning, and he pulled back. "It's best if you stay here. Let the angels investigate, and we'll do likewise. Don't do anything rash."

"Like break out of this cell," I said.

Uncle Kenny nodded. "If you try to run, it will only look worse for you. Stay here, be as cooperative as you can, and we'll sort it out."

I ground my teeth. I couldn't do that. I'd go crazy sitting in this cell while the angels bumbled around and pieced together a case against me. Not that they'd have to try hard.

I expected my growing anger and frustration to unleash Frank, but I felt nothing from him. Maybe he wanted me charged with this crime. A horrifying thought struck me. Could he be behind this?

"Wiggles, I was myself when I left the apartment?"

Wiggles cocked his head. "You were spaced out but not out of control. I wondered if Frank might have taken over, but he can't come through when you're asleep. It was definitely you. Frank wasn't in charge last night."

I felt around inside my head, trying to find Frank. Maybe he had some clue about what was going on. There was no sign of him. It felt like he'd gone. That was impossible.

My head spun. What had happened to me? Whatever it was, I'd lost my memory, and my demon was absent. Had Frank really disappeared? Was he the reason this was happening?

I shook my head. Right now, I felt stuck, alone, and I was about to be charged with murder. Something had to shake loose, or I was going away for a very long time.

Chapter 5

I talked through the events of the previous night with Uncle Kenny several times as we tried to find anything that would help me unpick the mystery. It didn't work, and Uncle Kenny left with the promise that someone would come see me soon.

Wiggles decided to stay. I was glad to have the company, even though he was fast asleep and snoring in the corner.

The door opened. Dominic walked over to the cell. He carried a pizza box. "Hey, Tempest. I thought you might be hungry."

Wiggles jumped up and hurried over. "We're always hungry. Have you brought enough for all of us?"

Dominic nodded. "Sure. There's enough to go around."

Although I didn't think I was hungry, my stomach grumbled as the delicious smell of melted cheese drifted over. "I could eat a slice."

Dominic passed around the pizza before taking his own slice. "Tempest, I've got to tell you, your family sure is persistent. They keep asking to see you."

"I'm glad to hear it," I said.

"One of them is always in the waiting room," Dominic said.

My eyes narrowed. "Why aren't they being shown through? Surely, I'm allowed visitors."

"Erm, well, technically that's true. Dazielle doesn't want you to see too many people."

"Let me guess; she wants me to sweat. She thinks if I'm isolated, I'll confess to what happened."

He shuffled his feet. "Something like that. She knows how close you are to your family and that you won't want to be away from them for long."

"I'll be away from them for a long time if I get charged." Although I wasn't impressed by her tactics, it didn't surprise me. Even though I'd helped Dazielle with previous cases, I always knew she didn't trust me. "I bet she's jumping up and down with glee about what's going on."

Dominic shook his head, his expression sincere. "Not really. She's more concerned than anything."

"Concerned! About me?"

"About the whole thing," Dominic said. "When we got to the crime scene, everything seemed straightforward. There was the body, and your fingerprints and bloody footprints all over the place. And your pajamas, which are really cute by the way, were also covered in Toby's blood. Plus, you tried to escape when I found you."

"About that. I didn't mean for the spell to go off in your face. My magic misfired."

He waved a hand in the air. "It's no problem. I could tell all wasn't right with you."

"No kidding. I'd just woken up lying next to a dead body."

"Of course. That would unsettle me as well. It wasn't just that. You had a strange look in your eyes. I could tell something was wrong."

I finished my slice of pizza, and Dominic handed me another one. "Did you tell Dazielle that?"

"I did. She said you were most likely panicking."

I sighed. "I should never have run. That was a mistake, but I didn't know what else to do."

"It's not looking great for you. We all thought you'd done it at first," Dominic said. "Most of the angels still do."

"You don't anymore? Have you got new evidence to suggest somebody else is involved?" Were the angels doing a proper investigation and not simply happy I was locked away?

"We haven't found anything useful at Toby's house." Dominic glanced over his shoulder as if he knew he shouldn't be telling me this. "There's something weird about the body."

"Weird how?"

"It's still warm."

I sat up straight. "Toby's been dead for at least fifteen hours. He shouldn't still be warm."

"Cassiel can't figure it out. She's run tests to work out why he isn't cooling, but she can't get to the bottom of it."

"He's definitely dead?"

Dominic chuckled. "I know you don't think much of us, but we know when someone has died. It's sort of creepy, though. It looks like he might wake up at any second."

"You've checked he has no pulse? He's not in some sort of hibernation spell?"

"He's not breathing. He has no heartbeat. Toby Matlock is D.E.A.D."

"Have you found the murder weapon?"

"Not yet," Dominic said. "I know you don't remember much about that night, but do you recall seeing anything that could have been used to kill him when you woke up?"

"Nothing," I said. "I know it's a claw-shaped object, but I didn't see anything like that."

"That's a shame."

"What else is odd?" I asked. "Other than Toby being warm."

Dominic leaned closer. "There was a letter on Toby's desk. Addressed to his brother, Nolan."

"I didn't know he had a brother. What does the letter say?"

His expression became grim. "It must have been written recently. It was short. Toby said that he felt under threat and was no longer safe in Willow Tree Falls. He asked his brother to visit him."

"What do you know about Nolan Matlock?"

"I know nothing, but we had a look into his background. Like Toby, he's a warlock, but he doesn't have the ability to manipulate minds."

"Does Nolan know what's happened to his brother?"

"Yes," Dominic said. "He's been in the village for hours. He arrived and identified Toby's body. He's staying at the hotel. Nolan wants to stay at Toby's house, but it's still being searched. And you left quite a mess behind. It's going to take serious elbow grease to get those stains off the carpet."

"I didn't mean to." I glowered at him. "Remind me to be more careful the next time I murder someone."

His blue eyes widened.

"That was a joke."

"Oh, of course."

"I wouldn't have been there at all if I'd had any say in the matter."

Dominic tilted his head. "Did someone coerce you into doing it?"

"No! Because I didn't do it."

"And it wasn't Frank?" Dominic asked.

I shook my head. "I don't think so. Going back to this letter, did Toby mention why he didn't feel safe?"

"Your name was mentioned," Dominic said. "He asked that his brother visit and assist with a difficult matter."

"What matter?" I asked. "Toby had nothing to fear in the village. He could control anybody he wanted to."

"He wouldn't use his mind manipulation magic without a person's permission," Dominic said. "He knows that breaks the rules."

"Toby Matlock didn't care all that much for rules," I said. "And he has used his mind manipulation magic without permission. He's used it on me several times."

"Did you report it to us?"

I gritted my teeth. Of course, I hadn't. "No. But Toby took a lock of my hair. That's evidence to show he didn't play by the rules."

"I guess so. I don't see how it will help in this investigation."

"It will show you he couldn't be trusted. Perhaps he used his magic on other people. This attack could be revenge for that. Whoever killed Toby set me up to take the fall. I'm an obvious suspect. It makes it too easy for you."

"But who? And what did they do to you?"

I tipped my head back and stared at the ceiling. "I'm drawing a complete blank."

The door leading into the cells slammed open. Dazielle strode through, her frown deepening as she saw Dominic chatting to me.

"You're not paid to flirt with the prisoners."

Dominic jumped to his feet. His cheeks blazed bright red. "I was giving Tempest her lunch."

"Prisoners don't get pizza for lunch," Dazielle said.

"I didn't know I was a prisoner," I said. "You haven't charged me with anything."

"Give it time." Dazielle thrust her chin up. "Dominic, get back to work."

His gaze was apologetic as he glanced at me before hurrying away.

"Have you made any progress?" I asked Dazielle.

She stopped, her hand on the door. "So far, we have the main suspect in custody."

I sighed. "What about Toby's body?"

Dazielle turned slowly. She shook her head. "Dominic can never keep quiet around you. What about it?"

"Why is it still warm? That's not natural. It suggests magic's involved."

"We haven't ruled out that possibility, but it's early days in the investigation. You'll have to sit tight while we work."

"Dazielle, let me help. You know I'm good at this."

"That's not happening."

"What about Toby's brother?"

Her eyebrows rose slowly. "You know Nolan?"

"I've never met the guy. I didn't even know there was a Nolan Matlock until a few minutes ago. Why was Toby writing to his brother and telling him he didn't feel safe? Doesn't that look suspicious to you?"

"It only confirms what everybody already knows. You hated Toby."

"He didn't care what I thought of him," I said. "Why leave such a prominent message on the desk for everyone to see? It stinks of a set up."

"What's to say he left it for anyone? He was intending to send it to his brother but died before he had the chance."

"Nolan could have useful information. Maybe they didn't like each other. He has to be a suspect."

"Why don't you ask him yourself?"

I sat up straight. "You're kidding with me?" There was no way Dazielle would let me interview possible suspects.

"Not really. Nolan's here. He wants to see you."

I stood and took a step back. "Why does he want to see me?"

"Perhaps he wants to ask you why you murdered his brother."

Chapter 6

I paced as I waited for Nolan to arrive. Dazielle had refused to let me out to talk to him in case I used my magic to escape.

Not that I felt able to do so. I was drained and running on empty. There was no sign that my magic was returning to full strength, and Frank's energy still seemed absent. I'd had that demon inside me for such a long time that it felt like a part of me was missing. Although, if a side effect of all of this was that he'd finally left, that was one good thing to take from this nightmare.

The door leading into the cells opened again. Dazielle led in a huge, broad-shouldered man. His jet-black hair was slicked back, and he wore drain pipe pants and a suit jacket that strained over his substantial muscles.

"Tempest, this is Nolan Matlock," Dazielle said.

My gaze ran over him. "You look different to your brother."

Nolan's fierce dark gaze met mine as a small smile appeared on his face. "I've heard that once or twice. My brother always said that he got the brains, and I got the muscles." He turned to Dazielle. "Thank you for accompanying me in. I would like to speak to Miss Crypt on my own."

Dazielle glanced at me. "Very well. She's not a threat. You may speak with her."

Nolan waited until Dazielle had left before turning to me. His gaze ran slowly from my head down to my toes and back again.

I stiffened but stared back. What was he expecting to see behind bars? Some deranged killer who had slain his brother?

Nolan glanced down as Wiggles approached and sniffed his leg. "You smell like Toby. Not quite so pungent. More bearable."

"How interesting, a talking dog," Nolan said. "Does he do tricks?"

"I can belch the national anthem," Wiggles said.

Nolan arched one eyebrow. "That's quite a talent." He settled in the seat and placed his hands in his lap. "So, Tempest Crypt. I've heard your name on several occasions from my deceased brother. You weren't friends."

"I expect you also know why that is," I said. "I didn't want him marrying my sister."

"Your mission has been accomplished," Nolan said. "I doubt your sister is into corpses."

I tilted my head. "You weren't close to Toby?"

"What makes you say that?"

"The shocking lack of grief." Here was a man who had shed no tears in the last twenty-four hours.

Nolan shrugged and plucked a piece of lint off his pants. "Toby's charm wasn't for everybody. We had come to blows on occasion. He could be a little... self-righteous at times."

"When was the last time you saw him?"

His smirk changed into a grin. "I see you're looking for other people who might have wanted my brother dead."

"I didn't kill him," I said. "Somebody out there did. Aren't you curious to find out who that might be?"

"From my conversation with the angels, they're convinced that they know who did it."

"They're wrong," I said.

"I admire your determination to keep up this charade. You're only putting off the inevitable."

There was the Matlock sleazy charm I'd come to loath, echoed in Nolan's tone. "Things look lousy for me, but I'm not stopping asking questions until this is resolved and my name's cleared."

"It will be resolved soon enough," Nolan said. "I believe your family protects the demon prison in the village. Perhaps there will be a space for you there. I imagine the residents will be delighted to discover Tempest Crypt in their midst. I wonder how many minutes you'll survive."

"They won't sentence me to go into a demon prison," I snarled. "Even the angels aren't that stupid."

"You could be right. But they aren't the brightest creatures in the book."

"Someone else must hate Toby," I said. "You're his brother. You knew him well. Did he have any enemies?"

Nolan rubbed the stubble on his firm jaw. "It's not the first attempt on Toby's life. It's simply the first successful one."

"Other people have tried to kill Toby? Who? They need to come here. One of them might be involved."

"It's a possibility that they had another go," Nolan said. "The only name he's been cursing for some time now is yours. He said you were interfering with his plans."

My hands flexed as frustration spun through me. "I didn't do this."

"I hope you did. You have my grudging respect for achieving something that a number of people have failed to do."

"You also wanted Toby dead?"

Nolan simply smiled. "I will, of course, feel his loss. But his death leads the way clear for me to undertake certain activities."

"Like what?"

"I'm his closest living relative. I'll acquire his assets."

"That makes you a suspect," I said. "You have a great motive for killing Toby. I don't know how wealthy he was, but I know he owned property and that he stole money from his previous partners, Marianne, Ava, and Olivia."

"Of course, the charming ladies he spent time with before he became involved with your sister."

"I've been trying to find them," I said. "I want to talk to them about what Toby did and what he took from them. They're missing. I think Toby might have harmed them."

"You amuse me, Tempest," Nolan said.

"I'm glad you find me so entertaining."

"You're guilty of this. Everyone can see it."

"So, why am I fighting to get out of here?"

He sat forward. "You're not fighting that hard. I haven't heard that you've tried to blast your way out of here with magic. In fact, the angels were muttering about how well behaved you've been. Having problems?"

"Nothing you need to worry about." I wasn't going to admit to this guy that my magic was on the blink.

Nolan shrugged. "If you want to find other people who'd like my brother dead, the succubi are the ladies you need to speak to."

"Succubi?" My eyes widened. "Toby was dumb enough to deceive succubi."

"Dumb. Brave. He didn't care if he offended them."

"What do you know about them?"

"I've met them all. They're beautiful women and powerful magic users. One of them took a shine to me."

"And Toby stole from them all?"

"He received generous gifts from them." Nolan smirked. "Of course, I grew up with Toby. I'm well aware he's not always to be trusted. He always had a way with the ladies. There was something about him they found most appealing."

"Most likely his mind manipulation magic," I said. "When you have someone under your influence, you can do what you like with them."

"Quite possibly that had an influence. My brother is unusual in his gift. It often skips generations. I didn't inherit that talent."

"Does that bother you?" I asked. "Were you envious of your brother because he could manipulate people?"

"Not envious. I'm not without my own ability."

"You still haven't told me when you last saw Toby."

"We rarely met in person, but we'd often communicate. He had an old-fashioned interest in letter writing. I've read the one he was planning to send before his death. You were mentioned."

"So I've heard," I said. "Did you find that unusual?"

"I suppose I did. Toby rarely admitted to being bothered about another magic user. You got under his skin."

"Because I was stopping him from getting his hands on Aurora?"

"Yes, the lovely Aurora. She sounds charming. My brother landed on his feet by marrying her."

"They weren't married," I said.

"It sounds like they were as good as," Nolan said.

"Getting back to the three succubi," I said, "what happened between them? What did Toby do?"

"I don't know the full details. All I know is that Toby had a relationship of an intimate nature with them."

"At the same time?"

"I really couldn't say. He entertained each lady for a short period until he realized she wasn't right for him. The tale he told is that they each gave him a generous parting gift."

"A substantial amount of money," I said. "That would be the last thing I'd do if I got dumped."

"As I said, my brother has a certain charm about him. Women like him. They do anything he asks."

"These succubi must have felt slighted. It's a great motive for wanting Toby dead."

"I agree, but they had no complaints."

"Not true. They all submitted statements to the angels complaining of his behavior," I said.

"I didn't realize the angels could talk about ongoing investigations."

I looked away, not willing to reveal that Dazielle had been letting me look at the case files. "It doesn't matter how I know that. I also know that they withdrew their statements. Did Toby make them change their minds?"

"If he did, I have no knowledge of that." Nolan smiled. "My brother didn't keep me informed of his nefarious love life. Although, I was planning to come to the wedding. I wanted to meet my new sister."

My nose wrinkled. "Do you know where the succubi are? They'll know more about Toby. Maybe they know who killed him." Or, one of them could even be the killer.

"It's funny you should ask. When I received the news of my brother's murder, I sent for them."

"Are they coming?" My heart skipped a beat.

"Of course. They wish to mourn Toby's death just as the rest of us do."

"I can see how deeply you're mourning," I muttered. "When are they arriving?"

"They'll be here this evening. I've booked them rooms at the hotel I'm staying at."

"Why are they coming? If they didn't like Toby, it makes no sense that they'd be keen to get here."

He smiled. "I may have mentioned a settlement due to them from Toby's will."

"He left them money?"

"I've not seen the will, so I have no idea, but I thought it was only right they be here. These ladies are motivated by money."

"And revenge?"

He lifted his hands. "They've had years to exact their revenge. When they heard the news about a possible payout, they were already packing their bags."

"You lied to them to get them here. Why do that?"

"Call it a small stretch of the truth. It's not outside the realm of possibility that he left them something. My brother was a generous man when it came to the ladies. That must be one of the reasons they were so charmed by him."

"He was generous unless he was stealing from them." I was puzzled why Nolan would make the effort to bring Toby's former girlfriends to Willow Tree Falls. Still, it was great news for me. With the succubi arriving, they'd be able to give me insight into Toby and what had happened between them.

With Nolan in town and Toby's three exes arriving soon, I felt like I was getting somewhere. It didn't feel like great progress, but it was all I had, so I grabbed hold of it.

Nolan's gaze ran over me again. "You don't strike me as the killing type. When my brother spoke about you, he said you were a fearless demon hunting witch who exuded dark energy thanks to your demon. I don't feel any of that."

My lips pursed. "What do you sense about me?"

"You feel like a scared, confused woman. I'm disappointed. I expected great things from you, Tempest Crypt."

"I'm sorry to let you down." His description wasn't far from the truth. I'd had moments in the last few hours when I thought I'd fall apart. My power was drained, my limbs ached, and my dominant feeling was one of confusion.

"My brother always exaggerated. You are one of his over exaggerations. You're just another witch. There's nothing special about you." Nolan stood. "Maybe the angels really do have the wrong person."

I didn't care about the insults. All I cared about was that Nolan considered me innocent. "Tell them that. Tell them you don't think it was me."

"Why would I do that?" He headed toward the door. "If the angels don't consider you the killer, they might turn their attention toward me."

I glowered at him. "Did you do it? Did you have anything to do with your brother's murder?"

"I'm an innocent party. I'm here to grieve for my dear brother. And, of course, oversee his estate and ensure it's fairly distributed. It's just a shame I arrived too late to meet Aurora."

"What do you mean? Aurora's around." Although, when I thought about it, Uncle Kenny hadn't mentioned her. Neither had the angels. A ball of dread settled in my stomach.

"You really don't remember anything about that evening?" Nolan shook his head. "I can't decide if you're an extremely good actor or an excellent liar."

"I'm neither. Tell me what you know about Aurora." I grabbed the bars, my knuckles white.

"Your sweet little sister has disappeared."

Chapter 7

The floor felt like it had tipped underneath me. I stared at Nolan. "Say that again. Aurora's missing?"

"That's correct," Nolan said. "No one's seen her since Toby's death. There are rumors she could be involved, and that you worked together to get rid of him."

My heart stuttered. Aurora had gone missing? "I have to get out of here. I have to find Aurora." I thumped my arm against the bars. "Let me out."

Nolan raised a hand. "That is outside of my ability."

"Aurora has nothing to do with this. She'd never hurt anybody."

"It seems a strange coincidence that her fiancé is dead and she's missing." Nolan tilted his head. "Perhaps you also killed her."

A distressed cry shot from my mouth. "I wouldn't do that. I'd never hurt Aurora." My head swiveled toward Wiggles. "Did you know about this?"

He ducked his head. "Your mom said to keep quiet. She said you'd only panic when you discovered Aurora is missing."

"You should have told me."

"You're in a cell," Wiggles said. "What can you do?"

"Break out and look for my sister." I kicked the wall of the cell. "Get Dazielle."

Nolan shrugged. "There are people searching for her. I believe your family is involved, and many of the residents are assisting. If you have done something to her and hidden her body—"

"I haven't done anything to her, and I'd never hide her body. She's alive!" My word shot out on a panicked breath. What had happened to Aurora? Was this to do with Toby? Had he hurt her, and I'd discovered it and killed him in a blind rage? Had I blanked it out because I'd been too shocked to accept that my sister was dead?

I shook my head. I couldn't think like that. She was alive. Aurora would be found, and she'd be fine. She was spooked, that's all.

The door to the cells opened. Dazielle looked in. "I heard shouting. Is everything okay?"

"I made the mistake of informing your prisoner of Aurora's situation," Nolan said.

Dazielle glared at him. "I did ask you not to say anything before you came in here."

"That doesn't matter," I snapped. "What are you doing to find Aurora?"

"If you'll excuse me," Nolan said. "I must attend to the preparations for my brother's burial."

My glare fixed on Dazielle as she closed the door after Nolan had left. "What's going on?" My words came out shaky. I couldn't make sense of any of this.

"Tempest, calm down," Dazielle said.

My foot slammed against the bars. "I have to help in the search."

"You're not doing that," Dazielle said. "If you don't calm down, I'll restrain you."

I growled at her. "I'd like to see you try."

She advanced toward the cell. "Don't tempt me."

The fight flooded out of me, and I rested my forehead against the bars. "Tell me what's going on. I don't know anything about Aurora."

"The evidence suggests otherwise."

I lifted my head. "What evidence?"

"We know you had a feud with your sister."

"Of course, she was making a terrible marriage match. I wouldn't kill her because she was marrying the wrong guy."

"You haven't spoken to her in some time. Your family confirmed that."

"I don't speak to you on a regular basis. That doesn't mean I want to kill you."

Dazielle's lips pressed together. "That's debatable. There were signs of a struggle in the kitchen. Although there was no blood, things were knocked over as if someone was fighting. Did you fight with Aurora when you went to Toby's house?"

"I'd never hurt my sister." I struggled to get my panicked thoughts under control. "Let's just say for a second that I did kill Toby. I'd have done it because I wanted to protect Aurora."

"Is that a confession?"

"No! What I'm trying to get you to see is that I'd do anything to keep my sister safe. It makes no sense that I remove the biggest problem she has in her life and then kill her."

"Perhaps she defended Toby and got in the way."

"Is there evidence of that?"

"We're still investigating."

"Which means no." Heat exploded up the back of my neck. Could Frank be making a return? It didn't feel like him. It felt more like my own rage was making me see red.

"Wiggles, you were with me in the house," I said. "Did you see Aurora?"

"There was no sign of her," Wiggles said. "While Tempest was being all spaced out and weird, I went and had a look for snacks in the kitchen. Aurora wasn't in there."

"Was there already a mess in the kitchen?" I asked.

"There were a few things knocked over. I was more interested in the trash."

"We can't take the word of your hellhound," Dazielle said. "He's always going to be on your side."

"He's telling the truth," I said. "Aurora wasn't in the house. I'd even begun looking for her when you arrived. Maybe Toby's done something to her."

"They're supposed to be married in a few weeks' time." Dazielle twisted her mouth to the side. "You're telling me this is a lover's quarrel gone wrong? You want to shift the blame for this murder onto your sister?"

"Of course not. Neither of us are involved. Aurora wasn't there, but she could have woken up to what Toby was doing. If she tried to get away, he'd have stopped her. Have you searched the house thoroughly? Maybe he's got her locked up somewhere, or she's unconscious in a room so you don't know she's there."

"We've searched every room," Dazielle said. "She isn't in the house."

"What about her things? Is there anything missing like clothes or cosmetics?"

"It doesn't appear that she's gone away anywhere." Dazielle stepped closer. "Listen, Tempest, I know how hard this is for you. Toby wasn't a good guy. What you've done is extreme. Confess to it, and I'll see if I can get you a deal. Maybe we can argue that your obsession with Toby tipped you over the edge."

"I'm not unbalanced."

She was silent for a second. "We can use Frank as an excuse."

"You're suggesting that I'm either crazy or my demon made me do it?"

"Not crazy but unhealthily obsessed. That makes people act out of character. The judge might be lenient."

"I'm confessing to nothing." I gritted my teeth. "Focus on finding Aurora. She has to be your priority."

"We're investigating her whereabouts, but we're also continuing our investigation into Toby's murder."

"She was being manipulated. Aurora's vulnerable. You can't abandon her. Wherever she is, she needs help."

"And when she's found, she'll get it," Dazielle said.

I was getting nowhere with Dazielle. I could plead and beg all I liked, but she wouldn't let me out of this cell to look for Aurora. The only thing I could do was concentrate on clearing my name. The sooner I did that, the sooner I could get out of here and join the search.

"Do you know about the succubi?"

"Succubi?"

"Yes! The three women Toby stole from are succubi."

"That's news to me."

"Nolan knows where they are. They're coming to Willow Tree Falls. You have to speak to them. They'll know all about Toby. They can tell you the truth about him. And they all have great motives for wanting Toby dead. Don't be too quick to discount other suspects just because of how you found me."

"Covered in the victim's blood and running away from the scene of the crime, you mean."

I grimaced. When she said it like that, it sounded terrible. "Talk to them when they get here. Find out what they know about Toby. Find out if they had a grudge against him. For all we know, they could have come to the village and bumped off Toby."

Dazielle's lips pursed, but she nodded. "When they arrive, I'll talk to them."

"And keep an eye on Nolan as well. It's too much of a coincidence that Toby left a letter on his desk for his brother just before he died. Nolan's planning to scoop up all the money. That's another great motive for killing Toby."

"I have my eye on Nolan Matlock, but he's not going anywhere. As you say, he's interested in what he can get out of this. No one knows where Toby's will is. For now, everyone will have to wait for their share of his assets. Nolan and the three succubi have motives, but none of them were found in your position."

"Framed," I said. "That's how I was found. I don't remember who did it, but it will come back to me." At least, I hoped it would, along with my magic. I didn't mind if Frank never put in an appearance again, although it felt weird not having him lodged at the back of my head.

"We'll speak to everybody," Dazielle said.

"And let me out?"

Dazielle shook her head. "You're in here for a while longer."

"I'm no good to anyone in here. I can't sit around and wait for you to pass judgment on me."

"That's all you can do," Dazielle said. "Get some rest, Tempest. You don't look so hot."

I grabbed a handful of the tunic I wore. "White's not my color."

"I mean, you look exhausted."

"You'd be a mess if you were wrongly accused of murder," I said. Although Dazielle probably wouldn't. Angels always looked immaculate.

I slumped back on the bed as Dazielle left. The same feeling of being stuck and helpless filled me.

"Is there anything I can do?" Wiggles asked. "We can sing sea shanties if you like."

"Sea shanties?"

"You know. Songs sung by salty old alcoholics who lived a dangerous life on the open waves."

"What do you know about that?"

"I study."

"You study how to steal doughnuts."

"Among other things." Wiggles sucked in a deep breath. "Ohhhhhh, there was an old sea dog with a smelly green duck. Who loved nothing more than to drink and to—"

"No singing," I said. "But you can help. Follow Nolan. Watch his every move at the hotel and see what he's up to. He's a Matlock, and I don't trust him. And the second you see three women arrive at the hotel, let me know. It will be the succubi. I need to speak to them as soon as possible."

"Mission accepted," Wiggles said. "I'll be your eyes and ears while you're locked up."

"It won't be for much longer." I said the words more to reassure myself than Wiggles. If Dazielle had her way, I wouldn't be getting out of here for the next hundred years.

Chapter 8

The previous night, I'd barely slept. It wasn't that the cells were noisy, but I'd tossed and turned all night trying to figure out what had gone down at Toby's house.

It was only just dawn when I finally abandoned any pretense of sleep and stood from my small bed. I could already feel myself getting cabin fever.

I'd only been pacing for a few minutes when the door opened and Cassiel poked her head in. "Fancy some visitors?"

"Who's here?" I shook my head. "It doesn't matter. I'll see anybody."

Before Cassiel could say another word, Mom and Granny Dottie hurried in.

"Tempest!" Mom hurried over. She tried to put a hand through the bar but retracted it and winced before she could reach me.

"Don't touch the prisoner," Cassiel said. "It's for your safety that the magic is there."

"She's my daughter," Mom said. "Tempest won't hurt me."

"It's fine, Mom. I'm glad you came. Is there any news on Aurora?"

"You're not supposed to know about that." Mom brought over two seats for her and Granny Dottie and sat in front of me. "I didn't want you concerned about your sister when you need to concentrate on getting out of here."

"There's nothing yet," Granny Dottie said. "Don't worry. We'll find her. Aurora will be fine."

"Dazielle was interrogating me yesterday," I said. "She thinks I'm involved with Aurora's disappearance."

"That's nonsense. We all know you're innocent." Granny Dottie pulled a large box out of her bag. "These have been checked by the angels." She pulled off the box lid and passed around some iced buns. "We need sugar in this time of crisis."

The bun looked delicious. It was the first time I'd felt hungry since I'd been shoved in here.

Granny Dottie hesitated before grimacing. "No magic is stopping me from feeding my granddaughter." Her hand shook as she forced it through the magic, angry sparks flickering up her arm. She got the bun almost all the way through, and I grabbed it.

She pulled her hand back and shook it. "Those angels have nasty magic surrounding you. There's no need for it. What do they think you're going to do?"

"They know exactly what I'll do," I said. "I want to break out of this place and help you look for Aurora."

"We're doing everything we can to find her." Mom's smile looked strained.

"I wish I could help." I took a bite of my iced bun, but its sweetness didn't do anything to soothe me. It would take more than an iced bun to fix this mess.

"We've gone over what happened dozens of times, trying to figure this all out," Granny Dottie said. "You seemed okay when I was in your apartment. You were tired, but I assumed that was because you were ill."

"There wasn't anything about me that seemed out of character?"

"Nothing. I stayed and watched over you, finished my cream horn, had another cup of tea and then left. Nothing you did made me think you were planning on sneaking out in your pajamas and heading to Toby's house."

"As I told Uncle Kenny, that evening is a blank. All I can think of is that someone used magic on me. They made me do this."

"Who was it?" Mom's eyes sparked with rage. "You let us know, and we'll wring the truth out of them."

"I'd give you a name if one sprang to mind," I said.

"I've asked in all the stores. No one saw you that night," Granny Dottie said. "They're all shocked by what's going on."

"People don't think I'm guilty, do they?"

"Don't mind what other people think," Mom said swiftly. "We know the truth." She glanced over her shoulder. "Granny told me your idea about Toby manipulating Aurora into opening our prison. Are you certain about that?"

"Not a hundred percent, but Toby wanted something out of their relationship. We have a powerful resource in the demon prison. If someone broke it open, everyone is in for a world of hurt."

"We think you're onto something," Mom said, her voice lowering. "The demons are restless."

My heart thudded. "Somebody down there is expecting to get out?"

"It's possible," Granny Dottie said. "But the demons who almost broke out were different ones."

"Demons? Multiple demons on the attack?"

Granny Dottie nodded. "It's been a riot over there, keeping everyone under control. I've not had a chance to finish any of my cross stitch."

"And they almost broke out?" I leaned nearer. "How close did they get?"

"I've never seen anything like it," Granny Dottie said. "It's as if they know we're distracted. With you here and Aurora missing, our focus isn't where it needs to be."

"Are the demons working together?"

"They never do that," Granny Dottie said. "Demons are selfish and single-minded. They always focus on themselves. That's why their escape attempts are so feeble. If they formed a demon army and worked together, we'd have a challenge. The fact that demons are inherently selfish is a bonus for us."

"What if a few aren't as selfish as we think?" I asked. "These near misses sound serious."

"We've got a handle on it," Mom said. "But our resources are divided."

"Not for much longer," Granny Dottie said. "Your cousins are on the way. They'll help with the prison and keep things under control."

"That's good." I felt a flicker of relief. Raine and Azura could handle a few disruptive demons. "It'll help to have them here."

"Don't worry about the prison. Focus on getting your name cleared," Mom said. "We'll deal with the rest."

I looked at my hands. "Speaking of demons, I might have a problem with mine."

"Is something wrong with Frank?" Mom asked. "I'm surprised he hasn't made more of an appearance with you being in here."

My stomach fluttered with uncharacteristic nerves. "I don't think he can."

"Frank must be aware that Aurora's missing," Mom said. "He must also be thrilled that Toby's dead."

"If either of those things are true, he's not showing his excitement." I looked at them. "I think Frank's gone."

They both gasped. Mom was the first to smile. "That's amazing. How did you get rid of Frank?"

"I have no idea. When I woke up in Toby's house, I couldn't feel him. It was so strange. Whatever happened to me, it's knocked Frank out of action. Usually, I can summon him, but nothing I do will bring Frank to the fore."

"At least some good has come out of this." Mom sat back in her seat and sighed. "You're free from your demon."

I smirked. "Only to get locked behind bars. This isn't freedom."

Granny Dottie didn't look so convinced. "Frank only dies if you do."

I jerked back and stared at her. "I'm very much alive."

"From what the angels said when they brought you here, you weren't in great shape. You were covered in injuries. Can you remember anything about what happened?"

"Those injuries are a mystery," I said. "You can't think I was injured so badly that I died." The possibility swirled in my head. Had I been attacked and died briefly before coming back to life? It didn't seem possible. But if I died, Frank died. It was the reason he kept me alive whenever I got in trouble. The alliance had always been uneasy and never one I enjoyed being a part of, but it would explain why he'd gone.

Granny Dottie shook her head. "If I could get my hands on you, we could try memory recall magic. It might jog your memory. Somebody else must have been in that house with you and Toby. Somebody knows what happened."

Doubt flooded through me. I'd heard plenty of times that people considered me dark and dangerous because I carried a demon inside me. I never believed them. I'd always followed a slightly darker path than other magic users, mainly because of Frank, but I always kept that restrained.

Had I failed somehow? Had the dark side taken over? Or maybe it was Frank? Had he finally succeeded? He'd taken over while I was ill, hunted down Toby and killed him, and then taken Aurora.

"What's wrong, Tempest?" Mom asked. "You've gone ghost-white."

I blinked rapidly. "You do believe me when I tell you I'm innocent?"

"Of course!" Granny Dottie said. "You didn't do this."

"What about Aurora? Frank's always wanted her. He never lets me forget that one day I'll make a mistake. I'll slip up and Aurora will pay the price." I looked at Mom and saw the tension deepening the lines on her face. "What if that happened? I messed up. I let Frank take control. This is the result. Frank did something to Aurora."

Mom grabbed Granny Dottie's hand. "No, I won't believe that. I can't. Nothing bad has happened to your sister. She'll show up. Everything will be fine. You'll get out of here, and this whole mess will be cleared up."

I wanted to believe her. I wanted to believe that everything would be okay, and I wasn't involved, but the more I thought about it, the more I realized that I might be.

It made sense to me when I put the pieces together. Frank had left me because he'd gotten what he wanted. Toby wasn't the real target in this whole mess; it was Aurora. Somehow, Frank had slipped through my defenses. He'd gotten to Aurora. My brain froze at the possibility.

Maybe Toby had tried to defend her when I'd arrived at the house with Frank in charge. He might have died protecting my sister. My body shook as I thought through this gut churning scenario.

"Tempest, are you listening to me?" Mom asked.

"Huh? No, not really." I'd been trapped inside my thoughts, frozen with the horrifying possibility that I was to blame. "I need some time on my own."

"You don't want us to stay?" Granny Dottie asked. "It's not good for you to be on your own. You need your family around you."

That was the last thing I needed, especially if I'd hurt Aurora. "I'm tired. I didn't sleep well last night. I need to rest."

"Oh, well, of course." Mom stood, her hand still gripping Granny Dottie's. "Don't worry. Everything will be fine. We'll be back to see you soon."

I nodded, not able to speak as I watched them go. I dropped my head onto my knees and allowed a single tear to fall.

Was I hiding from the truth? Should I confess to this murder after all?

Had I killed Toby when he'd tried to save Aurora from me? Was I responsible for two deaths?

Chapter 9

I'd been grouching and snapping at anyone who'd dared look in on me. I needed time to think but being alone with my thoughts wasn't helping.

"Are you sure you don't want to see Queenie?" Dominic asked. "She's bribed me with all sorts of things to get in to see you."

I smiled at that comment. Auntie Queenie would have all kinds of tricks up her sleeve to tempt Dominic. Even so, I didn't feel like company. I wanted to wallow. I wanted to feel sorry for myself, and I needed to get a handle on my thoughts and figure this out.

"Tell her I'm fine and not to worry. She can come back tomorrow. I'll be in the mood for company then." Maybe. I hoped I would.

"Right you are." Dominic disappeared, and the door shut behind him.

I'd just slumped on my bed when Dominic reappeared. I sighed quietly and twisted my head to look at him. "What now?" I sat up straight as I saw the worry in his eyes.

"You have another visitor."

"I don't care who it is. I'm not seeing anybody."

He swallowed loudly. "It's Rhett Blackthorn."

My eyes popped open. Rhett was inside Angel Force. He avoided the angels like they had the plague. He must really want to see me. Even though I was tempted to see his gorgeous face, I resisted. Not even Rhett could help me.

"Let him know that I appreciate him coming, but I'm lousy company. He doesn't need to be here."

"You want me to tell Rhett to go away?" Dominic's wings trembled around him.

"He's not so bad when you get to know him. Just be polite and you'll have no trouble." As a fallen angel, Rhett came with a lot of baggage, and that included a deep dislike of the angels who looked after the village.

After tugging at his collar, Dominic disappeared through the door.

I settled back on my bed, drawing my knees up and resting my chin on them. Even if I had magic and Frank made an appearance now, I wasn't sure I'd break out of this cell. I was no longer convinced I was innocent. Something terrible had happened in Toby's house. Something that I might be responsible for. I needed to stay here until I worked out what I'd done and if I'd hurt anyone.

My thoughts strayed to Aurora, but I shut them down. A worrying ball of dread was still lodged in my stomach. If I had killed Aurora, then I deserved everything I got.

I glanced up at the sound of several thumps outside the door. There was a startled cry and the sound of breaking glass. I lowered my feet to the ground and slowly stood, my hands clenched and my eyes on the door.

A second later, the door slammed open. Rhett strode through, his dark eyes blazing with anger and his fists clenched.

Wiggles trotted in behind him, a takeout bag in his mouth.

"Rhett! What did you do?" I glanced over his shoulder as the door shut behind him.

He shrugged, and some of the anger left his face. "I needed to see you."

"You fought your way through the angels to get here?" Even though it was a foolish move, I couldn't help but feel a little gooey inside. Rhett had fought the angels to get to me. It was weirdly romantic.

"They said you didn't want visitors." Rhett grabbed the chair, spun it around so the back faced me and sat. "I didn't believe them."

Wiggles spat out the takeout bag. "Hey, Tempest. I got us treats."

"Great," I said. "Rhett, Wiggles, and treats. My life is complete."

Rhett's eyes tightened a fraction. "Did you really not want to see me?"

I sighed and settled on the floor next to the bars. "It's not just you I can't be around right now." I tapped the side of my head. "Something's gone wrong. I don't believe I'm innocent."

Rhett clasped his hands together, and his knuckles cracked. "Don't even think that. Everyone knows you're innocent."

"I don't. I hated Toby."

"But you love Aurora," Rhett said. "You wouldn't do anything to hurt her. That includes killing that sleazy warlock. You didn't do this, Tempest. You have to believe that."

I glanced at the door. "I'm trying to. How much time do we have?"

"You've got loads of time." Wiggles nosed the bag toward Rhett. "He knocked out all the angels."

A startled laugh shot out of me. "You did?"

Rhett shrugged again as he opened the bag Wiggles had shoved toward him. "There were only a few."

"You didn't hurt Dominic, did you? He's ditzy but harmless."

"If you're referring to the blue-eyed wonder currently taking a nap by the reception desk, he'll be fine. He'll wake with a sore head and a story to tell his buddies."

I blew out a breath. "I hate to say it, but they're only doing their jobs. They've got evidence to hold me. I'm stuck here."

Rhett pulled out six doughnuts and placed them on the bag on his knees. "What will it be?"

"I'm not hungry," I said.

"You've got to eat," Rhett said. "How about snickerdoodle?"

"Sure, whatever you don't want."

"Most of them are for me," Wiggles said. "I've been working hard following Nolan Matlock."

"What's he up to?" I asked.

"Nothing exciting. He went back to the hotel for a while then walked to Toby's house. I watched as he tried to get in, but the angels aren't allowing access."

"He must be trying to find a copy of Toby's will," I said. "Maybe he's desperate for the money he thinks is coming his way."

"Desperate enough to kill his brother?" Rhett arched an eyebrow as he placed my doughnut on the paper bag and went to slide it through the bars.

"Be careful," I said. "The angels have some spiteful magic surrounding me."

"It shouldn't be a problem," Rhett said. "I'm used to—" His back arched as he made contact with the magic.

"Oh, crud! Wiggles, help him." I watched helplessly while Rhett spasmed as the angel magic flowed up his arm.

Wiggles grabbed Rhett's arm with his teeth and pulled it out of the magic.

Rhett hissed out a breath as he shook his hand. "Holy mother of demons! What are they using to keep you in?"

"I thought it might affect you more than others, given your fallen status," I said. "Granny Dottie was able to pass something through to me with nothing more than a painful sting."

"Wiggles, you try," Rhett said.

Wiggles jerked his head to the side. "Are you kidding me? I'm a hellhound. I'm much meaner than you."

"Just try it, pooch," Rhett said. "Tempest deserves a doughnut."

Wiggles grumbled under his breath as he marched to the bars. He nudged the bag toward me. It slid along a couple of inches before Wiggles yelped and backed away. "It stings my nose."

"Don't bother," I said. "I can live without doughnuts."

"No stinking angel magic is besting me. We're getting through this magic." Wiggles tried again, this time using his paws to push the doughnut. It slid another inch before he growled and his fur stood on end like he'd been electrocuted.

"Maybe you're right," Rhett said, watching Wiggles with an amused smile on his face. "You must be much meaner than I am. That magic is beating you."

"One more go." Wiggles backed up. He wriggled his butt before charging toward the doughnut. He slammed into it, smashing his face into the bars, before bouncing off. "Ouch! Ouch! Ouch! That's the last time I'm doing that." Scorch marks marred his fur.

"Wiggles, give up. You're not getting through, and neither is that doughnut." I looked forlornly at the squashed remains of the doughnut that hadn't made it through the bars.

"Those feathery freaks have better magic than I realized," Wiggles grumbled as he settled down to eat his own doughnut.

I watched them eat, trying not to salivate. The doughnuts looked amazing. "What else has Nolan been up to?" I asked Wiggles.

He swallowed his doughnut. "He's mainly scoping out the house. He went back three times. I figured he's trying to find a way in without the angels noticing. The security is tight there, though. No one would let him in. He's back at the hotel for now."

"If he's hankering to grab the cash, he could have issues with debt."

"That's a good motive for wanting to kill his brother," Rhett said. "Nolan could have debt collectors chasing him and he got desperate. Even if he asked Toby for help, he wouldn't have gotten it. I imagine Toby was the kind of brother who wouldn't loan any money without conditions."

"And I imagine Toby's conditions were never fun," I said.

"You can guarantee that," Rhett said. "So, what's our next move to clear your name?"

I shook my head. "You need to stay out of this."

Rhett chuckled grimly. "You're my girl. There's not a chance I'm staying out of this. I've had the gang out looking for Aurora ever since we found out what happened."

My chest grew warm knowing he was looking out for me. "Have they seen any sign of her?"

"Not a thing. It's so weird. It's like she's vanished. The last time anyone saw her was three days ago in the village. She was picking up supplies and talking about making dinner for Toby. Patti saw her walk past Sprinkles on her way to Toby's house."

"And what happened next?" I asked more to myself than the others. "You don't just vanish. And Aurora has power. If someone tried to hurt her, she'd fight back. Her magic is pure, but it's still strong."

Wiggles polished off his second doughnut. "If I could get inside Toby's house, I can sniff around and see how old her scent is. Maybe she left before... the incident."

"You mean, me killing Toby?"

A growl rumbled in Rhett's chest. "You didn't do it. We'll find Aurora, figure out who killed Toby, and get you out of here. I bet in a couple of days, this will all be over."

"Most likely because Dazielle has charged me with murder," I said.

Rhett licked sugar off his fingers as he shook his head. "It's not happening. And if you do get charged, I'll break you out."

"And get arrested yourself," I said. "What then? We go on the run? We leave behind everything we have in Willow Tree Falls? I can't abandon my family, and you can't abandon the gang. We have lives here. We won't be happy being on the run from the angels."

"Besides, Tempest will never leave me behind," Wiggles said. "I can't leave the village."

"That's right," I said.

"I'd be happy if I was with you." Rhett reached a hand toward the bars but stopped and scowled. "It could be fun, the two of us on the road together. There's always plenty of room on the back of my bike for you."

I loved the way Rhett was looking out for me. He had absolutely no doubt that I was innocent. For a fallen angel, he had a sweet side.

"As great as it is to have you here," I said, "it won't be long before the angels wake up. You'll need to be gone by the time they do."

Rhett looked at the door. "I'll knock them out again if I have to, but maybe you're right. I need to check in with the guys and see how the search is progressing. You never know. We might be sitting here chatting and they've already found Aurora."

"I hope you're right. Let me know if you find her. I can't relax until I know she's safe."

"Of course, you'll be the first to know." Rhett stood. "I'll leave you to it. Have fun in there." He winked at me before cracking the door open and sneaking out.

I watched Wiggles with envy as he finished off another doughnut. "Describe the doughnut to me."

"Sugary heaven. Imagine the best doughnut from Sprinkles and times the sweet, mushy yumminess by a hundred."

My stomach growled.

"You can have your own box of doughnuts once you're out," Wiggles said. "Oh! And you'll be pleased to know that the succubi have arrived."

"How long have they been here?"

"They arrived half an hour ago," Wiggles said. "That's why I came back."

"What are they like?"

Wiggles belched as he trotted closer, sugar sprinkles on his nose. "Smoking hot. I mean, out of this world gorgeous. They have long willowy limbs, manes of hair that shimmer in the sunlight, and their eyes glow. Oh, and they all have huge boob—"

"Enough with the physical description." Succubi were renowned for their beauty. They used their looks to attract men and exploit them. Some succubi killed to gain power while others just enjoyed toying with their prey and using them to get everything they could.

"I had to force myself not to reveal my hiding spot as they walked into the hotel. Even I could feel their allure. They're like magnets. I wanted to go and ask for a lot of belly rubs. The dirty kind."

My nose wrinkled. "You need to keep an eye on them. They're most likely here for the same thing as Nolan. He enticed them with a promise that they'd get something now that Toby's dead."

"They're after Toby's crown jewels," Wiggles said.

"It's possible. And they know all about his jewel collection. They could be the reason he's dead."

"Shall I tell the angels that they've arrived?" Wiggles asked.

My shoulders slumped. "Even if they are involved, they're not going to admit it, especially not when I'm the scapegoat stuck behind bars. If they did kill Toby, the chances are they set me up to take the fall."

"I smell the unpleasant whiff of defeat." Wiggles cocked his head as he studied me. "It's not like you to go down without a fight. I know you think you had the flu before all this happened, but what if it was more than that?"

"Like what?"

"You were acting oddly the day before you got sick. I kept having to repeat myself every time I asked you something. It was as if you were physically in the room, but your mind was elsewhere."

My brow wrinkled. "I don't remember that."

"Sure, you don't remember most of that time. You were spaced out and weird, just like Aurora is when she's around Toby. Then you got sick, took to your bed, and that was it. You headed out to Toby's, knocked me out, and did whatever you did. Someone was in charge of you."

I ducked my head. "I've been wondering about that myself. I know you didn't sense Frank that night, but could it have been him? Did Frank finally win?"

Wiggles shook his head. "This wasn't Frank's doing. But someone was influencing you."

"Could it have been Toby? He's done it before, and he has that lock of my hair. That would be a useful tool to influence me." I shook my head. "But why use it to get me to kill him?"

"Even though I didn't see it, I'm sure you didn't kill him," Wiggles said. "You beat on him a bit, but I missed the finale."

"That's not super helpful."

"How are you feeling now? Do you still feel spaced out?"

My mouth twisted to the side. "Honestly, not great. I'm okay, but my magic's drained, and it doesn't feel like it's recharging. I can barely do a basic spell. My magic has faded. And Frank, well, I don't feel him. I don't even want to hope that he's gone, but what if he has?"

Wiggles' ears sprang up. "That makes sense. Toby wasn't killed with magic. He was physically attacked. If your magic was drained when you attacked him, that would have been the only way you could have killed him."

"Wiggles! You're not helping. Remember, I'm supposed to be innocent."

"Oh, sure, I know that. But if someone else was in charge of your movements, maybe that drained your magic, so they had to use your body as a weapon. You slashed and punched Toby until he died."

"Which still means I killed Toby."

Wiggles' nose wrinkled. "No, this stinks of siphon magic."

I lifted my chin. "That's not a bad idea, but it's a rare gift. I've only met a handful of people who have the ability to siphon magic. To take magic forcibly requires a huge amount of power. No one in Willow Tree Falls can do it."

"It would explain what happened to your magic. And if someone has done that to you, it would be the reason you felt sick. Maybe you weren't suffering from the flu. Somebody took your powers from you and drained your energy."

"I don't know. It's a stretch. And what about Frank? Would someone draining my magic take him as well? Surely, taking my power would have made him stronger. With my magic on the fritz, he would take over and do what he's always wanted to do."

"Maybe whoever drained your magic also drained Frank. The two of you are joined at the hip. Perhaps our magic using siphon got more than they bargained for when they drained you. They could have taken some of Frank's ability. That would have been quite a kick when they received it."

"We need to see about Nolan and these succubi. We have to find out if any of them have this ability. If they do, it makes sense that they're involved in taking my power and using me to take the fall for

Toby's murder. Whoever can siphon magic is the killer."

"I'll look into it," Wiggles said. "It won't be easy to get anyone to confess to having that ability. No one likes a magic siphon. Those people give me the creeps."

The door to the cells slammed open. Dazielle charged through, anger radiating off her as her wings fluttered.

"Eek!" Wiggles squeaked. "We've been rumbled."

Dazielle stopped outside the cell, her arms folded across her chest. "Did you have anything to do with what happened to my angels?"

"I've been in my cell the whole time," I said. "Hand on heart, in this instance, I'm not guilty."

Her eyes narrowed. "We know it was Rhett who slammed through my angels to get to you. Did you tell him to do that?"

"I'm saying nothing," I said.

Dazielle sighed, and her nostrils flared. "That's it. This comes to an end now. Tempest Crypt, I'm charging you with Toby Matlock's murder."

Chapter 10

I stared into Dazielle's defiant eyes. "You've given up? You really think I did this?"

"The only thing we don't have is an eyewitness and your confession," Dazielle said. "But we have enough evidence that makes it clear you're involved."

"You're not sending Tempest to jail." Wiggles stood in front of my cell, his teeth bared and his eyes glowing red.

"Don't get involved, hellhound," Dazielle said. "Feel grateful we don't charge you with aiding and abetting."

"Leave Wiggles out of this," I said. "You saw for yourself that he'd been knocked out. He did nothing to Toby."

"And you did?" Dazielle stared at me, the silence stretching out for an uncomfortable length of time.

It was time to be straight with Dazielle and share my concerns about my involvement in Toby's death. I sucked in a breath.

Wiggles growled a warning as if he knew what I was about to say.

"It's okay," I said. "Dazielle, maybe I am involved."

"You admit to killing Toby?" Dazielle inched closer but stopped as Wiggles snarled.

"Something happened to me that night. I did something, and I don't remember what it was. I'm not innocent."

"We already know that," Dazielle said. "It's why you're being charged."

"Don't say anything else," Wiggles warned me. "They don't have enough to charge you."

"You're wrong," Dazielle said. "We can hold Tempest for as long as we need until this is resolved. You're being charged with murder. You'll get a fair trial. The evidence will be presented to an impartial jury. They'll make the ultimate decision on your fate."

I shrugged. I couldn't fight back, not from inside the cell. "I'll take the trial."

"Step aside," Dazielle said to Wiggles, "unless you want me to ban you again."

"Wiggles, it's fine," I said.

He growled again but edged away. "You didn't do this. Someone set you up."

I knew that, but we were out of time to prove it. "What are you going to do with me?" I asked Dazielle.

"We're moving you out of Willow Tree Falls. There's too much interference going on in this case."

"You mean Rhett and my family?" I shook my head. "I'll tell them to back off, but I'm not leaving Willow Tree Falls."

"You don't have a say in the matter," Dazielle said. "It's standard practice that we move criminals to a different location. These are simply holding cells."

"You're sending me to jail?"

Dazielle nodded. "Don't worry. We're not sending you to the demon prison."

I scowled at her. "If you did, you'd have every Crypt witch descend upon you."

"That sounds like a threat."

"It's a guarantee."

Dazielle glowered at me. "Let's do this nice and quietly. You can have legal representation if you want it. I suggest you do. It's your word against insurmountable evidence at this point."

A wave of fetid air shot from Wiggles' mouth. He stood on the tips of his paws, his hackles raised as smoke drifted from his nose.

"Hey, buddy, you need to calm down," I cautioned him.

"They're not taking you." A growl rumbled low in his chest. "You aren't leaving Willow Tree Falls. You're not leaving me. What about the siphon theory we're working on?"

That was the problem. At the moment, it was just a theory. "It won't be for long. We'll find the truth."

"We've already found it," Dazielle said. "Let's move. I'll have transportation pick you up in thirty minutes. I don't want any more incidents involving my angels being injured. In case you've forgotten, we're still searching for your sister. I can't send out injured workers."

"Have you found her?" I approached the bars.

She shook her head. "There's still nothing. But you causing problems is taking resources away from the search. Do the right thing, Tempest. Come quietly and don't kick up a fuss. Once you're out of here, I assure you, the majority of my angels will look into the disappearance of your sister."

I pinched the bridge of my nose. I couldn't stand in the way of them finding Aurora. "I won't fight you. Let's get this over with."

Dazielle looked at Wiggles. "Tell him to move."

I smirked and shook my head. "You've been around Wiggles long enough to know he doesn't obey orders if he doesn't like them."

Wiggles took a menacing step toward Dazielle, his head lowering as he did so. "You're not taking Tempest."

Dazielle's wings extended, brushing against the walls outside the cell. "Try to stop me."

Wiggles hunched onto the ground before launching at Dazielle, his teeth aiming for her throat.

"Wiggles! No!" I smashed into the bars and was stung with angel magic. That didn't stop me as I kept kicking them.

Dazielle slammed against the wall as Wiggles punched into her chest. Her wings wrapped around him. All I could see was a squirming mass of hellhound and feathers flying as they battled.

"Don't hurt him," I yelled. "He's only protecting me." My heart pounded, making my head throb. I couldn't lose Wiggles, not on top of everything that had happened.

The door to the cells slammed open. Dominic stood there, his eyes widening as Dazielle hit the floor and rolled around with Wiggles still encased in her wings.

"We've got an emergency," Dominic said as his puzzled expression followed Dazielle.

"You're telling me," I said. "Stop Dazielle from smothering Wiggles."

Dominic blinked rapidly. "No, that's not the emergency."

"It is!" Dazielle yelled at him. "Get the angel net. We need to deal with this hellhound."

"But it's the—"

"Do it. Now!" Dazielle said.

Dominic looked at me before turning and racing out of the room. I watched him go, worry trickling through me. What had he come to tell Dazielle? Was there another problem in Willow Tree Falls? Could this day get any worse?

Wiggles appeared out the bottom of Dazielle's wings. He rolled across the floor, spat out a mouthful of feathers, leaped onto his feet, and threw himself at her extended right wing. He caught it between his jaws and shook it, feathers flying everywhere as Dazielle shrieked.

Ignoring the stinging pain of the angel magic, I forced my hand through and grabbed the back of her shirt. I yanked her against the bars. "Stop fighting."

"I'll stop fighting when your insane hellhound lets go of my wing." Dazielle squeaked as something could be heard tearing.

I winced as I heard a sickening crack of bone.

The room was full of feathers and the sound of growling as Dominic returned with Jophiel. They held a glowing net between them.

"Catch." Dazielle swung her injured right wing.

Wiggles flew through the air and landed in the angel net.

Jophiel sealed the net, trapping Wiggles inside. He squirmed, growling and cursing as they watched him with wide eyes.

"Like Tempest, that hellhound is a menace," Dazielle said as she inspected her damaged wing.

I let out a sigh of relief as I saw that Wiggles didn't seem injured. "Calm down, buddy. This isn't helping our case."

Wiggles snorted, and a burst of flames flickered through the angel net.

"Get that hellhound out of here," Dazielle ordered Dominic and Jophiel. "Make sure he doesn't get back through the front door."

"We're on it, boss." Dominic hurried out with Jophiel, Wiggles swinging in between them, trapped in the net.

Dazielle brushed at her ruined shirt and tugged at her wings.

"You know he's not a bad hellhound," I said quietly.

"That defies the definition of a hellhound. They're meant to be bad."

"He's worried about me."

Dazielle grunted. "Perhaps. The pets we own can be protective of us. He still shouldn't have done it."

"He's scared. We all are," I said.

Dazielle glanced up at me, and a trickle of what looked like sympathy moved across her face. "I wish it hadn't come to this, Tempest. I was beginning not to hate having you around. You often interfered, but you had good insight on some cases you've helped with."

"What's your instinct telling you about me?" I asked. "Do you really think I murdered Toby Matlock?"

Dazielle swiped her uninjured wing across her forehead. "It's telling me to trust the evidence. I saw you at the crime scene. You looked guilty. You were running. And, we found no one else there at the time of the murder."

"What about Nolan?" I asked. "He's been trying to get into Toby's house. What's he after?"

"And you know that how?" Dazielle looked at the door and sighed. "Of course, Wiggles told you. Well, perhaps he has, but that doesn't make him guilty. Nolan was nowhere near Willow Tree Falls when Toby was killed."

"Or the three succubi?" I suggested. "Do you know they've just arrived in the village? Why not question them before shoving me into jail and writing me off?"

"Tempest, despite what you think of me, I know how to do my job," Dazielle said. "Those women aren't involved. They're here for the reading of Toby's will."

"And what about the will? Any sign of one?"

She scowled at me. "We're working on it. But for now—"

The door slammed open again. Dominic burst in.

Dazielle wheeled on him. "For the angel's sake, stop racing around like an over-excited toddler."

"I was trying to tell you earlier," Dominic said, "there's an emergency in the village."

"What kind of emergency?"

"It's the demon prison." Dominic looked at me.

"The prison! Has somebody been hurt?" My heart raced again.

"We're not sure what's going on," Dominic said, "but your family called for reinforcements. They're asking for our help."

They never did that. The cemetery was our domain. It had to be really bad for them to ask for help from the angels.

"What's the problem?" I was almost shouting, fueled by panic and my inability to do anything to help.

"Take two other angels and go to the cemetery," Dazielle ordered. "Assess the situation and help if you can."

Dominic shook his head. "They've asked for all the help they can get. Three angels won't cut it."

"You have to go," I said. "My family won't be exaggerating if they've asked for every angels' assistance."

"Who told you this?" Dazielle asked Dominic.

"Queenie," Dominic said. "She appeared in the office. She's already gone. She said she couldn't risk being away from the prison for too long."

Dazielle ran a hand down her face. "Very well. Assemble all available angels. We'll fly over there now."

"Let me help," I said. "You know I have skills when it comes to demons."

Dazielle was by the door. Dominic had already raced ahead of her. "No, you can't help this time. You stay here."

"I know the prison," I said. "My family needs me. I have to help."

"You can help by causing no more problems." Warning filled Dazielle's eyes. "If you put a foot out of line, I'll know about it. This isn't over, Tempest. I'll be back to transport you to jail as soon as I can." She walked out of the room, and the door shut behind her.

I only just managed to repress the scream that bubbled up my throat. I thumped my head back against the wall several times. I had to get out, but without my magic or Frank, I was stuck and alone.

My hands curled into fists. I couldn't sit here and wonder if my family was being massacred by the demons as they escaped the prison.

"Is anybody there?" I yelled. "Someone! Get me out of here."

There was no answer.

"Wiggles! Where are you?" If he was free from the angel net and could hear me, I knew he'd come back. Maybe he'd also gone to the cemetery. He knew a few tricks when it came to fighting demons.

I paced the cell, listening for an angel on the other side of the door who could tell me what was going on. They wouldn't have left the building empty, would they?

A flood of cold air filled the room. It was followed by a clicking sound.

I stopped pacing and stared at the door. That sounded like the lock had just opened.

I crept closer to the bars and waved my hands against them. The magic barrier had gone. I shoved my hand straight through the bars. There was nothing, no magic holding me in place. I grabbed the cell door and pulled. It opened.

Stepping out into the corridor, I looked around. Was this a trap? Was it a test by Dazielle to see if I'd do as she ordered? She must know that was a mistake. I'd ignore her a million times if it meant I could get out and help my family.

Another cold chill flooded the room, and I shivered. Something was going on inside Angel Force, and it felt nothing like the sharp burst of angel magic.

I inched to the door and opened it. I stopped moving the second I heard footsteps.

Whoever was out there wasn't in a hurry. They were shuffling along, moving at a slow pace, and taking their time.

Sucking in a breath, I pulled the door wider. I stepped into the main office of Angel Force. I kept my back against the wall as I looked around. The place was deserted. Chairs were shoved back and mugs of coffee abandoned. The angels had been in a hurry as they'd raced to the demon prison. The thought only made my gut churn.

I hurried through the office toward the reception area. This was a big risk. Leaving was a clear sign of my guilt, but this could be the only opportunity I had to escape and clear my name. I had to take it.

As I reached the reception, I inched the door open. Standing by the main front doors were two figures dressed in black cloaks, their features concealed by hoods. One was limping. It looked like a man. He was taller than the other person and leaned heavily on them.

I moved through the doorway, creeping toward them. As they reached the main door, the shorter of the two black-clad figures pulled it open. They turned, and a pair of brilliant green eyes met mine. For a second, there was alarm in their gaze before their eyes narrowed.

"Hey! Who are you?" I took a step forward.

The figure's arm shot out. A blast of hot magic slammed into my chest.

Grunting in pain, I stumbled back against the wall, my head hitting the door frame. I groaned as I slumped down.

"Stay here," a quiet female voice murmured.

Oh, crud, she was coming to finish me off. My magic was pitiful. I could do nothing to defend myself. I looked around, hunting for a weapon. My gaze landed on a pile of angel balls in the corner, behind the desk. The angels used them to play bat and ball with their wings. They landed quite a bruise when they made contact. I'd experienced it myself when one had hit me on the forehead.

I ducked behind the desk, ignoring the throbbing ache in my chest from where the magic had slammed into me. I scrambled over on my hands and knees and grabbed a handful of angel balls. I held two up, waiting for my attacker to appear.

Footsteps grew close. My breath hitched, but I forced myself to focus. I might not have my magic, but I wasn't going down without a fight.

"Hurry! Someone's coming," an exhausted sounding man said. "We have to get out of here. They can't find us."

I tilted my head. That voice was familiar. Despite the bone-weary tone, I'd heard that person speak before.

There was a quiet sigh before the footsteps retreated. The door slammed open and then shut. I was alone.

I lowered my hands, my arms feeling like lead and my head pounding. Why would someone break into Angel Force? What were they stealing?

I tensed as the door opened again and hurried footsteps approached. My attacker was back. She'd decided to take me out, after all. I raised an angel ball again and let it fly as she rounded the corner.

Granny Dottie clicked her fingers. The angel ball stopped an inch from her nose. She batted it away and stared at me. "What are you doing down there?"

"I thought you were here to kill me." I let out a sigh. "What are you doing here?"

She smiled smugly as she held her hand out. "Springing you out of prison."

Chapter 11

"You broke the magic around my cell?" I grabbed Granny Dottie's hand and pulled myself up. "Shouldn't you be at the cemetery?"

"We can't talk in here." Granny Dottie hurried toward the exit, her warm hand clasped in mine.

"Oh, I get it. You made up the story about the demon prison being under threat to get me out." Of course, this was all a ruse to distract the angels.

"Oh, no. The demons are revolting."

"Sure. They're always revolting."

She snorted a laugh. "Too true, but they're all trying to break out. We have to go."

We hurried out into the late evening gloom.

"Wait!" Granny Dottie swiped a hand over us, and I felt the familiar tingle of her magic. "We don't want anyone to see what we're up to. The whole village is preoccupied with events at the prison, but we still need to be careful."

"We have to get to the prison and stop the demons."

"You're not going anywhere near the prison, my girl." Granny Dottie continued to hurry me along.

I dug my heels in and stopped walking. "It sounds bad."

"I'm here on your mom's orders." Granny Dottie's expression softened. "We know you're having trouble with your magic. You wouldn't be able to stand up to a baby demon, let alone the things creeping out of the gaps. If you went into that cemetery now, you'd be killed in seconds. We saw the opportunity to get you out and took it. Now you're out, you can find Toby's killer, Aurora, and clear your name."

I scrubbed my forehead with my fingers. Granny Dottie was right. I'd be a hindrance if I tried to fight the demons with my malfunctioning magic.

"You see, it makes sense," Granny Dottie said. "You keep your head down and don't draw attention to yourself. You can't do anything from inside that cell. Out here, at least, you have a chance."

"I wouldn't have been there for much longer." I let Granny Dottie lead me away. "Dazielle has just charged me with Toby's murder."

Granny Dottie shook her head. "Foolish angel. The lot of them are dumber than a sack of rotten potatoes. We were worried something like this might happen."

"Where are we going?"

"Into the forest." Granny Dottie grinned at me. "I've got reinforcements. Everyone wants to help."

"I don't want people taking risks on my behalf," I said. "It's bad enough you came to break me out. The angels might not be smart, but they'll know someone in the family got me out."

"I wasn't leaving my granddaughter in their incapable hands any longer," Granny Dottie said. "It took all your mom's persuasion to stop me from blasting a hole in that place and taking you as soon as they put you in that cell."

I couldn't help but smile. That was typical Granny Dottie style.

Once we were deep enough into the trees, Granny Dottie dropped her cover spell.

The second she did, Wiggles popped into view on the path, his tail wagging. "You made it."

"As if you had any doubt about that," Granny Dottie said.

"I hope the angels weren't too rough on you," I said to Wiggles.

He grunted. "Their cards are marked. I won't forget what they did to me. They'd better guard their lunch pails very carefully from now on."

I pulled up short as Fallon and Suki also stepped into view. "What are you doing here?"

Suki flexed her substantial biceps. "I'm not abandoning my boss when she needs help. Fallon's agreed to work with me on this, too."

Fallon flourished a hand as she bowed. "I'm always at your service. My only price is a ride on your pony."

Wiggles growled, and I groaned. Fallon was obsessed with riding Wiggles.

"It's a fair exchange," Fallon said.

"We'll negotiate later," Suki whispered. "Not now. We don't have time."

"Suki's right," Granny Dottie said. "We've got the jump on the angels, but it's only a short lead. We have to work fast."

"Then you'll need my help." Rhett appeared. He smiled at me. "How are you doing?"

I hurried over, not caring who saw us, and wrapped my arms around him.

He hugged me tightly, his mouth by my ear. "Hold it together. We're almost done. We can fix this."

I pulled back, blinking tears out of my eyes as he kissed me. I was full of gratitude that people hadn't given up on me. They didn't think I was a killer.

Granny Dottie cleared her throat. "As handsome a hunk as Rhett is, now isn't the time for canoodling. Let's get Tempest somewhere safe then make a plan of action."

Rhett kept hold of my hand as we hurried through the forest, entering the densest part where the path vanished and the foliage grew dense and wild.

"Where are we heading?" I asked.

"There's a place I know," Rhett said. "The gang uses it sometimes. You'll be safe there. The angels don't know about it."

As we hurried along in the gloom, I tugged on Granny Dottie's arm. "When you were at Angel Force, did you see those two people leaving?"

She glanced at me and shook her head. "It was just us. There were no angels there."

"No, these people weren't angels. That's why I was waiting to attack when you found me. Whoever it was, they didn't want to be seen. It was two people dressed in black. One of them looked injured. It was a man and a woman. Are you sure you didn't see them leave through the front door?"

"I must have just missed them," Granny Dottie said. "What were they doing?"

"I'm not sure. The woman blasted me off my feet and was coming to finish me off. If you hadn't got there, I doubt the angel balls would have done me much good."

Granny Dottie scowled. "What were they up to?"

"I've no idea. I don't think it was another prisoner breaking out. I was the only one in the cells."

"We can't worry about them now," Granny Dottie said. "We need to focus on clearing your name and finding your sister."

"We're here." Rhett led us into a gloomy cave that seemed to go back a long way.

"You light a fire," Granny Dottie said to Rhett. "I'll put a cover spell over the entrance, so no one can see us."

Rhett ducked in front of a shallow pit, clicked his fingers over the kindling and wood already in place, and a flame burst to life. The light illuminated our faces as we stood around staring at each other.

I felt like I had to say something meaningful. "Listen, I appreciate everyone helping. You know this won't be easy. If the angels find out you're helping—"

"You let us worry about that." Granny Dottie rubbed her hands over the flames. "We know what we're doing. We also know that you're innocent."

"And we're not going to stop helping you until we've proven that." Suki nudged Fallon with her knee. "Isn't that right?"

Fallon's intense gaze was on Wiggles. "I'll help."

"You're not riding me, wood nymph." Wiggles growled at her.

Fallon tilted her head from side to side. "I have my uses, but I also have short legs. We might need to flee this place. If I ride you, pony, I won't be left behind. My services are valuable to you."

Wiggles continued to growl low in his chest but didn't say anything.

Rhett slung an arm around my shoulders and squeezed. "I've got all of my guys out looking for Aurora. We've covered almost the whole village."

My gut clenched. "Still no sign of her?"

"Not yet, but she'll turn up."

"Aurora's a strong magic user," Granny Dottie said. "She'll protect herself. Maybe she's hidden until this blows over. If she was at the house when Toby was attacked, she could be in shock."

"Toby's had her in his thrall for such a long time," I said. "I've no clue how her magic's holding up. It might have been compromised. I'll help you look for her."

"I disagree." Granny Dottie raised a hand to stop me protesting. "You focus on clearing your name."

"Aurora could be in danger," I said.

"She might be, which is why we're concentrating on her," Granny Dottie said. "You'll be no good to anybody if you get yourself arrested again. You make sure the angels know you're innocent and then you can help find Aurora. By then, she'll most likely be found, and you won't need to worry."

As much as I hated to agree, Granny Dottie was right. I turned to Rhett. "Promise me you'll keep looking for her. Don't worry about me. I can handle this mess. I have to know my sister's safe."

He kissed the top of my head. "Of course. We'll focus on finding Aurora."

"Where have you tried looking?" I asked him.

"Her apartment. Heaven's Door. We've also been in every store in the village asking about her."

"Have you searched the forest?"

"Every inch of it," Rhett said.

"With my help," Fallon said. "If it wasn't for me, half of the biker gang would be dead."

Rhett glowered at Fallon. "We need to talk about your magic traps. My gang has been using this forest for years. We need to know where your traps are."

"That will spoil the whole purpose of the traps," Fallon said. "Maybe your gang needs to be better at detecting dangerous magic."

"My gang shouldn't need to worry about exploding webbing, arrows in the back, or big holes you've dug."

"They must be used to people wanting them dead," Fallon said. "This will keep them on their toes."

Suki stepped between Fallon and Rhett. "I'll make sure the dangerous magic is kept to a minimum."

Fallon opened her mouth, but Suki slapped a hand over it.

Rhett's fingers flexed, and he glared at Fallon.

"You don't think Aurora's left the village?" I asked Granny Dottie. "If she saw something bad happen in Toby's house, she might have gotten scared and think it's not safe here."

Granny Dottie nodded. "We'll expand the search if we haven't found her by the end of tomorrow. If we have to go outside the magic barrier, she could be anywhere."

I dropped my head against Rhett's shoulder. "What if she saw me passed out on the floor next to Toby's body and freaked out, thinking I'd done that to him?"

"It's no good with what ifs and buts," Granny Dottie said. "We could do that all night and not get anywhere. As soon as we find her, we'll ask her what she saw. Until then, you know what you need to do."

I nodded. "Clear my name."

"And I need to get looking for your sister," Rhett said. "I'll go join the guys." He pressed a kiss to my lips before leaving the cave.

Granny Dottie glanced around the group. "Fallon. Suki. Can you give us a little privacy? Keep a watch outside to make sure no one knows we're here. I need to talk to my granddaughter."

They both nodded and hurried away.

"What is it?" I asked.

Granny Dottie's gaze was intense as it ran over me. "When I touched your skin, I felt something."

"What did you feel?" My heart thudded.

"Tempest, where is your magic?"

I swallowed and felt my bottom lip tremble. "It's not working properly."

Granny Dottie took hold of both of my hands. "Child, your magic is almost gone. Somehow, it's been taken."

I glanced down at Wiggles and tightened my hold on her hands. "We did wonder about that."

Wiggles nodded. "A magic siphon. That's what I thought. Someone got to Tempest and took away her ability."

Granny Dottie's jaw clenched. "No one has ever taken a Crypt witch's powers before. It can't be done."

My eyes widened. "But it has. It's happened to me."

"Let me focus for a moment." Granny Dottie pinched my hands so hard they ached. Her forehead wrinkled in concentration as her eyes fluttered closed.

I tried to calm my racing heart as I watched her tap into my energy. Granny Dottie would know what to do. She'd have a solution for this. She'd better, because I had no clue why my magic was so weak.

With a sigh, she opened her eyes and dropped one of my hands. "It's not all gone. You can get your power back. It will take time, and we don't have that."

"How long?" If I went crazy with the spells, I often felt a little tired, but after a good night's sleep, I was back to normal. Right now, I felt anything but normal.

"Weeks. Maybe months to get you back to full strength."

"I'm no good to anyone if I can't use my magic," I said.

Granny Dottie cupped my cheek. "Yes, you are. You're not special just because of your magic."

My nose wrinkled. "How did this happen?"

"I've heard of rare individuals who siphon magic without touching a person. They'd need something that belongs to you, so they can form a connection. And it would take time. The effects wouldn't be immediate."

"I said you were acting weird for days before the whole slaughtering Toby thing happened," Wiggles said. "Whoever did this has been slowly zapping your magic without you realizing it."

"It's true. I felt odd for days before I got sick."

"I don't think you were ever sick, not in a physical sense," Granny Dottie said. "You were invaded."

"That used to happen to me before I was a hellhound," Wiggles said. "Remember that time I got a flea infestation, and you had to fumigate the apartment?"

"Don't remind me." I grimaced. I'd been scratching for weeks, convinced they hadn't all gone. "What do I do without my magic?"

Grannie Dottie patted my cheek. "You don't need to be without magic. I'll gift you some of mine."

"No, that'll leave you vulnerable," I said. "You need your magic to help deal with the prison. In fact, you shouldn't even be here with me. You should be dealing with the demons."

"I know. That's my next stop." Granny Dottie smiled. "But that's what I'm here for, to indulge my granddaughter. Take my magic. It will make you feel better. Then you can defend yourself when you find Toby's killer. It will also give you a chance against the angels when they start to look for you. And they will. When they get back and find you gone, they won't stop hunting you. You have to be ready for that."

I blew out a long breath. I didn't want to take her magic. Granny Dottie was an immensely powerful witch, but she was an aging one. Although, I'd never say that to her face. Witches lived longer than humans, but they weren't indestructible. Age caught up with them, eventually.

Her lips pursed. "You can't refuse my gift. I'll take offense."

"Okay, just a little of your magic."

Granny Dottie chuckled as she led me back to the fire and held my hands over the flames before linking her fingers with mine. "Don't you worry about me. I'm a lot stronger than I look." She winked at me as warm pulses of energy flooded from her arms and into my fingers.

Bright red and green sparkles spun around me, lacing up my arms and over my head. I always loved the feel of Granny Dottie's magic. It felt bright, alert, and a little naughty. And it was strong. She was flooding me with energy.

I wriggled in her grasp, trying to get free and break the connection. I didn't want her giving me too much.

She ignored me and continued to pour her power into me. Finally, she broke the connection and stepped away from the flames. "How do you feel?"

Flexing out my fingers, I saw the sparks of her magic fade into my skin. "Good. Better. My head's not hurting, and my stomach's stopped flipping."

"That's a good start," Granny Dottie said. "Use my magic wisely. You only got a small burst. It will drain if you overuse it. And be careful around other magic users. I'd do a recall spell on you to see if we could dig up any memories of what happened that night, but it will weaken you, as will other spells. This burst of magic you have is only temporary."

"I'll be cautious," I said.

She walked around the fire and hugged me tightly. "Stay safe, Tempest. I have to get back to the cemetery. Use your allies wisely. Don't do this on your own. With the whole of Angel Force out looking for you soon, you'll need all the help you can get."

I returned her hug and buried my nose into her jasmine scented hair for a second.

She pulled back. "Where are you going to start?"

I chewed on my bottom lip before nodding. "I know where to go. We have to go back to the scene of the crime. We need to go to Toby's house."

Chapter 12

I watched as Granny Dottie left the cave and merged into the gloom of the forest. I felt torn. A part of me wanted to go with her. I wanted to stand side-by-side with my family, defend the prison, and get the demons under control. I also knew that Granny Dottie was right. If I showed my face when the angels were fighting the demons, it would descend into chaos. They'd turn their attention on me, and the demons would exploit their distraction. I couldn't let that happen. I had to keep a low profile, even though the thought made me sick with worry that I was leaving my family vulnerable.

I led the way out of the cave, Wiggles beside me, and Fallon and Suki trailing close behind.

"Keep up," I whispered as Fallon vanished from sight.

"If you let me ride your pony, I won't get lost in the forest." Fallon's voice sounded faint.

"You can't get lost in here. You live here. You know this forest as well as Suki," I said.

"My legs are short. I'm struggling."

"It's not happening, wood nymph," Wiggles said. "Your legs might be stumpy, but they work fine. Use them."

Wiggles and Fallon continued to debate the not being ridden issue as I hurried along with Suki.

"Are you sure you want to be here? The angels won't be friendly when they find out you're involved in this," I said.

"Don't worry about me," Suki said. "I'm not a big fan of the angels. Their feathers get everywhere. You always know when angels have been in the forest. Bits of feather and fluff stick to the plants. They shed far too easily."

"I'm also not scared of any angel who crosses my path," Fallon said from behind us. "If they come into the forest and try to take me down, they'll be sorry. My magic works on angels as well as anybody else."

We reached the edge of the forest. Although I was tempted to use a cover spell, I needed to keep my magic reserves in check. "Let's stick to the shadows. It's late, so there won't be many people about, but keep an eye out. If you see anyone, let me know. We need to keep out of their way."

We stayed in a single line, keeping to the densest of shadows as we made our way toward Toby's house.

"Ouch! You giant oaf. That was my toe," Fallon grumbled.

"Sorry. It's so dark," Suki whispered. "I can carry you if you like. I can't tread on you if you're in my arms."

"I don't want to be carried. I want to ride that pony."

"Enough!" I hissed. "If we get caught because you're bickering, it'll all be over."

"I'm just saying," Fallon said.

I glanced down at Wiggles, who was glaring back at Fallon. "Any chance?"

Sulfuric smoke belched from his nose.

"It would speed things up and stop Fallon from complaining," I said.

Wiggles muttered several rude words before nodding.

Fallon gasped. "You're going to let me ride you?"

Wiggles snorted. "If you promise not to say another word until we get to Toby's house."

"Oh! Of course! My mouth's closed. You won't hear anything from me." Fallon jumped in the air.

"And if I hear one yee-haw, that's it. I'm flipping you off and stamping on you."

"Absolutely! I won't say yee-haw." Fallon raced over and climbed on Wiggles' back.

"And keep away from my ears," Wiggles said. "They were sore for days after the last time you rode me."

"This is epic," Fallon whispered, her eyes wide. "Giddy-up, pony."

"And no giddy-up's," Wiggles said. "Remember the rule, no talking."

"Let's go," I said. I broke into a jog, and Suki matched my pace as I led the way to Toby's house.

"What are you hoping to find here?" Suki asked.

"Evidence of who really killed Toby," I said. "The angels might have missed something. Their focus was finding evidence to prove my guilt. I'll look for the opposite. We need to get inside and search the house. I also want to see if there's anything left behind that shows where Aurora went."

Suki nodded. "Your sister will be okay. Everyone's watching out for her."

"She has to be," I said. I wasn't sure what I'd do if I lost Aurora. There wasn't a reality I could conceive that didn't have my adorable, frustrating, wonderful sister in it.

We slowed as we reached the gated entrance to Toby's house. I looked around for any signs of angels.

"There's just that one by the front door," Suki whispered. "The rest must be over at the cemetery."

I glanced at her. "Did you go to the cemetery? What's it like?"

Suki's lips pressed together. "It's not so bad."

"Define not so bad."

"I mean, there were some cracks. Tiny cracks. A few demons were trying to get out." She kicked the ground with her toe. "I didn't see much."

"Suki," I said. "Tell me the truth."

She glanced down at me. "Granny Dottie told me not to. She said she'd hex me if I told you how bad it was."

I sucked in a breath, and my gaze went back along the lane. I so badly wanted to go to the demon prison and help.

Fallon poked me in the leg. "Are we doing this? My pony's getting restless."

I looked at Toby's house. "We need a distraction to get that angel out of the way."

"I can knock her out," Suki said. "One direct hit and she'll be out for the count."

"Maybe not. Wiggles and Fallon, you head into the garden. Make some noise so the angel comes to see what's going on," I said. "If we can get her away from the door, it'll give us time to slip inside. Nobody needs to be hurt."

"No problem," Wiggles said. "I know Toby's garden well. I've dug loads of holes in it."

"Giddy-up, pony," Fallon said.

Wiggles bucked several times as he tried to dislodge Fallon. "I warned you. It's stamping time."

"Trample on Fallon later," I hissed. "Go cause a distraction."

Wiggles' eyes glowed red before he strode off with Fallon still firmly attached to his back.

I edged closer to the house, watching the angel. Suki was glued to my side, one hand clutching my arm so tightly I was certain there'd be a bruise there tomorrow.

We got as close as we could without the angel spotting us before stopping.

We only had to wait a moment before an enormous crash sounded in the garden.

The angel spread her wings and turned toward the sound. She took several steps before pausing.

"Go on," I whispered. "Go see if there's an intruder."

The angel looked back at the house. Another thud sounded, and the smell of smoke drifted in the air.

That was enough to spur her into action. The angel hurried away from the door and around the corner of the house.

"Let's go." I raced toward the front door with Suki. I kept glancing into the garden, expecting the angel to appear at any second.

We weren't quiet as we got closer, the gravel crunching under our feet, but we had to move fast. Stealth wasn't an option. Suki reached the front door first. She grabbed the handle, and the door sprung open.

I raced into the dark hallway with her, and she eased the door shut behind us.

We both stood there panting and staring at each other in the gloom.

"We did it," she whispered. "We got past the angel."

"Let's hope Fallon and Wiggles stay out of her way." I gestured her along the hallway. "Let's start at the scene of the crime, where Toby's body was found."

As I crept along, I listened for any noises that might suggest someone was there. It all seemed quiet. Maybe there was only a single angel looking after Toby's house.

I eased the door to the study open. Moonlight flooded the room through the windows, filling it with an eerie white glow.

I gestured Suki over to the couch where Toby had been discovered. The only evidence that a murder had taken place was a dark stain on the carpet.

"What are we looking for?" Suki asked.

"It happened in here," I said. "Toby was on the floor behind the couch. I woke up next to him. I was on my back in my pajamas. Wiggles was over by the door on his side. It was too perfectly set up. It was staged. Maybe Toby's body was moved, or they killed him here and then laid me and Wiggles out to make it look like we were involved."

"Okay," Suki said slowly. "How can we prove that?"

I looked around the room and sighed. "I'm not sure. Wiggles said I came straight through the front door and Feodor, the zombie butler, saw me and didn't react. That means he must have expected me. He's vigilant about allowing guests in to see Toby. He's shut the door in my face several times."

"Does that mean Toby knew you were coming?" Suki asked. "If this zombie butler let you in, he must have been told you were on your way."

I nodded. "That's right. There's no way I'd have gotten past him otherwise. Wiggles said I was acting strangely. I wouldn't have been able to defend myself against the butler if he'd decided I wasn't to get in."

"Toby invited you here knowing that you planned to kill him?"

My eyes narrowed. "I didn't kill him."

"Oh! Of course. He must have been surprised to find you here wearing your pajamas. Maybe Aurora invited you."

"If she did, I don't remember that. We haven't spoken in weeks. She wouldn't suddenly invite me for a sleepover."

Suki looked around the room. "I don't like to say this, but what if Aurora's involved with killing Toby? What if she hurt him and called you for help? Would the butler have let you in if she'd told him you were coming?"

I thumped my forehead, wishing I could remember that night. "Aurora wouldn't kill anybody. But if she did discover that Toby was manipulating her, she'd have been mad as hell. She'd have confronted him. Aurora would expect him to tell the truth."

"Could things have gotten out of hand and she had to defend herself? Maybe Aurora killed Toby in self-defense and then fled." Suki ducked her head as if expecting me to thump her for suggesting that option.

I sighed. "Or she panicked. Like I did when I woke up next to a dead body. If that happened, which I don't believe it did, it's no surprise she's in hiding." I shook my head, not able to believe my little sister could be involved. "Let's try the kitchen. Nothing in here is triggering anything useful."

I led the way back into the hallway and into the kitchen. I risked conjuring a tiny light ball to help us look around.

"What about in here?" Suki whispered. "Do you remember coming in here when you visited Toby?"

"No, I've never been in Toby's kitchen. None of this is familiar. But the angels said there were signs of a disturbance. Perhaps Aurora fought someone in here. She argued with Toby and the fight moved into the study."

"Or she discovered the killer, and he took her," Suki said.

My stomach dropped. "Why take Aurora? Why not kill her?"

"Maybe the killer panicked, too."

There seemed to be a lot of people panicking over this mess. "The angels think I attacked Aurora." I walked around the large kitchen island several times, but no memories returned. I was certain I hadn't been in here.

I paused as I heard a scraping sound beneath my feet.

"Is there a basement?" Suki asked.

"I think so."

"It could be rodents." Suki's expression was doubtful as she watched me creep toward the kitchen door.

"We need to check it out. What if the angels haven't searched the basement? Aurora could be lying down there injured." I opened the kitchen door and froze. A pair of red glowing eyes stared back at me.

"What's up?" Wiggles trotted closer.

"Shouldn't you be outside distracting the angel?"

"She found herself in a bit of a situation," Fallon said, still sitting astride Wiggles. "She won't bother us for a while. Have you found the evidence you need yet?"

I pressed a finger to my lips. "Not yet. We're about to go to the basement."

"We heard a noise," Suki whispered. "It might be rodents."

Fallon smiled and rubbed her hands together. "I fancy a late-night snack."

I grimaced as I led the way along the corridor. I tried several doors until I found one with a set of steps leading into the basement. I poked my head in and listened. There were scraping sounds, and I detected a light. I waved with my fingers to let the others know to follow as I tiptoed down the stone steps.

Once I was halfway down, I ducked and peered through the gap. My eyes widened as I saw Feodor.

Wiggles pushed past, Fallon no longer on his back, and stood next to me. A quiet growl rumbled in his chest.

I shook my head. "Not yet. We need to see what the zombie butler's up to."

The cold stone steps quickly numbed my backside as we sat watching him. There was a stone table in the center of the room, and a long bench lined one wall. Feodor was laying out magic items and pieces of equipment. There was a pestle and mortar, bunches of dried herbs, and several glass vials. There was also a long, sharp knife with a leather wrapped handle.

Wiggles placed his front paws on my knee and leaned his nose against my ear. "It looks ceremonial."

"Maybe it's his night-time beauty routine." The zombie butler was made by magic, so perhaps he needed to rejuvenate every night.

"We should—" Wiggles' back paw slipped off the stone step.

I tried to grab him, but it was too late. He bounced down the stone steps, cursing, yelping, and breathing fire every time he rolled. He landed at the bottom on his belly with a loud belch.

The three of us froze and waited to see if he was okay.

Wiggles hopped up and shook out his fur. "Nothing to see here. I slipped."

"No kidding," I muttered.

A growl that didn't come from Wiggles rolled across the basement.

I ducked again and saw Feodor standing there, his mouth open and his hands clenched as he glared at Wiggles.

I gritted my teeth. They had a history. Feodor wasn't a fan of Wiggles. The feeling was mutual.

"Let me past," Fallon said. "I must defend my valiant steed." She hurried down the steps and strode toward Feodor.

Wiggles grabbed Fallon by the collar of her tunic. "Not so fast, tiny."

She wriggled free, and what sounded like a battle cry sprung from Fallon's lips. She launched herself into the air, her arms out.

Feodor swiped Fallon in mid-air with the back of his hand as if she were nothing more than an annoying fruit fly.

Fallon squeaked as she flew through the air and hit the ground.

Suki roared in rage. She shoved past me, almost taking me down the stairs with her. "Nobody attacks my friends."

"Suki, maybe you shouldn't." I hurried after her. Feodor in a rage was never fun to be around.

She glanced back at me, and I flinched. Suki in full-on rage mode was also a terrifying sight. I'd seen her take down a group of angels. Maybe she could handle a zombie butler.

Wiggles jumped to the side as Suki raced past. She didn't slow as she plowed into Feodor.

Her arm wrapped around the zombie butler's neck, and she took him to the ground, her elbow slamming into his chest.

Feodor rolled away and onto his feet. He was surprisingly lithe for a big guy. He lumbered toward Suki, his fists flying.

Suki sidestepped him and thumped him in the back of the head with the side of her palm.

Feodor stumbled and crashed into the wall.

"You go, Suki," Wiggles yelled. "Punch that mean bag of wind in the gut for me."

I stood by Wiggles as we watched Suki and Feodor brawl. The dirt floor shuddered every time they slammed into each other. It was like a clash of the titans. Suki had the upper hand. She was faster and more agile than Feodor, whose movements were growing sluggish. Maybe his magic was wearing out.

I glanced over to see Fallon flat on her back, blinking slowly as she stared at the ceiling.

I crept over and helped her up. "Anything broken?"

"Just my substantial pride," Fallon muttered. "He hits hard."

"He meant to," I said. "He's supposed to be a butler, but I think he serves many purposes."

"I could take him down," Fallon said. "I just don't have the right equipment."

"We'll let Suki handle this one," I said.

We ducked as Feodor threw a huge wooden barrel toward us.

"Good thinking," Fallon said as splintered wood exploded above our heads. "Suki has an effective punch. I taught her everything she knows."

As if to demonstrate, Suki landed a bone breaking uppercut on Feodor's jaw.

He staggered back, his arms waving as he tried to keep upright.

She hit him again. Feodor collapsed backward. He didn't get up.

Wiggles raced over and jumped on Feodor's chest. "When will you ever learn? You can't beat us." He bounced up and down on Feodor several times.

I walked slowly toward Suki, who stood over Feodor, glaring down at him. I felt rage radiating off her. She'd need a few moments to calm down and return to the sweet-natured Suki I was used to.

"Wiggles, let's take a look around," I said. "There could be something useful down here."

Wiggles bounced once more on Feodor's chest before striding to the table.

Fallon grabbed Wiggles and squeezed him tightly. "I'm glad he didn't hurt you, my little pony."

Wiggles struggled out of her grip and backed away. "Yeah, I guess the same goes for you."

I left them to make up while I walked to the long bench and investigated the items. There was a stone dagger, a bowl containing different crushed herbs, a long piece of gnarled wood that looked like a wand, a dried claw from an animal, and a bottle of what looked suspiciously like blood. There were also three demon hammers. They operated just like the sticks I used to beat down demons who tried to escape the prison. I'd not seen one in years.

I traced my fingers over the cold metal, and it thrummed. They still held power.

"This has ritual written all over it," I muttered. "What kind of ritual was the zombie butler planning?"

"That's a sacrificial altar," Fallon said as she walked over with Wiggles. She gestured over her shoulder with her thumb.

I glanced at the stone table. "Feodor wouldn't do anything without instruction from Toby. Who did Toby plan to sacrifice?"

"Who said it has to be a sacrifice?" Suki walked over, wiping her forehead with the back of her hand. She smiled at me and nodded.

I patted her arm. "Nice work."

She blushed and scuffed her feet in the dirt.

I looked over the objects again. My heart sped up. These things could be used for sacrifice but also for restoration magic. "You don't think..." I turned to the stone table. I walked over and placed my hands on it. It hummed with old magic, none of it friendly. "You don't think Feodor was instructed to bring Toby back to life?"

"By whom?" Suki asked.

"It could be an instruction left by Toby. In the event of his death, Feodor was to use a restoration spell. The order would have kicked in as soon as Toby died. Feodor must have snuck back in here to set things up."

"Are we going to see a zombie version of Toby wandering around Willow Tree Falls?" Wiggles shuddered. "It's like my worst nightmare. A sleazy, smug zombie with terrible facial hair slowly rotting on the street. Who needs that?"

"He definitely won't be his old self if Feodor brings him back," I said. "He's been dead for days. Toby would come back a very different person."

"He wouldn't even be a person," Fallon said. "He'd be something out of a horror movie. The shell of the man who used to live here. His magic would be warped and dangerous."

"Toby was already that." I frowned and rubbed the back of my neck. "We don't want an even more warped version of him here. We can't let Feodor go through with this."

"He's not going anywhere for a while," Suki said. "We can bind him and leave him down here. He won't get away."

"We need to destroy as much of this as we can," I said. "There's no way we're having Toby Matlock return to Willow Tree Falls."

"Although, if he did come back, you can't be charged with his murder," Wiggles said.

My eyebrows shot up. Would that work? If Toby came back as an undead version of himself, was he dead or alive? "Nope. We need this stuff gone."

Everyone got to work. Suki and Fallon discovered some strong cable and wrapped Feodor in it. I worked with Wiggles to destroy the herbs, get rid of the blood, and separate the rest of the artifacts, so they'd be hard to find.

I felt better after we'd done that. We might have come to the wrong conclusion about Feodor wanting to bring back Toby, but I couldn't risk that happening.

"We need to explore the rest of the house and make sure there's nothing the angels missed in their search for Aurora." I glanced down at Feodor, who appeared to be sleeping peacefully, despite his multiple bindings.

"We'll split up," Wiggles said. "We can search more quickly."

I'd just made it to the bottom of the stone steps when I heard the basement door open. I gestured everyone back, and we ducked and pressed against the wall.

Light footsteps hurried down the stone stairs.

They stopped, and I heard a woman gasp. "What's been going on here?"

Wiggles ducked his head out before nudging me with his nose. "It's a succubus. I recognize her from the hotel."

The footsteps continued down the rest of the staircase. When her feet hit the basement floor, I didn't hesitate. I lunged and grabbed her around the neck.

The intense smell of vanilla filled my nose as I held on tight. I was almost blinded by the woman's luxurious mane of midnight black hair.

She grabbed hold of my arm but didn't fight. Instead, she squeezed me as if feeling for something. Her touch felt more like a massage. It made me relax, and my limbs grew loose.

"What are you doing here?" I hissed in her ear. The smell of her perfume was so intense it made my eyes water. It also made me want to take another breath.

A deep throaty laugh came out of the woman. "Well, well, well. Tempest Crypt. Shouldn't you be behind bars?"

Chapter 13

My grip loosened on the succubus. I kept hold of her arm and shoved her against the wall. For a second, I couldn't breathe as I took in her appearance. She was stunning. Her skin was luminous as if she was lit from the inside by a warm, amber light. Her hair fell in a silken wave down to her waist. Her large dark eyes stared at me with an amused gleam in them. Her full lips were pursed and glistened with a red gloss.

My gaze ran down her form fitting dress that showed her curves off to perfection.

When I finally pulled my gaze back to her face, she was smiling broadly. "It's a pleasure to meet you, Tempest." Her gaze went over my shoulder. "And friends."

I cleared my throat. I had to stop staring. She was a succubus. She was supposed to be temptation personified. I was just surprised to discover that I was tempted by her.

"How do you know who I am?"

"I know all about you," she said. "Everybody's talking about the amazing witch who killed Toby Matlock."

"They're not telling the truth," I said. "Who are you?"

"Marianne O'Hanrahan," she said. "And who are your charming friends?"

Wiggles bounded over, his tail wagging. "Wiggles at your service."

"What an adorable creature." She scratched his belly. "You must get all the bitches looking like that. Such a handsome fellow."

His tongue lolled out. "I do okay."

"This is Suki and Fallon." I introduced the others. "They're forest guardians. Suki also works at my bar."

Marianne inclined her head at both of them. "It's lovely to meet you."

"Now the introductions are over," I said, "care to explain what you're doing creeping around a dead man's house?"

She smiled and rested one hand on her hip. "Of course. I'm here for the will. I received notification from Nolan Matlock that I'm entitled to a share of Toby's assets. You may not be aware, but Toby and I had a meaningful relationship for a number of years. He always assured me that he would take care of me after his passing."

"So, you remained friends even after your romantic relationship ended?"

She shook her head and waggled a finger in the air. "No, that's not how we play this game." The melodic tone of her voice made my heart pound. "You ask a question, and I answer, and then you reciprocate. It's only fair."

I should tell her I didn't have time to play games. Instead, I found myself nodding. "What do you want to know?"

"What are you doing here? The last thing I heard about Tempest Crypt, she was safely behind bars, arrested by the angels after fleeing the crime scene covered in Toby's blood."

"There's some truth in that," I said. "I was arrested, but I'm innocent. My turn. Were you still friends with Toby even after you split up?"

Marianne shrugged, and her hand traced across her ample chest. "We kept in touch after our relationship ended. It wasn't always easy to remain friendly with Toby. He always looked out for himself, but I never wanted to sever ties with him."

"So, what—"

"Play the game, Tempest. My turn. How did you break out of Angel Force?"

I tilted my head. "I had a friend help me. She decided I was better able to clear my name if I wasn't stuck in a cell about to be charged with murder."

"Interesting. You have powerful friends."

"I do. As do you. You didn't come here alone, did you?"

"I'm here with my fellow succubi," Marianne said. "We've known each other for years and are close. My turn. Did you murder Toby Matlock?"

I shook my head. "I'm eighty percent sure that I didn't."

"Eighty percent?" Suki stared at me. "You think you might have done it?"

"My memory's blank. The evidence is convincing, but I can't be sure. I don't think I did it."

"But you did hate Toby," Marianne said. "I'd heard from him recently, and your name was mentioned. He said you were being difficult. He said he needed to deal with a significant problem before he was free to move on with the next adventure in his life."

I glowered at her. It sounded like Toby had badmouthed me to anyone who would listen. "I had good reason to dislike Toby. I didn't trust him."

"My sisters and I are undecided whether to congratulate you or kill you for your actions," Marianne said. "Our feelings about Toby are... complicated."

"Why would you like to do either?" My fingers flexed.

Marianne smirked. "Toby had a dark side."

"I know that," I said. "I've experienced it first-hand."

"How exciting. What did he do to you?"

"Used his mind manipulation magic."

She tilted her head. "And you aren't in his thrall?"

"That's a deeply disturbing idea. I'd never be under Toby's thrall."

"Then you're more exceptional than the feeble magic you currently possess suggests. People who are manipulated by Toby develop strong feelings of attachment. It happened to me and my sisters."

"You're not actually sisters," Wiggles said. "I've seen you all. You look totally different. Hot but different."

"Sisters in the sense that we're all succubi." Marianne smiled indulgently at Wiggles. "We share the same abilities. We've also experienced losing someone we loved deeply. We formed what we like to call the Widows Club. We remember the wonderful times we spent with Toby."

"That sounds like therapy," Wiggles said. "You must have found it distressing getting up close and personal with Toby Matlock."

Marianne's laugh sounded like silver bells tinkling in the wind. "Not at all distressing. Toby's a vigorous partner."

I placed a hand on my stomach. "Moving past Toby and how vigorous he was, tell us about his dark side. I understand he left you. I've also read the report you submitted that claimed he stole from you."

She arched a groomed eyebrow. "How would you have access to such confidential things?"

"I'm doing my own investigation on Toby."

The brightness faded from Marianne's face. "I confess I changed my story to ensure Toby wouldn't get in trouble. He did steal from me. My thoughts on that matter are muddled."

"What's made them muddled?"

She sighed. "My experience with Toby exposed me to his power. Sometimes, I believe that I gifted him that money, then I remember it's not true. Our relationship was complicated."

"He manipulated you?"

"Toby stole from me and from my sisters."

"Why would he need your money?"

"I care nothing for the money." Marianne waved a silver ring covered hand in the air. "I have plenty of that. Toby stole valuable magic artifacts. I'm a collector. I had a wonderful display of relics."

"What kind of relics?" Wiggles asked.

"Teeth. Desiccated skin. Bones. A few mummified limbs. I even have a head. All from powerful magic users. I have a room dedicated to them."

"Jeez, lady. Why not have a normal hobby, like crocheting or fire breathing, or even deep-sea diving. Why collect creepy old leftover bits from the dead?" Wiggles asked.

"Because those creepy leftover bits hold power." Marianne winked at me. "I returned home one evening, expecting to find Toby there. He'd gone, along with most of my magic items. He denied taking them, but I knew the truth. You see, Toby had a secret."

"What was his secret?" I took a step toward Marianne.

She smirked. "I want something in return for revealing his secret."

My eyes narrowed. "What do you want?"

"One kiss."

"From whom?" I glanced at the others. Suki shrugged at me, Fallon looked like she was half asleep, and Wiggles looked puzzled.

"Tempest Crypt, you are something of a beauty yourself. If I'd not known better, I would have mistaken you for a succubus." Her gaze drifted to my mouth. "That's my price. A kiss from you."

"I'll pass. I've got a boyfriend," I said. "He's very male. A real stud."

"I won't tell if you won't," Marianne said. "Unless you don't want to learn the truth about Toby?"

Marianne was gorgeous. I wasn't even going to try to deny that. I guess one kiss wouldn't be so bad.

"No funny business," I said. "Closed mouths only."

Marianne grinned. "Whatever is your preference. I've always been an admirer of the Crypt witches. When we entered the village, we were alarmed to learn that your family is engaged with a problem at the demon prison. Is it always so active?"

"It definitely isn't," I said. "Most of the time, we sit around munching sandwiches and playing cards. Would you know anything about Toby being interested in the prison?"

"Not a thing. He always had his fingers in lots of pies, though." Marianne beckoned me closer. "Are you ready to be kissed by a succubus?"

"I'll do it if you don't want to," Wiggles said. "I'm not averse to kissing humans. I should warn you, I use a lot of tongue."

Marianne placed a hand over her heart as she looked at Wiggles. "You are a charming little hellhound, but you're not my type. It's all the fur, you see. It would stick to my lip gloss."

Wiggles grunted. "I'm here if you change your mind."

She tickled him under the chin. Marianne's gaze met mine. Something predatory lurked beneath the surface of those sparkling eyes.

I swallowed, my nerves making my heart hammer. It was a kiss. It meant nothing. So why were my palms sweating?

I'd do this if it meant I could find out what Toby was up to. "Just one more thing. I—"

Marianne pressed a finger to my lips before yanking me toward her. "The time for talking is over." She tilted her head and pressed her full mouth to mine.

The room spun. The lights dimmed, angels sang, and my senses kicked into overdrive as Marianne's warm lips touched mine. A hundred images flashed through my mind. They were all of us together, smitten with each other, holding hands, taking romantic walks on the beach, living together, spending the rest of our lives in blissful harmony.

With a monumental amount of effort, I placed my hands on Marianne's shoulders and pulled away. I staggered back, staring at her in alarm.

She smiled at me. "Was that your first time with a succubus?"

"And my last," I gasped. "That's quite a kiss you've got there."

"A succubus shows you what you desire. And you have a lot of desires in you."

I shook my head. I didn't want any of that. Not with Marianne. "You got what you wanted. Now talk. Tell us about Toby's dark side."

Her fingers played against her lips before she nodded. "Toby was a black magic trader."

"I've sensed dark magic on him." I was careful not to look at Marianne's mouth. That kiss had felt indecent. I couldn't stop thinking about it. It was a trick, but it didn't stop my thoughts from scattering back to those images of us together.

She smiled as if she read my thoughts. "At first, he dabbled. But as many dark magic users discover, it tainted him and darkened his beliefs. Toby became dangerous and unstable after trading a tainted black magic artifact. It was an ancient spell book. The darkness infected him. He grew power-hungry and would stop at nothing to get his hands on what he desired."

"Is that why you changed your story with the angels?" I asked. "Toby was threatening you?"

She ducked her head. "I cared for him, but he threatened me and everyone I care about. I had no option but to tell the angels I'd gifted him the money. I made no mention of the magic artifacts. If I wanted to stay alive and ensure those I loved weren't harmed, I had to stay quiet."

"You didn't trust Toby, though. Is that why you and your sisters disappeared?"

"Once the case was closed, we retreated and cloaked ourselves from this world. It was safer for everybody. I still spoke to Toby from time to time. He demanded it of me, but that was all the interaction we had."

"I can tell you're powerful," I said. "You should have stood up to him. Between you and your succubus sisters, you must have been strong enough to destroy him."

Marianne shook her head as she pulled up the sleeve of her gown. Tattooed on the inside of her wrist was a small red and black serpent. "Toby gave this to me. It meant he always had a certain amount of control over me."

"Why didn't you get it removed?"

Her laugh sounded bitter as she pulled her sleeve down. "I tried everything to get rid of it. I even burned it off once. The next day, it was back. Toby could manipulate me using this mark. He said if I ever betrayed him, he would turn me into a weapon and make me annihilate everybody I cared about."

I'd always known Toby was a sleaze, but he'd just dropped to a new level of pond scum. "And now?"

"I no longer feel his influence. That's all because you killed Toby."

"And if I didn't kill him?" I asked. "Toby had one hell of a hold over you. He could basically use you as a puppet to do as he wished. He stole from you and threatened you and those you love. Those are great motives for murder."

Marianne smirked again. "I'll admit, every word you speak is the truth. It's complicated. Even though a part of me hated Toby, I still loved him. He had a way about him that you cannot break free from. Once you've experienced life with Toby Matlock, it's hard to be content with anybody else."

"It must be tough to wipe the images of that creepy little goatee beard swooping in for some smooching," Wiggles said.

Marianne giggled. "I've remained single for many years because I've never found another individual who lives up to Toby's standards."

"Standards that weren't true," I said. "Toby could have manipulated you into believing anything about him."

She tilted her head. "And again, you speak the truth."

I cleared my throat, uncomfortable under Marianne's intense gaze. "So, where were you when Toby was murdered?"

"With my succubus sisters. We've built ourselves a commune away from everybody else. It hovers between the magic and human communities. Nobody knows where we are. It kept us safe and away from temptation."

"And Toby left you alone?"

"For the most part. So long as we remained there, he didn't threaten us and rarely bothered us. We were living in a different realm when Toby was killed. My sisters will support my alibi."

I huffed out a sigh. "If you didn't do it, then who killed Toby Matlock?"

"If you want me to believe it wasn't you," Marianne said, "then I'd look at his brother, Nolan."

"Do you know Nolan well?"

"A little. He was often around when I was seeing Toby. They had a dreadful relationship. Nolan was particularly cruel to his brother."

"When I saw him, he admitted that they weren't close, but he admired his brother."

"Don't believe anything Nolan has to say," Marianne said. "He was always jealous of Toby's success. He wanted the same as Toby. The houses, the money, the women. And most of all, he wanted his mind manipulation ability. It's such a rare gift. Toby got fortunate; Nolan didn't. Not that he isn't a strong warlock, but nothing on Toby's level."

"Is Nolan having financial problems? He seems keen on getting his hands on Toby's assets."

"The houses are valuable, as is the money. I'm sure Nolan will be most interested in the magic artifacts. They were both power-hungry men, always greedy for more and never content. If you're looking for who will benefit the most now that Toby's dead, then it's Nolan. If you're claiming your innocence, then Nolan is the killer."

Feodor groaned. We were out of time. We had to get out before he alerted the angel outside or broke through his bindings and squashed us.

"We still haven't searched the rest of the house," Suki said.

"There's nothing here," Marianne said. "I've been browsing for a while. Toby hid nothing of value in these walls."

"We need to see Nolan, anyway," I said. "We have to find out if he's lying."

"I can guarantee that he is." Marianne sauntered over to Feodor and rolled him onto his back with her high-heeled boot. "I never did like Toby's butler."

"Play with him if you like." Marianne's alibi would be easy enough to check when I spoke to the other succubi. For now, she was in the clear, but I didn't trust her.

Marianne waved a hand at us. "The very best of luck with your search. I'll deal with this fellow. You go find yourself a killer."

"Thanks." The others hurried to the stone steps, but I paused at the bottom.

Marianne glanced at me and raised her eyebrows. "I know you don't want to leave my side. I have that effect on everybody."

I grunted as I raced up the stone steps. That kiss had made my head spin. I'd need to be careful around these succubi. A few more kisses like that, and I'd be forgetting all about my relationship with Rhett.

Chapter 14

"That's a nice color on you," Wiggles said as we raced to the back door.

I glanced at him. "What do you mean?"

"The hot red lipstick."

I swiped the back of my hand over my mouth. It came away smeared with Marianne's lip gloss. My cheeks flushed. "That was nothing."

"It looked like something to me," Wiggles said.

"I only did it to get the truth about Toby. It was worth it. We now know he was working on the dark side of magic. He stole magic items and sold them to the highest bidder. I bet the angels don't know anything about that."

"Are you going to tell them?" Suki asked as we reached the back door.

"Not yet," I said. "If I show my face, they'll take me down." I snuck open the back door and peeked out. The way was clear.

We hurried into the gloomy early morning light. We crept through the garden, keeping to the shadows as much as possible.

I poked my head around the side of the house. There was no angel by the front door. Whatever

Wiggles and Fallon had done to her, it had been effective.

"Let's go to the hotel and find Nolan," I whispered.

As we raced past the front door and away from the house, I noticed a new addition to Toby's stone dragon collection. He'd always had two dragons looming over visitors, but now a third sat there. It was smaller than the others, its claws stretching skyward as if trying to reach the stars.

I turned and raced away with the others. To get to the hotel, we needed to pass several houses and stores. I had no choice but to use my limited magic as a cover spell. I included Wiggles under the spell. If anyone saw him trotting along on his own, they might get suspicious.

Suki and Fallon tried to act nonchalant as they strolled along together, making out that it was completely normal to take a walk in the early hours of the morning.

When we got to the front door of the hotel, I stopped. "You two stay out here," I said to Fallon and Suki. "I'll go in with Wiggles. I know the owner. Tabitha often sleeps in the back room, so I'll need to sneak past and check the guest book to see where Nolan is. If you see an angel coming or anything suspicious, let us know."

"No worries," Fallon said. "We'll slay anybody who interferes."

"No slaying," I said. "Distract them. Stop them from coming in but make sure they leave alive."

"You're no fun," Fallon said.

"I'm already wanted for one murder," I said. "Let's not make it any more."

Fallon grumbled under her breath as she positioned herself by the door.

Suki patted my arm. "Don't worry, Tempest. I'll keep an eye on her. Fallon's still in training. She gets a bit enthusiastic over the killing side of her job."

That didn't reassure me. I headed into the hotel, keeping the cover spell in place. I tiptoed to the reception desk with Wiggles and peered at the guest check-in sheet.

I jumped as a loud snore echoed from the back room. Tabitha Dimples lay under a pile of blankets on her reclined easy chair.

I saw Nolan's room number and gestured for Wiggles to follow me. We hurried up the stairs to his room.

"How will you handle this?" Wiggles asked. "If it's any help, I've got a painful build-up of gas. We could gas him into talking."

"Hold on to the gas," I said. "It's never fun when you discharge in confined spaces. Hopefully, Nolan will be so shocked to see me that he'll talk."

I tried the door, but it was locked. I risked an unlock spell, and it worked. Even using just a basic cover spell and this unlock spell had made me feel tired. My borrowed magic wouldn't last for much longer.

We crept into the dark room. I eased the door shut. I could hear someone breathing deeply as if they were asleep.

I didn't have time to be delicate about this. I flicked on the overhead light and strode into the main room.

Nolan opened his eyes and blinked in surprise. He went to get out of bed.

I raised a hand. "Stay where you are. I don't want to know if you sleep in the nude."

"Tempest! What are you doing here? Did the angels let you go?" Nolan eased into a seated position, his eyes wide as he stared at me.

"In a manner of speaking, they did," I said. "I don't have much time. I'm looking for Toby's killer."

Nolan's eyes narrowed. "And you think you'll find him here?"

"You have a lot to gain from your brother's death," I said. "Where were you when he was murdered? You never did tell me."

His brow furrowed. "I don't have to answer to you. I've already told the angels everything I know. I'm looking at my brother's murderer."

"I've been framed."

"A likely story." Nolan shifted the pillows behind his head. "Everyone knows the rumors about the witch who hosts a demon. You have your own dark soul, Tempest Crypt. You're not as innocent as you make out to be."

"That's what I'm here for," I said, "to prove you wrong."

Nolan's hand shot out from under the covers. A fireball flew toward my head. I dived out of the way and hit the floor.

I heard a yell and a muffled thump.

"You move, and the gas goes off," Wiggles said.

I jumped to my feet to discover Wiggles had pinned Nolan to the bed. His butt was over Nolan's face.

"I'm primed and ready to go," Wiggles said. "You won't survive this gas attack."

I pressed my lips together to stop from smiling. Anyone who'd experienced Wiggles' gas problem would know not to move.

"Get this beast off me," Nolan spat.

"Answer the questions and you're free to go."

Nolan writhed under Wiggles. "I'm not afraid of this mutt."

"Hellhounds have their own unique scent. If you wish to experience it, keep on wriggling," I said.

Nolan gagged. "Good grief. What's he got inside him?"

"That was just a taster, my friend," Wiggles said.

Nolan slumped back on the bed. "Fine, I'll talk. Please, no more gas attacks."

"Someone's pointing the finger at you for Toby's murder," I said. "I want to know if there's any truth behind that."

"They're lying," Nolan growled out. "Let me guess. It's one of the succubi? They never liked me."

"It doesn't matter who it is," I said. "You'll benefit from Toby's death. You're likely to get all of his assets. Then there are the magic artifacts. Do you have plans for those?"

Nolan shifted in the bed. Wiggles pressed his butt closer to his face, and he stopped moving. "I have no idea what you're talking about. This has to be Marianne's work. She's such a bitter old succubus."

"You're not a fan of Marianne?"

"A long time ago I was. She was supposed to be mine," Nolan said. "I met her first. We went on several dates before I made the mistake of introducing her to Toby."

"You were jealous that your brother stole Marianne?"

"Why would I be jealous?" Nolan scowled. "Marianne's nothing special to me."

I recalled our kiss. "She has a certain allure."

"That's because she's a succubus. That stunning hair and striking figure is all a facade. Marianne's over three-hundred years old. Strip away her magic and you'll see what a wizened old crone she really is."

I felt queasy having just locked lips with her. "You're still jealous that your brother got his hands on the wizened old crone and you didn't?"

"She never loved him," Nolan said. "Toby got all the women because of his ability to manipulate them. Marianne only thought she was in love with him. It was the only way he could ever get a woman like her."

"Did Toby always manipulate the women he wanted?"

"He got whatever he desired," Nolan said. "If he asked a woman out and she turned him down, he shifted tactics. He'd find a way to manipulate her. Toby was sneaky and used his ability subtly. He'd try a gentle bit of manipulation so as not to spook them. As they became used to the feel of his magic, he grew bolder. He'd use it more frequently until eventually it became second nature to them."

Wiggles grunted. "I never trusted that warlock."

"Without his mind manipulation working through them, they felt like something was missing. They grew to love Toby, but it wasn't a natural love. Now, everyone he manipulated will be free. There will be many people feeling odd right about now. With my brother dead, his hold is gone. They won't understand what's going on."

"Everything you're saying gives you a great motive for wanting Toby dead," I said.

"Why bother when you did the job for me?"

"What if I didn't?" I asked. "Toby would never have suspected his brother of coming to kill him. He'd have let you into his house with no problem. You'd have had easy access to him."

"I wasn't in the village when Toby was killed. I got the call from the angels to let me know what had happened. Besides, I don't have Toby's manipulation skills. Toby didn't even allow family into the house unless we had an appointment. Have you met that nightmare of a butler?"

I thought briefly to Feodor trussed up in Toby's basement. "We've met a couple of times."

"He was doing Toby's bidding, the same as everyone else he manipulated. I'm different to Toby. If I want something, I have to work for it."

"Which must be frustrating," I said. "Were you frustrated enough to kill?"

"Why wait until now?" Nolan asked. "Toby's always been the same. Nothing's changed recently."

"Tell me more about his manipulation skills," I said. "Do they work better when he has an object that belongs to you?"

"That's right." Nolan shifted beneath Wiggles. "Is there any chance you can get this dog off me? He's uncomfortably warm."

"I'm sitting tight, buddy," Wiggles said. "You keep on talking."

Nolan sighed. "Toby's ability worked because he made a psychic connection with a person. He could do it from a distance, but the effects were minimal. Someone with a strong will could overcome his suggestions, particularly if they went against their moral code. Where his skill exceled was when he had a part of you."

"Like some hair?"

"Sure. Hair, eyelashes, fingernails. Something that was once joined to your body. He could make the link, and his influence would be much stronger. He also used to fashion objects and use them in the same manner, providing he could get the person to wear them."

"What kind of objects?"

"For women, it was always jewelry. Anything they'd wear all the time."

My eyes widened. That could be how Toby had such a strong influence over Aurora. He must have swapped her magic eraser pendant with a duplicate. Aurora rarely took her pendant off, but she occasionally had it cleaned and the magic recharged. Toby could have grabbed it and replaced it with one that he made himself.

"What about the tattoos on the succubi?" I asked him. "Do they have the same effect?"

"How do you know about those?"

"I've been asking around."

"They do," Nolan said. "That's not just ink. There's magic tattooed on their skin. Toby kept hold of the succubi in case they could serve him in some useful manner."

"That must have made them hate him."

"You'd imagine so, but they were always quick to say how amazing he was." Nolan squirmed on the bed. "Tempest, I'll admit to not being fond of my brother. He was deceitful and twisted. He was alive a long time and had lost his grip on the real world. He thought everybody owed him and he was entitled to take what he desired. He barely thought through the consequences of his actions. When you've been alive as long as he has, time doesn't matter. The whims of ordinary people are just an annoyance."

"Hold on, I figured your brother was old, but you're making him sound ancient. Exactly how old was Toby?"

"We're a long-lived race of warlocks. We also know how to use magic to extend our timeline. It's always been a Matlock talent, although I don't have that gift."

"How long has your brother been manipulating his own timeline?"

"Toby was three-hundred and seventy-eight when he died."

My head jerked back. "I'm surprised he hasn't been driven mad. Using that much magic to keep you alive—"

"Will warp your mind. It makes you deluded and believe you are godlike. Toby was becoming unstable. I'd had concerns about him for some time. I intended to speak to him about this issue, but it's too late. The problems he was causing by manipulating his own mortality are over. I say again, I respect you for being able to dispense with him."

"And I say to you again, it wasn't me." I rested my hands on my hips. "Since you claim to be innocent, and I didn't do it, you must have an idea who did."

Wiggles bounced on Nolan's chest. "We're running out of time. I'm about to blow."

Nolan scowled at Wiggles' butt. "Speak to the succubi. They're bitter over what Toby did. Despite what they say about being fond of him, they've wanted revenge for decades."

"They're not involved," I said. "Marianne said they were all together. They exist in some kind of temporal realm to stay out of Toby's way."

"So says Marianne," Nolan said. "Those succubi stick together like frogspawn. If you get one of them to crack, they'll all talk. They're loyal to each other, providing it serves them."

My brows lowered. "You're suggesting they're all involved in what happened to Toby?"

"If it wasn't you, then you're not looking for one killer; you're looking for three. And those three are very powerful, ancient magic users."

It was possible the succubi were covering for each other. Marianne called the others her sisters. My family would do anything to protect me. Maybe it was the same for the succubi.

"Tempest, I can't hold it in any longer," Wiggles said.

"Then stop trying." My gaze went to the door.

Nolan gagged as Wiggles finally gave up, and the room filled with his toxic excretion.

I clamped my fingers over my nose. "Let's go, Wiggles. The other two succubi are in the hotel. We need to talk to them."

And I needed to discover how deep the succubi bonds ran. What would they do to protect themselves?

Chapter 15

"What are we going to do about Nolan?" Wiggles asked once we were safely on the other side of Nolan's hotel room door. "As soon as he stops retching, he'll run to the angels and tell them where you are."

"Wait here a second." I used a cover spell as I hurried down the stairs and out of the hotel. "Fallon, I need you inside."

She jumped and grabbed her chest. "Tempest! I almost died of fright."

"I have to stay hidden. You need to guard a suspect," I said.

"I'm happy to guard anyone. Whoever it is, if they step out of line, I'll ensure they breathe their last breath."

"No! Just watch and make sure Nolan doesn't leave his room. You don't need to terminate him."

"If he attempts an exit, I shall cut him down with my blade, and cut out his—"

"No cutting out anything," I said. "If Nolan makes a run for it, convince him to stay in his room, but keep him alive. He's not in the clear yet."

Fallon saluted.

"Suki, any sign of trouble out here?" I asked.

"It's all quiet."

"Stay out here and keep watch. Let's move, Fallon." I hurried back through reception with Fallon and back up the stairs. I stationed her outside Nolan's door before I began my hunt for the remaining succubi with Wiggles.

The first two rooms we tried were empty. The third we had a success. I stood at the end of the bed looking at the blonde temptress splayed out on the pillows. She was as heart-stoppingly beautiful as Marianne.

I had to remember they were ancient, haggard crones under the magic. She wasn't beautiful or desirable. Nope, I didn't find this succubus as appealing as Marianne. No way.

I raised a small light ball over the bed and cleared my throat.

The succubus blinked her brilliant blue eyes open and gasped. She clutched the sheets over her chest. "I'll give you anything you want. Money, jewels, just take it. Don't hurt me."

"We're not here to hurt you." Wiggles trotted around the side of the bed. "Which sexy succubus are you?"

She stared at him, her mouth slightly open. "Olivia Dearhart. How do you know me?"

"I'm the one being accused of murdering your ex-boyfriend," I said.

"You're Tempest?" She blinked slowly. "My word! I'd scream for help, but I'm too scared. What do you want with me?"

"Cut the act," I said. "If you're anything like Marianne, there's nothing delicate about you."

Olivia's lips pursed before she smiled and shrugged. She reached over and flicked on the bedside lamp. "You can't blame a succubus for trying. It's amazing how people let down their defenses when they think you're some weak little thing. And who's this cute fur ball?" She ruffled Wiggles' head.

"Wiggles. Hellhound at your service."

"You're gorgeous." She tickled his tummy. "So, you broke out of the cell to see little old me?"

"I'm seeing everybody connected to Toby's murder," I said. "You and your sisters have an excellent motive for wanting him dead."

"Ah, so it would appear to an outsider. Toby always was a tricky one."

"He took your money and magic as well?"

"My, my. People have been flapping their lips." Olivia lifted Wiggles onto the bed, flipped him onto his back and rubbed his belly. "What if Toby did take my things?"

"You must have wanted revenge."

"I did for many years. I felt betrayed by my one true love."

"You must also have known that Toby was manipulating you. Do you have the same tattoo as Marianne?"

Olivia scowled. "Marianne's such a gossip. Although, she always did have a soft spot for raven haired beauties. How did you get her to tell you so much?"

"Tempest kissed her." Wiggles squirmed on his back as Olivia continued to pet him.

"Wiggles!" I hissed at him.

Olivia's eyes gleamed. "I can see why you'd appeal to her."

I shrugged. "The tattoos?"

Olivia lifted her wrist to show another snake tattoo. "The snake's power died along with Toby. It has no influence over us anymore."

"And where were you when Toby was killed?"

She smiled. "With my sisters. The first we knew about it was when we felt a simultaneous rush of relief. It was as if somebody had clicked their fingers and drawn a veil back from our eyes. We all realized that Toby had tricked us. My snake has always caused me problems. I could feel it shifting under my skin. The second Toby died, that stopped. I was free."

"What did Toby take from you?" I asked.

"I collect magic infused gems," Olivia said. "I fashion them into jewelry. Some are too powerful to be worn in public. They hold old magic. Toby always admired them. I acquired a particularly rare piece that he was fascinated by. In fact, he was so interested in it that I became suspicious. I decided to keep it separate from the rest of my collection and moved it into a safe. The next thing I discovered, Toby had vanished, the jewel was gone, and I was left alone and much poorer."

"You must have hated him for such a betrayal."

Olivia sighed as she stroked her fingers through Wiggles' fur. "I wish I did. But even with his influence gone, I still loved him."

"How can you love someone who cheated, lied to you, and stole from you? Toby Matlock wasn't all that special."

"We were together for years. Toby will always have a special place in my heart. You can love and hate a person at the same time. I sadly did. I was the most upset when I learned of his death. The other two, not so much. They'd had longer to get over their loss. I was the last true love of Toby's life. I'm sure he felt the same way about me."

I snorted. "He didn't act like he did."

Her eyes narrowed. "Toby promised to take care of me. I will always feel affection for him. Love is a hard thing to shake."

"You may have cared for Toby, but he'd moved on. I doubt he even remembered you."

"That's a lie," Olivia hissed. "When the time was right, he would have realized his mistake and returned to me. I had time to wait. I was in no hurry to force him back to me."

"No, you misunderstand me," I said. "Toby was about to marry my sister, Aurora."

Olivia's hands fell onto the bed, and her face paled. "Another lie."

"No, that's why I was investigating him. I didn't trust him. Aurora would never fall for a guy like Toby unless he coerced her."

Olivia bared her teeth. "I know about your sister and her involvement with Toby. He cared nothing for that little witch." The tone of her voice was pure bitterness.

"The marriage was going ahead. Despite everything I did, Aurora's head wouldn't be turned."

"Then you're as naïve is your sister," Olivia said. "Toby would never settle for such an average magic user. She meant nothing to him. She simply had something he wanted."

"He told you that?"

Wiggles coughed. "Anytime you want to start the belly rub again, I'm right here."

Olivia dragged her nails through Wiggles' fur. "You're a persistent little thing."

"I aim to please," Wiggles said.

"What did Toby tell you about Aurora?" I asked.

"He barely mentioned her. I became aware of their entanglement through another source. Of course, I was furious and demanded to know what was going on. Toby shrugged it off. He said it was a business transaction. Aurora had fallen passionately in love with him, and he was being careful not to reject her until they'd finished their business together. The wedding would never have happened. You killed Toby for no reason."

I didn't bother to correct her. "You said he wanted something that Aurora could give him. Was Toby interested in our demon prison?"

Olivia's mouth fell open before she snapped her jaw shut and laughed. "Of course! I wondered what Toby's focus was. He'd been working on a project for months, amassing magic items and wealth, but it was never enough. He always wanted more. I assumed he'd simply become reckless. Sometimes, people with power simply want more power. But it makes sense now. A demon prison and the inhabitants in it are a valuable resource."

I sucked in a breath. "So, it's possible Toby wanted access to the demons in the prison. Did he get paid to break out a specific demon?"

"He'd never take on a small job like that," Olivia said. "Toby wouldn't even break a sweat cracking open the prison."

"He might," I said. "My family is harder to get around than you would imagine."

"And yet he so easily influenced your sister into wanting to marry him."

My fingers flexed. "I didn't say we were infallible. If he went up against us all, he wouldn't stand a chance. We'd never let Toby near the prison."

Olivia shook her head. "He is something else. Toby wants your demons. He's always believed he can control anyone and anything, no matter how powerful. If he owns a piece of them, he thinks he can manipulate them for life."

My heart stuttered. Had Toby been insane enough to believe he could control every demon in the prison? "That's not possible. We're talking about thousands of demons. The demons would have killed him if he'd managed to get the prison open."

"Toby wouldn't have considered it impossible," Olivia said. "He'd mastered his craft and amassed huge amounts of magic that he surrounded himself with. Have you been inside his house?" She laughed. "Of course, you have. That's where he died."

"I never noticed anything odd about the place."

"That's because he's crafty. Toby placed magic infused items everywhere. Some of them might look like antiques or vases, objects you'd expect to see. He activated the magic within them. When you step inside Toby's house, you're walking into a giant magic trap of his making. You wouldn't stand a chance against him inside that house. You're lucky to be alive, Tempest. You're only alive because he decided that's the way things should be."

"My gratitude is endless." I leaned against the wall. "But something went wrong with Toby. The dark magic got the upper hand."

Olivia tutted. "Naturally. No matter how powerful you are, you mess with the wrong kind of magic and it addles your brain. He may already have attempted to open the prison and failed. So, he moved to his Plan B and found a weak link in the Crypt witch coven. That must be why he wanted your sister in his life. Could she have given Toby access to the prison?"

"Aurora knows how to get inside, but she'd never share that with Toby." I tried to sound convincing, but I wasn't fooling myself. Aurora was besotted with Toby. Nothing was ever too much trouble.

"He'd have convinced her to do anything. She wouldn't have considered it strange if he asked to see the prison. For all you know, she might have taken him inside and shown him the delightful demons waiting for him." She laughed again. "Who'd have thought it? He really was quite mad."

My head pounded at the possibility of an insane Toby Matlock trying to control an army of demons.

"It's a shame he didn't get to carry out his life's ambition," Olivia said. "He would have been quite something, leading an army of dangerous, unstable demons. He could have taken over the world."

"Luckily for us, he's dead," I said. "He's not going to become master of the demons any time soon."

"This is true," Olivia said. "And it gives you a great motive for killing him. Not only was he mistreating your little sister, but he was threatening your family's work. He wanted to crack open a prison that's supposed to be impenetrable. If I were the angels, I'd be looking straight at you as the killer."

I crossed my arms over my chest. "The more I learn about Toby, the more convinced I am that there are others who wanted him dead more than I did. You don't try to amass a demon army without coming to the attention of unpleasant individuals. There are demons on the loose who won't appreciate the idea of a warlock in control of such an army. Maybe one of them learned of Toby's intention and slipped into Willow Tree Falls to deal with him."

"And the great demon hunter, Tempest Crypt, didn't notice when a dangerous demon entered her village and assassinated a resident?" Olivia shook her head. "If that is the case, then I'm disappointed in you."

She was right. I'd know if there was a demon skulking around the village.

"If you're pleading innocence, and I know it wasn't me, who would you point the finger at for killing Toby?" I asked.

Olivia's smile slipped. "It's obvious. If you didn't kill him, then I know exactly who murdered my Toby."

I took a step toward the bed. "You want to share their name with me?"

"You already know her. His charming fiancée killed him. Your sister, Aurora, found out the truth about what Toby was intending to do and stopped him."

My gut clenched, and I hesitated before leaping to Aurora's defense. Even if she was involved in what happened to Toby, I wouldn't let her take the blame. If she had killed him, she must have been desperate or acting in self-defense. When she was found, and I learned the truth, whatever that was, she wouldn't go to prison.

"Don't go putting that idea into the angels' heads," I snarled.

"You don't like the idea that your innocent little sister is a cold-blooded killer?" Olivia grinned. "We all have secrets, Tempest. Perhaps your sister isn't as good as she claims to be."

"For someone who claims not to know much about Aurora, you have a strong opinion about her." I stepped closer. "Or perhaps, you're jealous. Did you see my sister and Toby together and realize that he'd forgotten about you? Did you do something about that?"

Olivia hissed out an angry breath. "You know nothing about my relationship with Toby. What we had was special and unique. We were like the Romeo and Juliet of the magic community."

"You mean, both dead?"

"I mean, hopelessly devoted to each other. Finding love against the odds. Not seeing anybody else as worthy of our love."

Olivia sounded dangerously deluded. "You talk like you're still in a relationship with Toby. He must have ditched you years ago."

"Our love is eternal." Olivia's lips pursed. "Even though he pretended otherwise, I knew the truth."

"Either that, or you need to get out more," I said. "Find yourself a new guy. It might distract you from focusing on somebody you can't have. Someone who didn't want you."

Her lips thinned. She grabbed Wiggles and yanked him to her chest, wrapping one arm around his belly and another around his throat. "If you want this disgusting thing to live, you'll leave now."

My eyes narrowed. "Get your hands off my hellhound."

Olivia growled at me. "Watch your step, Tempest, or you'll lose someone you love, as well. Aurora's already missing. Are you prepared to risk this little beast's life?"

Wiggles yelped as Olivia's hand tightened around his throat.

"Keep quiet, mutt."

I grimaced as Olivia's beauty slipped, and I saw the withered hag behind her mask. There was nothing beautiful about her true form. Her skin was parchment thin and stretched over prominent bones. Her large eyes were set deep in her head, a crazed glint in them. This was a succubus on the edge of control. Had Toby pushed her over the edge? Had Olivia decided she could no longer have him around if she couldn't have him all to herself?

My gaze didn't leave Wiggles as he continued to squirm in her iron-tight grasp. "Let him go."

"I'll let him go once you contact the angels and turn yourself in," Olivia said. "Until then, I'm keeping him as collateral. Go back to the angels, confess what you've done, and you can have this foul-smelling beast back."

"You're squeezing me way too tight, lady," Wiggles squeaked. "We barely know each other."

"Be quiet, or I'll—" Olivia jerked away, dropping her hold on Wiggles. "Eurgh! What have you done?"

The rotten smell hit me a second later. I pinched my mouth and nose together. More of Wiggles' gas had discharged, turning the room into a toxic zone of nasal depravity.

My eyes watered as I caught hold of him, and we backed toward the door.

"You're not getting away." Olivia choked on the stench.

"That'll teach you to squeeze a hellhound with a mildly irritable bowel," Wiggles said, his front paws draped over my arm.

Olivia conjured a fireball and raised it over her head, one hand covering her mouth.

My eyes widened as I turned and ran to the door with Wiggles. Fire and gas were never good friends.

I heard the fireball discharge and threw myself on the floor on top of Wiggles. There was a blinding flash of light, and heat washed over me.

After a few seconds, I lifted my head. The walls were blackened with smoke, and the curtains smoldered.

Wiggles wriggled out from underneath me. "Hold on. You're on fire." He jumped on my back, extinguishing the flames in my hair.

"Thanks!" I rolled over, and he jumped off me.

A growl sounded from the bed. I clambered to my feet and peeked around the corner. Olivia lay flat on the bed, a charred version of her former self. Her eyes met mine, and she scowled.

"Are you feeling better now?" I asked. "It feels good to let off steam now and again."

She sucked in several breaths before slowly sitting upright. I could already see her injuries healing. Her magic was powerful. As her hair slowly restored to its luxurious former glory, she shook her head, and a sharp smile crossed her face. "I do have a hothead. Toby always said my temper was fiery."

"Quite literally," I said.

She chuckled, all signs of her anger gone. This was one crazy succubus. "You have an impressive weapon, Wiggles. You bested me."

"My gas is the stuff of legends," Wiggles said. "Squeeze me at your peril."

"Lesson learned," Olivia said. She was already almost back to her former beautiful self.

"Did I touch a nerve?" I asked, ready to race for the door if she started throwing more fireballs.

Olivia smoothed her hands over her glossy hair and sighed. "I will admit to being a little jealous of your sister for taking Toby's attention. I harbored a hope that he only wanted me. He was an exceedingly charming man, who could have any woman he wanted."

"Not always willingly," I said. "Toby's mind manipulation had gotten out of hand."

"Even without that ability, he had a way to charm a person. He charmed me the first time we met. I'll never forget it." Olivia sighed again. "Perhaps your sister isn't involved in this. Perhaps you aren't either. That's for the angels to decide. They seem to be looking very closely at your family, though."

"It won't be the first time the angels have made a mistake," I said. "This time, they definitely have."

"If that is so, I wish you luck in your pursuit to find the killer. I won't give up my belief that it was Aurora who killed my Toby. You are welcome to prove me wrong."

"It'll help if I can speak to the final succubus," I said. "Where's Ava?"

"Ah, you might like to tread carefully with her. She runs even hotter than I do."

"I'll take my chances," I said. I also didn't have any other option but to question her to see if their stories tallied.

"She's in the next room. Be careful. She blames you for all of this."

"Oh, goody." We left Olivia recovering from her fiery encounter and headed back out into the corridor.

"Is everything good with you, Fallon?" I whispered. "Nolan hasn't tried to escape?"

"The scoundrel crept the door open at one point. I blasted him with a special fire cracker I found tucked in my pocket. He shot back in the room,"

Fallon said. "Do you wish for me to cut out his heart for such unscrupulous behavior?"

"No, he can keep his heart for now. Just stop him from going anywhere. We've got one more person to speak to and then we're out of here."

"I am yours to command. I'm keeping a tally of all the pony rides I shall get when this is finished."

"None." Wiggles glared at Fallon. "You get exactly none."

"Come on." I headed to the next room and used an unlocking spell to creep inside.

That was two unstable succubi confronted and one to go. And this one already hated me. This should be fun.

Chapter 16

We stopped on the other side of the hotel room door. A light was on in the bedroom.

I crept forward with Wiggles by my side. A gorgeous brunette with waist length hair sat up in bed with a book resting on her knees. She wore a black silken lace negligee, still had a full face of makeup on, and her bronzed skin shimmered as if it had been oiled.

This time, I wasn't buying how incredible she looked. Having seen the real Olivia, the succubi didn't seem so appealing.

Her huge, dark almond-shaped eyes met mine, and she gasped. "You!"

"Surprise! You know who I am?"

"My lover's killer." The book slid from Ava's knees, and she scowled at me. "How dare you come in here?"

"I'm desperate. I'm also here to prove my innocence."

"The angels have released you?" Her button nose crinkled. "They're idiots. The evidence against you is overwhelming."

"And how would you know that?"

She snorted delicately. "My darling Toby, annihilated by a dark witch with an attitude problem."

"Since we've never met, you're quick to draw assumptions," I said, "unless we have met before."

Ava glowered at me. "I've never met you."

"But you know me."

"By reputation only. All of it bad." Her sour gaze ran over me. "Who have the angels arrested if they believe you to be innocent?"

"Let's just say I'm out on a temporary license," I said. "The angels don't strictly know where I am."

"Ha! You've escaped the angels. They will be delighted to know that you are here." She reached to the bedside cabinet where a snow globe sat.

Wiggles raced over and knocked the globe to the floor. "Not so fast, cutie. We've got questions for you."

Her nose wrinkled again. "You stink! You need a bath."

Wiggles sniffed her foot and poked his tongue out. "And you need to stop bathing in perfume."

"This is my natural scent," Ava said. "All succubi smell as delicious as I do."

"Yes, everyone knows how gorgeous succubi are." I clicked my fingers to get her attention. "I wouldn't have escaped the angels if I didn't have something to prove."

"You mean your innocence?" Ava smirked. "You must be deluded if you think you didn't kill Toby."

"Then I'm deluded, because somebody else did. Why don't you tell me where you were when Toby was murdered?" I knew what her answer would be.

The succubi were covering for each other, but with limited resources, it was impossible to check if they told the truth about their whereabouts at the time of Toby's murder.

"The other succubi will confirm that I was with them," Ava said. "Our temporal realm has been our home for years. We live there peacefully. We have little interaction with the outside world and other communities. It's safer that way. Toby didn't like us talking to other people. He said we gossiped too much." She smiled and stroked a hand down her silken negligee.

"What did Toby take from you?" I asked. "I know from your succubus sisters that he took their magic items."

"What if he did? Toby may take whatever he desires from me," Ava said. "I willingly gave him everything he wanted."

I shook my head in disbelief. Even after everything Toby had done to these women, they still defended him. Even though Toby was a sleazy, wizened warlock, they wanted him to themselves. If he was still alive and declared his love for just one of them, they'd reunite with him in an instant. That was their weakness. I could use that to my advantage.

"I knew Toby well," I said. "I'm sure you're aware of his relationship with my sister."

Ava shrugged, and her features hardened. "Of course. I'm always aware of Toby's movements."

"Because of your matching tattoos?"

She rubbed the pad of her thumb over her wrist. "That's correct."

"Although Toby seemed fond of Aurora, he did mention your name. I got the impression you still had a place in his heart."

Her head whipped up. "He spoke of me to you? What did he say?"

I kept my expression neutral. "He talked of a former love whom he thought of fondly. He wondered if he was making the right decision by marrying my sister. Toby wanted the best for everybody and wasn't sure if he was committed to the marriage."

Ava's expression lit up, making her even more beautiful. "I always knew, deep in his heart, he had love only for me. He promised that he cared for me more than the others. He used to bring me little gifts and surprises. I'm certain he didn't do that for any of his other women. I was always the most important to him. I always knew that."

"Your relationship must have been intense."

"It was wonderful." Her large eyes glittered. "What else did Toby say about me?"

"He was looking for a way to reunite with you without upsetting the others," I said. "It sounds as if you and your succubus sisters are close. If you live together, that would have been difficult."

She waved a hand in the air. "They'd have been fine without me. They would still have each other. But I would have had Toby. Imagine how happy we would have been. We could have been free to show our love in public. No more sneaking around."

"Toby didn't like anybody to know about your relationship?"

"Toby was an influential man. He couldn't be seen burdened with an exclusive relationship. It would have crushed the hopes of other women who must fantasize about having such an amazing man in their life."

"It's hard to believe." I amazed myself by keeping the sarcasm out of my voice.

Ava's eyes narrowed. "Did you kill Toby for your sister? Did she ask you to destroy him because he was going to leave her for me?"

"No, nothing like that," I said. "We all wanted what was best for Toby. If he wasn't going to be happy in a marriage to Aurora, then I would have told him to leave her and be with you."

Ava smiled, and it felt like the whole room brightened. The smile faded as quickly as it had arrived. "But something went wrong. Did you fall for his charms? Did you make an advance on Toby and he rejected you? Is that why you killed him?"

"For the love of... no! I didn't do it." My attempts at deception were wearing thin. How long could I make believe that I thought Toby was a living dreamboat? Well, a dead dreamboat, now. "I'd like to find out who did."

"Give me your hand," Ava said.

I clasped my hands behind my back. "What for?"

"I can sense when a person is being honest," Ava said. "I need to touch you to see if you're telling the truth about murdering my love."

"So long as that's all you want to know." My heart sped up. If she was telling the truth, that would mean my innocence would be revealed. I could use this with the angels, buy myself time, and maybe not end up back in a cell.

"Come, come. I imagine you don't have long before you're discovered. If you've escaped the angels' imprisonment, they'll be looking for you. Let me help you." She tilted her head to one side and smiled.

I extended my hand. Ava wrapped her warm, soft fingers around mine. She closed her eyes and tilted her head back, exposing her long slim neck. Despite my best efforts, I had to admit she was probably the most beautiful out of the succubi.

"Ah, you're not immune to my charms." A smile traced through Ava's words.

"You're not horrible to look at."

"That is very true. I'm the succubus who attracts the most attention out of the three of us. I bear the burden well."

"Lucky you." I kept my gaze fixed on the wall and not on her beautiful face.

"How interesting. You believe you are innocent. I'm sensing confusion as to what happened that night with Toby, but you really believe you didn't kill him."

I swallowed. "Can you see what happened? Can you see how I got in Toby's house that night?"

"No, my powers don't extend that far. I'm not able to shift through a person's memories and experience actual events in their lives. I simply sense emotions and the truths and lies behind a person's words. From what I'm feeling from you, you're not sure. Your beliefs flash to total innocence one moment to guilt and confusion the next." Ava opened her eyes and glared at me. "There's a part of you that wishes you had killed Toby. Why wish death on such a wondrous creature?"

I was done talking up Toby Matlock. "There was nothing wondrous about him. Toby was a cheat and a liar. He manipulated my sister and changed her. He weakened her and used his magic against her. He used it on me. Toby's not to be trusted. How can any of you have loved him?"

Ava's grip tightened on my hand, and she yanked me closer. "You do not know Toby. You speak of a stranger. Toby was never like that. He was honest, compassionate, and wonderful."

"He stole money and magic from you," I said. "He dumped you on your butt and left you after he'd gotten what he wanted. That's the opposite of what you've just described."

With a snarl, Ava pulled me off my feet. I rolled onto the bed with a startled gasp.

She dropped her weight on me and pinned me down, her arm resting across my throat. "Maybe you're just good at hiding the truth. You did kill Toby. You lured him into a false friendship, fell in love with him, and when he rejected you, you snapped. You're a twisted, dark, evil witch. That demon inside you has ruined you."

I choked as her arm cut off my air supply. I struggled beneath her, but Ava was supernaturally strong, and I could barely move.

"Look into my eyes," Ava said.

I blinked up at her, and the world took on a softer glow. All I could see was Ava. Her beauty surrounded me. Her scent invited me closer. I sniffed some hair that had fallen down around my face. Why was I fighting her? I would do anything she wanted me to. She was perfection. She was—

"Ouch!" A sharp pain shot through my calf.

The magic Ava had been weaving over me broke as Wiggles' teeth sank into my leg.

Ava glared at Wiggles. "Back off, mutt."

Wiggles glared back and bit me harder.

"Holy demons and angels!" I winced but was grateful that the bite had shattered the illusion. "You succubi never stop trying to enchant with your silky hair, and amazing smell, and big, beautiful eyes."

Wiggles growled and shook my leg.

"Jeez, Wiggles, I get it. If you keep going, I'll lose the leg." I felt blood ooze through my pants. "I'm not in love with the succubus."

Ava smirked at me. "All you have to do is keep looking at me and your problems will be over. I'll make your death a happy one. You'll be thrilled to die at my hand. You will beg for me to end your life."

"There's not a chance of that." I bucked underneath her and got one hand free. I pressed it to her side and used a blast spell, having no idea how effective it would be.

Ava shrieked and rolled off me.

I gasped in air and rubbed my sore neck. "Wiggles! You can let go now."

Wiggles dropped his hold on my leg and jumped on the bed. "I tried biting her, but she didn't seem to feel it. It was like trying to chew through an old cow hide. Exactly how old is this hot chick?"

"Probably a few hundred years old." I looked at the puncture marks in my pants and felt my leg throb unhappily.

Ava sat on the floor, rubbing her injured side, her shoulders slumped. "Get out of here, killer. I'm done with you."

I rolled off the bed and backed away from her. "I'm happy to oblige. And just so you know, I'll keep looking for Toby's killer. It's not me or Aurora."

"Liar!"

"You saw inside my head. You know I'm innocent."

"I know that your mind is a mess. I'm also aware that your magic is broken. You're living on borrowed magic, and you have no clue what to do next."

Ava had me spot on. "I might be a mess, but that doesn't mean I'm giving up."

"You'd better run," Ava snarled. "We're coming for you. My sisters and I won't stop until you're defeated. You hurt Toby, and you'll pay for that."

This succubus was as unstable as Olivia. The air in the room filled with tension, and I felt the now familiar prod of Ava's magic approach.

I grabbed Wiggles. It was time to leave. I raced out of the hotel room and slammed the door shut. Something heavy thumped against the door, and I jumped away.

Fallon stood to attention. "I heard yelling. Does someone need slaying?"

"Not yet, but Ava's pushing her luck. Let's get out of here," I said.

We collected Suki from outside the hotel and made our way swiftly back to the forest.

I wasn't convinced of their innocence. Each succubus carried an air of instability and a hefty dose of manic jealousy. I also couldn't be certain that they weren't covering for each other. What if Nolan was right, and they were all in on this? I couldn't blame them if they were. If he'd messed me around like that, I'd want his heart on a stick.

There had to be away to figure out if they were telling the truth. I had to get them to slip up, but I couldn't figure out how to do that. They were close to each other and had closed ranks, but were they close enough to keep their silence if any of them made a mistake? I wasn't sure. All three of them simmered with jealousy and an unhealthy obsession with Toby. That I could use.

"Were your meetings with the succubi useful?" Suki asked, as we reached the forest edge.

"Partly. I'm not sure of their innocence. We need to decide on our next move before the angels find me." Because, when they did, I'd be too late. My chance to prove my innocence would be gone, and all the other suspects would escape.

Time wasn't on our side, but I'd keep fighting until the very last second.

Chapter 17

I'd managed a couple of hours of restless sleep, lying on the hard ground in the cave beside the fire.

Suki hurried in, carrying a sack, as I blinked my bleary eyes at her. "I thought we'd need something to eat."

I could have kissed her as she produced croissants, takeout coffee, muffins in all different flavors, and a huge tub of fruit salad.

We all ignored the fruit salad as we grabbed for the muffins and croissants.

"Thanks, Suki," I said around a mouthful of chocolate chip muffin.

"I had to be careful," Suki said as she settled on the ground with her own pile of food. "I got these from Sprinkles. Patti was suspicious as to why I was ordering so much for myself."

"You didn't tell her anything, did you?"

"Of course not! I said it was for the rest of the staff at Cloven Hoof."

I nodded. I trusted Patti. Even if she thought Suki was involved with helping me, she wouldn't mention it to the angels. Still, we needed to be careful. If the angels weren't already looking for me, they soon would be.

"What's our next move?" Wiggles asked, his muzzle covered in croissant crumbs.

"It's hard to rule anyone out without being able to check alibis," I said. "Nolan claimed to have been somewhere else at the time of the murder, but he could be lying. Although Dazielle thinks he's innocent."

"He had excellent motives for wanting his brother dead," Wiggles said.

I nodded. "And then there are the three succubi."

"Who you're completely in love with," Wiggles said. "You've made out with them all."

"One! I kissed one. It wasn't a make-out session."

"You rolled around on the bed with Ava."

"I was pinned to the bed and almost crushed to death by Ava. There's a difference." I glanced at Suki and Fallon. "It was their magic. It made me feel weird around them. Wiggles was no better. He fell for Olivia when she started rubbing his belly."

"Why not? Those nails of hers were amazing. They got right through the fur and gave my skin a good exfoliation. She'll have hellhound flakes beneath those nails for weeks."

I wrinkled my nose. "Anyway, it could have been them, either working together or one of them broke from the pack and decided she had to kill Toby. If she couldn't have him, none of them could."

"Do any of the succubi strike you as unstable?" Suki asked.

"Possibly Ava," I said. "Her mood change was unnerving."

"I'm going for Olivia," Wiggles said. "She choked me."

"She does have a murderous streak about her," I said.

"Who do they think did it?" Fallon asked me.

"Ava blames me. Olivia blames Aurora, and Nolan pointed the finger at all the succubi. Everyone's deflecting attention from themselves."

"Could they all be in on it?" Suki asked.

"I doubt Nolan would work with the succubi. He has a huge chip on his shoulder about Marianne. She picked Toby over him, and he's never gotten over it."

"Which means that Nolan gets an extra tick in the box for being the killer." Wiggles grabbed the last muffin. "He lost the woman he wanted to Toby. Nolan got his revenge and plans to win the girl back."

"His alibi must be solid enough for the angels," I said. "They'd have checked his along with the succubi. If the angels were suspicious about any of the suspects, wouldn't they be asking more questions?"

"You are talking about the angels of Willow Tree Falls?" Fallon asked. "Those beautiful but stupid creatures, who leave feathers wherever they go?"

I shrugged. "You could be right. With their attention fixed on me, they probably haven't done anything more than ask the basic questions. Surely they'd have checked where the other potential murderers were at the time of Toby's death."

"I refer you back to my first point," Fallon said.

I nodded. "We have to consider them all suspects. They all have something to gain, and they're all powerful."

"Do you have a feeling about any of them?" Suki asked.

"I'm leaning toward Nolan," I said. "The succubi each have a snake tattoo on their wrists. Marianne said that gave Toby influence over them. If any of them had tried to attack him, he'd have used that against them. Maybe having that tattoo prevented them from harming Toby. He must have realized that they'd want revenge if they came to their senses about him."

"What if they all attacked at once?" Fallon said. "A coordinated, lethal strike by three powerful beauties. He might have prevented one of them, but all three succubi going at him? That could have been too much. They could have laid a trap and ensnared him."

"It would be helpful to see Toby's body," I said. "When I woke up next to him, I didn't have a chance to study his injuries in detail. I couldn't tell you if he was attacked from the back as well as the front. Maybe they worked together, like a pack of wolves, to take him down."

"I'd have loved to have seen that," Wiggles said.

"Me too," Fallon said.

I tensed at the sound of footsteps outside the cave. Rhett rushed in, his dark hair windswept and his eyes tired.

I jumped up. "Is there any news on Aurora?"

He caught hold of me and kissed my cheek. "Nothing yet, but we haven't stopped looking."

"And the demon prison?"

He guided me back to the fire and sat next to me. "Everything's back under your family's control. It was an impressive battle. I saw some of it. Your family and the angels worked well together. Although, I noticed Dottie misdirecting a few spells that kept hitting the angels. There are plenty of scorched feathers."

I chuckled. "Granny Dottie's spells never misfire."

Rhett grinned. "That's what I thought."

"Is everyone okay?" I asked. "No one got injured?"

"Everyone survived just fine. No one in your family is hurt. They're still at the cemetery, worried it might only be a temporary reprieve and the demons are gathering their strength for another escape attempt."

I groaned. "I wish I could be there."

"They want you to focus on clearing your name. How are you getting on?"

"I got around to all the suspects last night," I said. "No one's ruled out just yet."

Rhett frowned and scrubbed a hand over his stubbled chin. "Then you're running out of time. The demon prison is stable, so the angels aren't needed anymore. That's why I raced back here. Dazielle was rounding up everyone, and they're heading back to Angel Force. They'll soon find out you're no longer in your cell."

My stomach clenched. I was almost out of time, and there were so many more questions I needed to ask.

"We need to move. Rhett, can you watch the succubi? They're all at the hotel."

"Not a problem," Rhett said. "I'll keep the rest of the gang looking for Aurora while I stake out the hotel. What do you want me to do if I see them make a move?"

"Just follow them," I said. "Don't let them know you're watching. Those women are... well, let's just say they have influence over everybody. Don't be fooled by their beauty."

He grinned as he wrapped an arm around my shoulders. "Are you worried I might be tempted by a gorgeous succubus?"

I shrugged. "I was."

Rhett raised his eyebrows as he chuckled. "Then I'll be sure to keep my distance."

"I need to take another shot at Nolan. He's got the most to gain. It would have been easy for him to get to Toby without raising any suspicion. The succubi, not so much."

"You need to be careful out there," Rhett said. "The angels will be everywhere when they know you've escaped. Dazielle cursed your name several times while fighting the demons. She's convinced of your guilt."

"She can be as convinced as she likes. I've got to keep looking for the real killer."

Fallon brushed crumbs from her fingers and stood. She cleared her throat and puffed out her chest. "I have a cunning plan. You need a disguise. A way you can move around the village without attracting the attention of the angels."

I arched an eyebrow. "What kind of disguise are you talking about? With the limited magic I have, I can't change my appearance, not for long."

Wiggles cocked his head as he stood next to Fallon. "That's not a terrible idea. We can transform you to a certain degree without using magic. You look pretty hot when you make the effort."

Rhett laughed. "Tempest always looks hot. Even when she's covered in demon goo."

Fallon rubbed her hands together. "I don't find Tempest appealing. She's too tall and lanky, but we can make the most of her physical attributes. Magic will do the rest."

I shook my head. "I don't have that kind of power. What I have is borrowed, and it won't last for much longer."

"We have power," Fallon said. "Although I'm not adept in witchcraft, Wiggles has magic, as does your leather clad lothario. They'll share. And, if you're able to, you may borrow some of my ability. I should warn you, though, my magic comes with a little spice."

"And mine," Suki said. "We have different magic abilities, but they're not so different. You might be able to borrow some of my strength if that will help."

I looked around the group and saw the determination in their eyes. "I'm still not certain what you want to transform me into."

"It's simple," Fallon said. "We disguise you as a succubus."

My jaw dropped. "There's no way I can pull that off. Have you seen them? They're out of this world gorgeous."

Rhett laughed again. "You've taken quite a shine to these women. I can't wait to meet them."

I glared at him. "Like I said, keep your distance. They're not to be trusted. Don't look in their eyes and don't let them touch you."

His grin broadened. "I won't disobey your orders."

I stared at Fallon. "I can't be a succubus."

"You can. I have access to makeup and fancy heels. That will help."

"What do you have those for?" I asked. There wasn't much call for stilettos when you lived in a forest.

"I didn't say I own them." She waggled her eyebrows. "I just know how to get some."

"I reckon you can pull off Marianne's look," Wiggles said. "Although, you're paler than her, you've got the same dark hair. We'll need to add some curves and a ton of makeup."

"That's not me." I shook my head.

"What other options are there?" Fallon asked. "Now that the angels are coming for you, you need to stay hidden. Why not use a disguise? You go out looking like this succubus and you might be able to trick Nolan into spilling the beans."

My mouth twisted to the side. It was a long shot, but it had possibilities, and it would confirm whether Nolan was working with the succubi. If I turned up looking like Marianne, his lost love, and talked about what had happened to Toby, he might confess something.

"There's one big problem," Wiggles said.

"Only one?" I asked.

"You have no idea how to be sexy."

Rhett chuckled. "That's not entirely true."

I gritted my teeth. Wiggles was right. I did a terrible job of being sexy. Launch a demon at me, and I was fine. Give me a fitted dress and heels, and I fell apart.

Rhett leaned over, his mouth by my ear. "You can do this. You can be as sexy as you like."

I looked into his eyes and nodded. "I guess I'm pulling out the sexy card."

"You have to," Wiggles said. "There's no other option. Now, all you need is a crash course in sexy."

Fallon clapped her hands. "Leave that to me. I'll grab us some makeup and heels, and we'll get started."

I groaned. What had I let myself in for?

Chapter 18

"Wiggle your hips more." Fallon stood behind me, her gaze critical as it ran over me.

I turned slowly and stalked back to her. The dress I wore made it hard to take long steps, and the heels made me feel like I'd lose my balance and break an ankle at any second.

"That's as good as it gets." I was also not used to my new magically enhanced figure. I ran my hands over my waist and hips. We'd been working on my new appearance for hours.

"Maybe you need more of our abilities." Fallon tilted her head. "You need all the help you can get."

"I'm not taking any more from you," I said. All four of them had donated some power to help me maintain my magic disguise. Suki and Fallon's magic had felt weird as it had seeped over me. It smelt like earth and grass with just a hint of warmth to it. When Rhett's power had filled me, it felt jagged and a little dangerous. Wiggles just smelt of sulfur, and his magic had felt hot like Frank's energy.

I stumbled in my heels. Sadly, they weren't made of magic. They were very real and very painful. I still had no clue where Fallon had magicked them up from, along with the makeup caked on my face.

I thought about Frank briefly. There was still no sign of him returning to pester me. I should feel relief that he'd gone. Having my magic drained must have taken him. It would take a while to get used to being on my own with no demon inside me.

"Go again," Fallon said. "You have to live sexy. Think sexy. Be sexy. Less stomp, more sex appeal."

I sighed and turned, deliberately swinging my new curvy hips from side to side.

"Imagine that you're holding something valuable between your butt cheeks." Wiggles was sprawled on the ground next to Fallon. "Or maybe, you could believe that you're holding in a really big far—"

"Yes! I know what you're about to say. No one can walk and do that at the same time."

"It's easy," Wiggles said. "I do it all the time. It just takes practice."

"I'm running out of time to practise," I said. My new shiny, dark hair whipped into my face as I turned. I pulled it off my sticky glossed lips. Being sexy was hard work.

I was glad Rhett wasn't here to see me in my new guise. He'd gone to the hotel to watch the succubi. I must look ridiculous. I felt the opposite of sexy.

"You make a great Marianne," Wiggles said. "I think it helps that you got up close and personal with her. You're really vibing on that succubus."

"Let's hope the vibe is good enough," I said. "Practice time is over. I need to go to the hotel and speak to Nolan."

"Wait! We need an experiment first," Wiggles said. "Practice on Tabitha before you meet with Nolan. She'll have met Marianne several times, so you'll see if she falls for your disguise."

"Good idea," I said. "Do I have to wear these heels to walk in?"

"A succubus always looks sexy," Fallon said. "The heels stay."

I glowered at her. "This had better work."

"You can thank me later," Fallon said. "I'll take payment in rides on your pony."

"No deal," Wiggles said. "Your riding days are over."

"We'll negotiate later," I said.

"Good luck," Suki said. "Are you sure you don't want us to come with you?"

"I'd better go alone. It'll look odd if Marianne is suddenly friendly with two local wood nymphs."

Wiggles walked to the opening of the cave with me. "I'm not letting Fallon on my back again. She holds on so tight that it almost strangles me."

"I thought you were enjoying being ridden."

"She's lucky I haven't thrown her off and stomped on her," Wiggles said. "I still might. I'm just waiting for the right moment."

I smoothed my hands over the fitted emerald green dress I wore one more time.

"Shoulders back, chest out, and chin up," Wiggles said. "Make eye contact with everyone and use that new sexy smile of yours. You'll knock them off their feet. Nolan will be putty in your hands. He'll confess to everything when he sees that va-va-voom cleavage."

I looked at my newly enhanced cleavage and grimaced. It felt so weird to be double my normal cup size. I needed to do this. Pulling off sex kitten for an hour shouldn't be tricky. My freedom depended on it, as did finding Aurora. I was certain, when we got to the bottom of this mystery and the real killer was discovered, Aurora would come out of hiding.

"Go get them, hot stuff," Wiggles said.

"You're not coming?" I asked.

"I'll lurk in the shadows, like a ninja king. I'll be around if you get in trouble."

Stumbling out of the forest, my toes already pinching from the impractical footwear, I tried not to hobble as I walked toward the front door of the hotel.

I felt someone's gaze on me and turned to see a shadowy figure on the opposite side of the road.

That had to be Rhett. I didn't acknowledge him, not wanting to give away his location.

I took a deep breath and pushed open the door.

Tabitha looked up from the counter. "Marianne! Back so soon?"

"I left something behind." So, Marianne wasn't in the hotel. That was both a good and a bad thing. At least, if she wasn't around, she wouldn't walk in and see me sweet talking Nolan.

Her gaze narrowed, and she peered at me over the top of her glasses. "You look different."

My heart skipped a beat. Had Tabitha already seen through the disguise? I smoothed a hand down my hair. "I can't think why."

"Weren't you wearing a different outfit when you left?"

Oh, crud! Of course, I had no clue what Marianne was wearing. "I had to change. I spilled something." I batted my huge lashes at her. "I can be so clumsy."

Tabitha laughed, and her hand fluttered across her chest. "I'm just the same. Although, I can't imagine anyone so sophisticated being clumsy."

I joined in the laughter. It sounded like bells ringing in the wind. The combined magic of my friends was awesome. "Oh, you'd be surprised. You must excuse me." I tried to glide toward the stairs and swung my hips as I walked up them.

I turned just before I was out of sight of Tabitha. She was staring at me, her mouth open. I couldn't decide if that was a good sign or not. I winked at her and gave a finger wave before hurrying to the top of the stairs.

Reaching Nolan's door, I knocked before doing exactly as Wiggles had instructed. I stuck my chest out, put my chin up, and plastered a sexy smile on my face. I looked straight into Nolan's eyes as he opened the door.

"Oh! It's you." Nolan scowled at me.

"I was at a loose end. Keep me company." Before he invited me in, I pushed past, making sure to brush against his arm.

Nolan shut the door and followed me into the bedroom. "Where are your sidekicks?"

"Out." I turned, cocked a hip, and rested a hand on it. I forced myself not to squirm as Nolan's gaze ran over me. Desire was clear in his eyes, but there was also caution.

"Do you want a drink?"

"That will be lovely." I gave him my biggest smile.

Nolan turned and stumbled over a chair before righting it and muttering to himself as he hurried to the drinks cabinet.

My disguise was having the right impact. I needed to make my next move carefully. It was possible that Marianne had spoken to Nolan about what had really happened to Toby. If I asked the wrong question, it would give away the game.

"What are your plans for the rest of the day?" I positioned myself on the edge of the bed and tried to make myself comfortable in the tight dress.

"I'm going to try to get into Toby's house again." Nolan turned, saw where I was sitting, and his jaw dropped. His hand shook as he passed me a glass of red wine. "What about you?"

"There's not much I can do," I said. "I hope this business with Toby can be cleared up quickly." I patted the space next to me on the bed.

Nolan launched himself into the space. He settled in close. It took all my willpower not to shuffle away.

"Once I get into the house and assess the situation, it will speed things up," Nolan said. "The angels can't need any more evidence."

"I'm glad to hear it. Now that clever witch is behind bars, I don't see the need for further delay."

"Clever witch?"

Oops! "I meant, Tempest Crypt."

"There's nothing clever about her," Nolan said. "Although, she could be a problem."

My fingers tightened around the glass. "Why will she be a problem?"

He smirked. "She didn't visit your room last night?"

I batted my eyelashes. "We did meet." I decided not to mention that we'd actually met in Toby's basement, not the hotel. Nolan might not know that Marianne had struck out on her own and was doing some snooping. "Tempest claims to be innocent."

"The evidence says otherwise," Nolan said. "And the angels think she's guilty. That's all that matters."

"And what do you think?"

"You know what I think." He took a sip of his wine.

"Do we need to do something about her?" I traced a finger down Nolan's arm.

He froze for a second and watched my finger. "The angels will have Tempest soon enough. She's too clumsy to be a real threat. She can only run for so long. The fact she's broken out of the cell is a bonus. It makes her look guiltier."

I decided to take a risk. "When the angels spoke to me, they were persuasive. They questioned my motive and everyone else's. They said we all have good reasons for wanting Toby dead. You don't think they consider us suspects?"

"As if. We don't need the angels poking around anymore than necessary. You can see how they've interfered with me discovering Toby's last wishes and ensuring everyone gets what they deserve."

"What are you planning to do when you get what you want from this unfortunate situation?"

"You mean, when I have Toby's assets?"

"I do. Have you got someone you want to spend your new wealth on?"

Nolan's eyebrows shot up, and his tongue traced across his bottom lip. "I've always yearned for a yacht. A super yacht. I plan to spend big once all the assets are liquidized. It will take time but will be worth the wait." He squeezed my knee. "How about you?"

"I don't know what I'm getting, do I?"

He tilted his head. "I haven't put an exact figure on things yet. There are a lot of variables. My brother always said he'd see his women right."

"You say that with such bitterness." I attempted a flirty laugh. "After all this time, can't you forget?"

"Forget that you left me for him?" Nolan's grip tightened on my knee, and the dress fabric rode up. "You've told me plenty of times that I was never the right one for you. In fact, I recall you saying that you only dated me to get close to my brother. That's hardly the behavior of a lady."

I placed my hand over his and removed it from my knee. "Everyone makes mistakes. Perhaps I made a mistake with you."

His nostrils flared. "Is my brother's influence finally fading now he's dead?" Nolan grabbed my wrist and stared at the snake tattoo. "While that is still in place, I fear he will always possess you. Even from beyond the grave."

"Maybe I no longer wish to be possessed by him." The clamminess of Nolan's hand made me squirm.

"Are you looking to have a room on my yacht?"

"You never know." I winked at him.

He smirked. "I have yet to decide if I wish to have just one woman in my life. Perhaps I will turn into my brother in other ways. He could have several women at the same time. They never complained."

"We never complained publicly," I said.

"I know how jealous you succubi get. It must have been a slap in the face when he played you at your own game."

I tried to look innocent. "Do you think Toby played us?"

"You're supposed to captivate men. He did that to you, Ava, and Olivia. He turned you into his obedient pets to do with as he desired. Nothing was too much of an effort, so long as Toby Matlock wanted it. I always admired you, Marianne. We could have had a wonderful future together."

"And not anymore? Have I missed my chance?" I batted my eyelashes again.

Nolan's gaze went to my mouth. "There was a time when I'd have done anything for you."

"And...." I leaned closer, pretending I wanted to kiss him.

He grunted. "Your charm is no longer so enticing."

My magic could only do so much. I looked like Marianne, but I didn't have the succubi ability to tempt men. My own natural charm was more sledge hammer than silken glove.

"You're saying you no longer want me?" I asked.

"Do you want me?"

I forced myself to stroke his arm again. "There's always hope."

"Hope that you'll fool me again." Nolan shook his head. "Not anymore. Although, you do owe me. Perhaps it's time I called in that favor."

The predatory look in Nolan's eyes made me jump up. He grabbed my hand and yanked me back down, pulling me so close that I could smell the wine on his breath.

"You've humiliated me for the last time. You come to my room, flaunting your curves and flashing those beautiful eyes, but I see the real you. Toby's gone, and you're scrambling to find somebody to be your protector. My brother won't help you anymore. You're on your own. You and those other hags."

"We're not hags," I spat at him. "And get your slimy hands off me." I batted away his hot little hands as they grabbed at my dress.

"Oh, no! This is the payment I want, and I'm taking it." Nolan tried to shove me back on the bed, but I kicked him in the shin with the pointed toe of my high heel. I kept kicking until he backed away.

Nolan launched at me. We rolled off the bed in a tangle of limbs and onto the soft carpet.

One sweaty hand wrapped around my throat while the other slid down to the long slit in my dress. It was a stupid, impractical dress. I couldn't get my feet free from the tangled fabric to knee him somewhere he'd never forget.

As his hand touched my knee, I felt a gut churning sickness. The room spun, and I grew lightheaded.

"What's going on?" Nolan's voice sounded faint, even though his mouth was inches from my ear. "Why are you shaking?"

My focus slipped, and I felt my magic disguise fading. It rippled over me in waves. I tried to push

Nolan off, but he wouldn't budge. I had to get away before he saw through the magic.

Nolan's eyes widened as he stared down at me. "Tempest!"

I jerked in his grip, continuing to feel dizzy and weak. The use of the magic disguise had drained me like I was a cheap battery. It should never have happened so quickly. The disguise should have been good for several hours.

A memory slammed into me, and I gasped. My eyes narrowed as I glared at Nolan. "We've been in this position before." A fuzzy image of him peering down at me passed through my head.

"I'd never debase myself with a Crypt witch." Nolan glowered at me. "Why are you in my room disguised as Marianne?"

I ignored his question. "Likewise, pal. But we've met before."

"I don't know you. The first time we met was at Angel Force."

"Yes, you do." The feel of his clammy hand on my throat had knocked something loose in my head. "You just siphoned my magic."

Nolan's grip around my neck tightened as his eyes flickered with alarm. "I'll call the angels and have you arrested again. How dare you sneak in and try to seduce answers out of me?"

"Tell me the truth!" I dug my nails into his hand. "You can take another magic user's ability, can't you?"

"You're deluded." Worry flickered in Nolan's eyes as he dropped his hold on my neck and scrambled to his feet.

"Wait!" I jumped up, staggering to the side as the blood rushed to my head. This guy had a strong ability. Glancing down, I saw that I wore nothing but a pair of black shorts, a tank top, and those stupid high heels. "This isn't the first time you've siphoned my magic. You took my power."

Nolan blinked rapidly and backed away. "You have no proof. I'm not a siphoner of magic. That's forbidden."

"Does the Magic Council know what you can do?" The Council didn't take kindly to unregistered siphons. Anyone with this ability was kept on a tight, unbending leash by them.

"That's none of your business." Nolan lifted his chin. "Leave before I bring the angels here. This is your only opportunity to escape."

I shook my head. I was going nowhere. "You did take my magic." I didn't care that my abilities felt kitten weak. I had to stop Nolan. He must have been at Toby's house the same time as I was. He'd framed me. I'd just found Toby's killer.

"It's not what you think. I can explain everything." Nolan continued to back away, his hands raised until he smacked into the wall behind him.

"Then explain. The way I figure it, you killed your brother. Toby must have told you what a problem I was. Did he suggest you get rid of me? Then what? You deceived him and figured this was a perfect opportunity to kill him and frame me?" I was thinking on my feet as I wobbled toward him on my heels.

"No to all of that." Nolan's face drained of color. "I admired my brother."

"You hated him. You must have known that the angels would look straight at me, given how much I despised Toby." I raised my hand, not sure whether to slap Nolan or fire magic at him and drain the meager amount I had left.

Nolan's eyes widened. "This isn't my fault."

I glared at him but didn't attack. He wasn't fighting back with magic. Nolan might be a magic siphoner, but it looked to be the only ability he had. Rare magic traits often came with side effects. It looked like Nolan was nothing more than a stealer of magic. When he had it, he couldn't use it.

"Whose fault is it? Are you working with someone else?"

He scrubbed a hand down his face, and his shoulders drooped. "Toby was a tyrant. You have to be glad that he's dead."

"I'm not disappointed. It frees my sister from a marriage to an unsuitable jerk." I grabbed his shoulders and shook him. "What I mind is being framed for something I didn't do. Admit that you killed your brother." I raised my hand as I took a step back. A jagged ball of flames appeared. It took all my focus to summon it. No matter how drained I became, I was taking Nolan Matlock down.

I jumped as someone thudded against the door. My flame flickered out.

"Nolan. It's Dazielle. Are you in there?"

I groaned softly. Not now. The angels couldn't find me. I was so close to getting a confession out of Nolan. I scanned the room, but there were few places to hide. Even if I did, Nolan would sell me out the second the angels came in.

I glared at him and saw an evil glint in his eyes. "Don't you dare. Keep your mouth shut and let the angels leave. We aren't finished."

Nolan smirked. "Help! I'm in danger. There's a murderer in here."

There was silence for a second before the door burst open. Angels flooded into the room, a dazzling blur of white and feathers.

I backed up and looked out the window. It was too far to jump.

Dazielle extended her wings, her gaze full of anger. "Tempest Crypt. What are you here for? Planning on killing Nolan next?"

Dominic and Cassiel joined her and stood on either side, their own wings extended. All I could see was a bank of solid feathers and muscle. There was no way through to the door behind them.

I raised my hands slowly to show I wasn't going to cause trouble. Not yet, anyway. Maybe I could get the angels to listen.

"Don't believe anything she says." Nolan hurried to Dazielle and grabbed her arm. "She was here to kill me. She's lost her mind. Now that she's killed my brother, she's gotten a taste for blood. Tempest won't stop. You must arrest her. She's not safe."

I glowered at Nolan. I'd expect nothing more from him.

"That's exactly what we're here to do," Dazielle said. Her gaze cut to Nolan. "Although, we didn't come here to hunt for Tempest. I'm glad we arrived when we did."

Nolan let out a big sigh and dabbed his brow with his fingers. "As am I. I wanted to contact you, but Tempest wouldn't let me. She was holding me hostage. She needs the severest of punishments. You should execute her right now!"

Dazielle's eyebrows rose. "Let's not get ahead of ourselves. Tempest deserves a trial."

"You shouldn't waste your time," Nolan said. "Her guilt is clear."

Dazielle glanced at him before shaking her head at me. "You made a big mistake fleeing your cell."

"Why did you come here?" I asked Dazielle. "If you're not here because of me, do you have something on Nolan?"

Nolan's head twisted to stare up at Dazielle. "That can't be true. I'm an innocent man. A grieving man."

Dazielle glared at me. "I'll deal with that in a moment. Tempest, will you come quietly?"

"I will, so long as you hear me out," I said. "Nolan killed Toby."

"She's lying!" Nolan said. "I loved my brother. I wouldn't want him dead."

Dazielle's fingers flexed, but she didn't dismiss my comment. "You do gain a lot by Toby dying."

Nolan gaped at her.

A sliver of hope ran through me. Did the angels also have doubts about what happened to Toby?

"Let me have ten more minutes with Nolan," I said. "He'll confess to everything. He was about to talk when you barged in."

Dazielle shook her head. "Any confession you force out of Nolan will be worthless. I imagine you were threatening him before we arrived." Her gaze ran over my lack of clothing. "Although, maybe you were using something else to get a confession."

I shuddered. "I wouldn't stoop that low. There's desperate and then there's downright dumb."

"She was tricking me," Nolan said. "Tempest had disguised herself as Marianne. She was trying to tempt me. When that didn't work, her true self was revealed, and she was about to strike. I must thank you angels. You saved my life."

Dazielle looked distinctly unimpressed. Something was wrong. Why was she hesitating in taking me down?

"Let me stay out of the cell. We can take Nolan to the station and question him together." I took a step toward Dazielle. All the angels' wings shivered as if they expected me to jump them.

"That's not happening," Dazielle said. "You're charged with Toby's murder. That still stands."

"How did you escape?" Dominic asked.

I pressed my lips together and shook my head. I wasn't getting Granny Dottie in trouble.

Dazielle sighed. "Not that it matters. I imagine you had help from the outside. I should have kept your family away from the cells. I was certain they were casing the joint every time they came in."

"I didn't see who got me out," I said. "Maybe you left the cell door open."

Dazielle snorted.

"We can work together on this," I said. "We've done it before. I know you want to see the best for the village. You know I'm not a killer."

"She is," Nolan hissed. "This witch cannot be trusted."

"All I know for certain is that you're trouble, Tempest, and you're coming with me," Dazielle said.

"I can't do that." I licked my lips. There was only one way out. It was through those solid wings. I'd been up close with angel wings several times. They weren't soft or comforting. They hurt when they hit you.

My gaze went from Cassiel to Dazielle and finally to Dominic. He was the weak link. He wasn't physically weak. He was almost as tall as Dazielle, but we were sort of friends. Dominic might not be so hard on me if I tried to get past him.

"Don't do it, Tempest," Dazielle warned as if sensing what I was about to attempt. "You won't get out of this room in one piece."

I couldn't let them arrest me. Once I was back in the cell, I'd be powerless. I had to try.

I faked a sigh and walked closer. "Fine. Take me back to the cells. But bring Nolan too. He's guilty."

Dazielle's head tilted, and her shoulders tensed. "You'll come quietly?"

"So long as you bring Nolan. There's something you need to know about him. His power is the reason all of this happened. He's the reason you think I killed Toby. He set this whole thing up."

"My ability isn't important. I've answered all your questions. You must silence this witch." Nolan spoke rapidly. "If I can be of any further assistance, I will. Here's your killer. Keep Tempest away from me. She has a murderous gleam in her eyes every time she looks at me."

"That's Tempest's default expression. Try not to take it personally," Dazielle said.

I pursed my lips. Dazielle had a point. My resting bitch face could look a little murderous.

Dazielle sucked in a breath to ask more questions. I couldn't wait any longer. I barreled into Dominic, using my weight to knock him off balance. It wasn't easy getting an angel to move, but he grunted in surprise at my unexpected attack and stumbled backward. For a second, I was blinded by a wall of wings but ducked and weaved and found myself at the door. I yanked it open, not looking back as I raced into the hall. I managed five steps before two powerful wings wrapped around me, and the air was pushed from my lungs.

"You're going nowhere," Dazielle growled in my ear. Her wings tightened around me as I bucked against her.

"I didn't do it." I kicked back, losing my hateful heels as I did so.

Dazielle's grip stiffened, and I felt my ribs creak under protest. "Tell me what you did when you got out of your cell. I know your family has been shielding you. We searched your mom's house but couldn't find any sign of you there."

I bet my family loved the angels snooping around. I was surprised to learn they'd even let them in. I still wasn't revealing my hiding place. "I had to investigate Toby's murder and clear my name."

"Tempest! Enough!" Dazielle squeezed so tightly that I saw stars. "I'm going to ask you one more question. I'll know if you're lying."

"How?" I wheezed. My chest felt like it was about to crack at any second.

"A pure being can always smell the truth."

I wanted to say something witty but could only focus on remaining conscious. "What's the question?"

"What did you do with Toby's body?"

Chapter 19

I stopped fighting Dazielle, too shocked to keep struggling. "Toby's body is missing?"

She sighed, and her hold on me loosened. I could breathe again. "That's why we're here. I have to tell Nolan that his brother's body's been taken. What did you do with it when you escaped?"

"I have no clue what you're talking about." I staggered away from Dazielle as she released me from her wings and sucked in several deep breaths. Those wings were lethal.

I saw Dominic and Cassiel guarding the stairs, but the fight had left me. I was so surprised by the news that Toby's body was gone.

Dazielle raised a finger. "Don't say another word. Let me tell Nolan what's going on." She looked over my shoulder to the other angels. "If Tempest makes one wrong move, you have my permission to knock her out. Don't be gentle. She doesn't deserve it."

I watched as she retreated into Nolan's hotel room and shut the door.

I turned and looked at Dominic and Cassiel, rubbing feeling back into my arms as I did so. I didn't want to fight them. I just needed to figure out the truth. This new piece of the puzzle had me stumped. "Sorry about slamming into you, Dominic."

He rubbed his stomach. "No hard feelings, Tempest. I'm made of tough stuff. You must have known you couldn't get past us."

"I had to try. I can't go back in that cell."

"You have to," Cassiel said. "And you have to tell us where Toby's body is."

I glanced over my shoulder. The door to Nolan's room was shut. "About that. Tell me more about his body. Dominic mentioned it was still warm. Did he stay warm?"

Cassiel shot an irritated glance at Dominic. "You shouldn't know about that. It's confidential information."

"You have to admit it's sort of odd," Dominic said, not picking up on Cassiel's annoyance. "A corpse shouldn't stay warm."

"Or get up and walk away," I said. "I know I've asked you before, but Toby was one hundred percent dead?"

Cassiel sighed. "He was. Toby wasn't coming back from what you did to him."

I waved my hand in the air, not bothering to correct her as to my innocence. "Did you do an autopsy? Did you remove his organs?"

"I didn't have the opportunity," Cassiel said. "It was scheduled for the day we had to go to the demon prison. Everything was set out, and I was about to begin the autopsy when I had to leave. I put Toby back in cold storage. When I returned, he was gone."

"Even when he was in cold storage, he stayed warm?"

Cassiel nodded curtly.

"Then he can't be dead!"

"I know a corpse when I see one," Cassiel said. "Toby Matlock was dead."

"Unless he was bitten by a vampire," Dominic said, "or a werewolf. He might have survived the process and returned a changed man."

Cassiel and I shook our heads.

"There were no bite marks of any animal or supernatural creature on Toby's body," Cassiel said. "I had completed my external examination. I'd taken samples and scrapings and checked all the wounds. He wasn't bitten. Toby hasn't risen from the dead."

"Nice try, Dominic." At least I had one angel who didn't automatically think I was guilty.

His smile almost dazzled me. "Thanks, Tempest."

"How do you explain him not going cold?" I asked Cassiel.

"I was investigating that curiosity," Cassiel said. "I would have figured it out. I can't do that now, until you tell me where you've moved him to."

"It makes no sense that I'd move Toby. What would I want with his body?"

"You killed him. You can answer that better than us."

I rolled my shoulders. It was time to do a little sharing with the angels. "After you all left for the cemetery, something happened."

"We know that. You broke out," Cassiel said.

"I did, but there was someone else in Angel Force. Someone who shouldn't have been there."

"Who?" Dominic asked.

"It was two people, a man and a woman. The man was struggling to walk. The woman had magic."

"Did she hurt you?" Dominic looked like he wanted to hug me.

I shook my head. "She tried, but they had to leave. This could have something to do with Toby's disappearance."

"This is a distraction," Cassiel said. "There was no one there. You're making this up, so we think that you didn't take Toby."

I sighed. I should just keep my mouth shut until I'd figure it out for myself. The two figures I'd seen leaving Angel Force were important. Could one of them have been Toby? How had he been brought back to life? And if he was alive, who was aiding him?

My heart fluttered as my thoughts flew from one possibility to another. Toby must be hidden somewhere in Willow Tree Falls, recovering from his ordeal. He wasn't dead. I felt more hopeful than I'd done since I woke up next to his body.

The door behind me opened. Dazielle stepped out and closed it quietly behind her. "Nolan's been informed about what's happened. He's not happy."

"Maybe Nolan took the body," I said.

"Outside now," Dazielle said. "We're not discussing this case. You try anything funny and you'll wake up back in your cell."

My hope faded as quickly as it had arrived. Dazielle wasn't looking for evidence to suggest my innocence. In her mind, I was guilty. It was only a matter of time before she put me away for good.

Dominic and Cassiel led the way down the stairs. I followed them, my bare feet protesting as I stepped on the cold ground outside.

Dominic held my high heels. He offered them to me, but I'd rather have cold feet than squeeze my feet back into them.

Four more angels stood outside. It was nice to see the welcoming party Dazielle had summoned. I looked around the group of angels. I wasn't getting out of this. Still, I'd give it one last try.

I turned to Dazielle. "Nolan can siphon magic. He drained my magic. He's involved in this."

"Save your breath," Dazielle said. "You need to focus on the upcoming case against you."

"Test Nolan. He used his ability on me in the hotel. He was telling the truth about me turning up disguised as Marianne."

Dazielle's lips pursed. "Why do such a thing?"

"To get Nolan to talk. He's been in love with Marianne for a long time. Disguised as her, I thought I could get him to open up. And he did. He revealed that he can drain another magic user. That's how my disguise failed. Nolan tried to weaken me to get what he wanted."

"I imagine he got a shock when Tempest Crypt appeared."

"That's beside the point. Nolan talked about me being a problem."

"He's got that right."

"No! When I was Marianne, he told her that I was being tricky."

Dazielle waved a hand in the air. "Stop! I will question Nolan and check his ability, but that means nothing in regard to Toby."

"It does," I said. "When I woke up next to Toby's body, my ability had gone. My magic was so drained that I couldn't even fire a blast spell correctly. You know what ability I have. Not anymore. My power is almost gone. I'm back to kindergarten level of spells." I glanced at the group of glowering angels. "And you'll all be happy to hear that my demon has also gone."

Feathers ruffled, and the angels mumbled to each other.

Dazielle stepped closer and towered over me. "You no longer host Frank?"

I shook my head. At last, I was getting through to her. "That's right. He's gone. When Nolan drained me of my witch ability, he also took Frank. Maybe he didn't realize that's what he was doing, but I haven't felt Frank for days. I've tried to summon him, but he's not there."

A glimmer of something evil flickered in Dazielle's eyes. "Prove it."

"How can I do that?"

"You could be faking it. How do we know your magic is weak? How can we tell that you no longer have a demon inside you who comes out when you get angry?"

The angels formed a circle, trapping me inside. I had a bad feeling about this. "What are you going to do?"

"We're going to see how strong Tempest Crypt still is." Dazielle smirked.

"Dazielle, maybe we shouldn't," Dominic said. "Tempest could be telling the truth. We should trust her."

Dazielle glared at him. "Are you disobeying me?"

His shoulders slumped. "Of course not, boss."

Poor Dominic. He was always looking out for me. I'd try to stay close to him. He might protect me from a few wing swipes. "What will you do if this test proves my magic has failed and Frank has gone?"

"Listen to you," Dazielle said. "I'll listen to your wild theories about who killed Toby and why you're innocent."

"How about you take me to the scene of the crime and let me look around properly?"

"Don't push your luck, Tempest."

"Or let me interview the other suspects? We'll do it together. You can lead, but I want in."

"That's not happening," Dazielle said.

"At least let me go to Toby's house with you," I said. "There are things you might have missed. Have you checked the—"

"Enough! Until you show us how weak you are, none of this matters. There's nothing to negotiate over."

My gut tightened as I saw the angry angels around me. Over the years, I'd annoyed most of them by not following the rules. It was payback time. Only Dominic looked sorry for me, but there wasn't much he could do to stop this.

He looked away as I met his gaze. I was in this alone, but I'd do it. If this meant Dazielle listened to me, I was prepared to be roughed up by the angels. I'd heal, most likely.

I shifted until I was in the center of the circle. "Go easy on me. After a few spells, I'll be powerless. And your wings hurt."

"We'll make sure you live. After all, you have a crime to pay for." Dazielle raised her chin as her gaze went around the group.

Their wings flared as one. My gaze shifted as I waited for the first blow to strike, trying to figure out where it would come from and how to defend myself.

I had one tiny advantage on my side. Angel magic was only to be used to help others and defeat evil. Technically, I was no longer bad. With Frank gone, I was just your average witch. I still knew the angels' power could sting, and their wings left a hefty mark. I had a fifty-fifty chance of getting out of this alive. They weren't great odds, but I'd take them.

Jophiel was the first to attack. She launched a ball of light. It skimmed past my ear before exploding behind me.

I staggered into a solid wall of angels and was shoved back into the center of the circle. I raised my head and came face-to-face with Dazielle. She placed a hand on my chest, and I felt a throb of heat pass through me.

For a second, it felt nice. Then pain exploded in my gut. I was knocked off my feet and landed on my back.

These angels weren't playing nicely. My fingers tingled with the remnants of the magic I'd been gifted. There wasn't much there, but I could make a few of them hesitate from striking.

I rolled onto my hands and knees, pretending to be stunned. I shot out my hand. A jagged flame spun toward Dazielle.

She shielded herself with her wings before extinguishing the flame. "You're holding back. Don't think you can trick us."

"I'm really not." I pulled myself upright. "That's as good as it gets. I'm not lying about my lack of ability."

Several light balls slammed into me at once. My skin itched and tingled as if I was covered in fire ants. I gritted my teeth and waited for the magic to subside.

A wing slammed into my back and shoved me to the ground again.

I rolled over, fire shimmering on my fingers as I tried to find my attacker. It wasn't cool to be hit from behind.

All I saw were angry expressions. It looked like the angels had some serious grudges they'd been holding onto.

I ignored the throb in my back as I stood and slowly rolled my shoulders. Nothing was too damaged, yet.

Jophiel's fingers flexed as if she was about to strike. This time, I didn't hesitate. I threw the last of my magic straight at her.

She lifted a wing a fraction of a second too late, and the ends of her perfect blonde hair ignited. She shrieked and flapped her wings around her.

I backed up and slammed into an angel. Wings wrapped around me, trapping me in a protective cocoon. I expected to be squeezed, but nothing happened.

"Don't worry, Tempest. I've got you," Dominic whispered in my ear as he continued to hold me tightly against his hard chest.

Whilst I appreciated the assistance, Dominic would get in trouble for helping me. "I'm okay. Dazielle is just flexing her muscles. She wants to show me who's the boss."

"Some of these angels aren't your friends," Dominic muttered. "You have a terrible reputation at Angel Force."

"It's deserved," I said. "Now, make out like you're trying to squish me to death with these enormous wings, or you'll be facing a disciplinary."

His breath huffed against my cheek, smelling of vanilla and a hint of cinnamon, before he dropped his hold on me.

I staggered forward, trying to make out that I'd been hurt. I was hit with more light balls.

I tried to fire up my own magic. Fragile sparks lingered on my fingertips before dying. I was out of juice and at the mercy of the angels. This was what it felt like to have no powers. To be normal. I hated it.

Something hot and painful slammed into my back. I splatted face first into the dirt. I rolled onto my back and flopped my arms out to the sides. "Do your worst." My gaze settled on Dazielle.

She tilted her head a fraction, indecision in her eyes. Did she finally believe me?

There were startled yelps as the circle broke apart. I was temporarily blinded by a blast of foul smelling flames and smoke.

Wiggles landed on my chest, his growl so loud that it made my ears ring.

He turned in a swift circle, bouncing on his paws as he moved, flames pouring from his open mouth. The angels backed away, their eyes wide as they watched him protect me.

I wanted to wrap my arms around Wiggles and hug him. I wasn't sure how far the angels had intended to go, but I had a feeling they'd just gotten started on bringing me down to size.

Wiggles clamped his mouth shut. He crouched on top of me, his fierce red gaze on the angels. "Everything okay?"

"Just about. You arrived right on time."

He blasted a jet of flame at an angel who'd been foolish enough to inch closer. "I couldn't figure out what the angels were up to at first when Dazielle dragged you out of the hotel and they surrounded you. Then I saw the fight begin. They're cowards. There are seven angels and one of you."

"And I'm having a bad day," I said.

"Sure, you are. Otherwise, these angels would be toast. Rhett wanted to help, but we all know that wouldn't end well. He's poised to attack if they don't back down." He growled low in his chest as Dazielle approached.

She raised her hands. "We don't want to fight anymore."

"It seems like that's exactly what you want to do." Wiggles snorted, and smoke drifted out of his nose.

"You should be ashamed. If it weren't for Tempest, Angel Force would be a laughing stock."

"Hold on a second—"

Wiggles growled, drowning out Dazielle. "She's saved your feathery butt so many times, and this is how you repay her."

"She's also been arrested for murder," Dazielle said. "And her help often comes with a big dollop of interference."

"That dollop of interference has solved crimes," Wiggles said. "You should be thanking her, not blasting her with your tingly, fuzzy light balls."

Dazielle's eyes narrowed. "How was I to know that she was telling the truth about her ability?"

I opened my mouth to speak, but Wiggles thumped a paw on my face. "It's time you started trusting Tempest. She's one of the good ones. Sure, she buys lousy dog kibble and makes me eat it instead of doughnuts, but she's usually generous when it comes to treats. I only have a small list of things I'd change about her. You could do a lot worse than to have Tempest Crypt on your side."

I rested a hand on Wiggles' back, feeling a little teary.

Wiggles grunted before removing his paw from my face.

"Do you believe me now?" I asked Dazielle.

Dazielle folded her arms across her chest. "I can't decide."

"Trust me. I wouldn't be able to fake not wanting to knock you and your feathery friends on their backsides. You attack me, I fight back. I can't do that anymore."

"We're keeping Willow Tree Falls safe," Dazielle said. "We can't have you on the loose when you're the prime suspect in a murder investigation."

"Pretty but dumb. That should be the Angel Force motto." Wiggles remained planted on my chest. He settled himself down as if happy to sit there for as long as it took to convince Dazielle that I wasn't the killer.

I decided that the safest thing to do was remain on the ground. At least this way, the angels wouldn't consider me a threat. "You agreed you'd listen to my theories about Toby's murder if I proved my magic has faded. You're not going back on that deal, are you?"

Dazielle glared at me for a second before nodding. "We'll talk. Back at the station. But first..." She lifted her chin.

A huge, sticky white net dropped on top of me and Wiggles.

"What the—"

"We're arresting Wiggles as an accomplice," Dazielle said.

Angels surrounded us as they wrapped the net around Wiggles.

"I'll burn your wings off if you don't let me go right this second." Wiggles snapped and snarled.

Dazielle held out a hand to me, which I ignored as I struggled to my feet. "You didn't have to do that to him."

"Wiggles is an even bigger problem than you," Dazielle said. "A little payback isn't a bad thing. It might teach him to stop stealing food every time he comes into Angel Force."

"He's a hellhound. He runs hot. He burns through food quickly. You can't begrudge him a leftover sandwich." I looked over to see Wiggles blasting flames at the angels through the net.

"If I could order it, I'd make him go to obedience classes for naughty hellhounds." Dazielle grimaced as she watched Wiggles.

"If he went, he'd be top of his class." I wouldn't change a thing about Wiggles. Well, maybe the gas issues, the pillow obsession, and the food stealing. Other than that, he was perfection.

Dazielle grunted. "Let's go to the station. I trust I don't need to shackle you."

"So long as you don't put me back in a cell, I'm sticking with you," I said.

I walked alongside Dazielle, the rest of the angels following us, still holding Wiggles in the net. He was using increasingly inventive curse words as he was bounced along between them.

Once inside the station, I was left alone in a room with Wiggles. I untangled the angel net, ignoring the sting from the magic as I removed the sticky substance from him.

He rolled onto his feet and blasted flames at the net until it was nothing but a charred mess. "Those angels have got issues."

"They know how to hold a grudge," I said. "Maybe don't steal their food from now on. They may tolerate you a little more."

"Forget that. I'm stealing double the amount of food. They owe me. It'll take me weeks to get the angel stink off my fur."

I settled in a seat, feeling exhausted but happy to be free. Well, sort of free. I now had an opportunity to prove my innocence. "Dazielle told me that Toby's body has gone missing."

Wiggles hopped around to face me. "No kidding. Who took it?"

"They think it was me. Nolan has to be involved," I said.

"Did he tell you anything useful when you were disguised as Marianne?"

"He thinks I'm trouble, and he wants his brother's assets as soon as he can. And Nolan siphons magic. He did it to me in the hotel, and I'm sure he drained me the night I woke up in Toby's house."

"When did that happen?"

"That's still a blank, but it has to be him. I just need to get the angels to believe it. If they start looking into Nolan instead of me, they'll uncover the truth."

The door opened. Dazielle walked in and settled at the table opposite me. "So, talk. We don't have much time. We still need to find Toby's body."

I took a few seconds to gather my thoughts. "Nolan Matlock did this. He has the ability, the motive, and he could have faked an alibi. He killed his brother."

Dazielle shook her head. "Wrong. His alibi is solid. A witness testified that they were with him at the time of Toby's murder. He's not involved."

"Alibis can be faked," I said. "What's to say that Nolan doesn't have something on this witness? Or he could have taken their magic and threatened not to give it back until they pretended to be his alibi."

"I have yet to test Nolan's powers to confirm he can even do that," Dazielle said.

"Then you need to get a move on," I said. "Magic siphoning is restricted. If he's using his ability to gain power over others, he has to be stopped. He did it to me."

"Your lack of ability is curious," Dazielle said.

It didn't feel curious to me. I felt vulnerable without my magic. I wanted it back.

"Let's assume that Nolan did fake his alibi," I said. "He's the perfect suspect. He's shown zero remorse over Toby's death. There's nothing but good things coming to Nolan now. He'll get everything Toby owned."

"Why now?" Dazielle asked. "If he hated his brother this much, why wait this long before doing something about it?"

"Because of me," I said. "I'm the perfect fall guy. Toby's been complaining about me. Nolan saw this as an opportunity too good to miss. He killed his brother and framed me. Everyone knows I wasn't a fan of Toby Matlock."

Dazielle pressed the tips of her fingers together. "The missing body is odd. It makes no sense that you would take it."

"Another odd thing about this mystery can be found in the basement of Toby's house."

"When were you in Toby's house?"

I winced. There was no point in hiding this information. "When I got out of the cell, I headed over there to take a look around."

Dazielle's eyes narrowed. "You were the one who disabled the angel standing guard?"

"That was all me," Wiggles said, "with the help of an accomplice who shall not be named, even though she's super annoying and insists on riding me at every opportunity. We caused a distraction, and Tempest went inside."

Dazielle hissed air through her teeth. "What about the basement?"

"It was set up as some sort of ceremonial room. There's a stone table and a range of powerful magic objects that we dealt with. I think someone's trying to bring Toby back from the dead. That's why the body's gone missing, which proves it can't be me. I'd never do that. I never want to see that guy again."

Dazielle jerked back in her seat. "And you think Nolan's involved with this? He killed his brother then changed his mind and took Toby's body to undo what he did?"

"Maybe not Nolan," I said. "There are three succubi in the village. They were all once passionately in love with Toby. I think they still are. And that's not all. I saw two people leaving Angel Force just as I got out of my cell. It could have been a succubus who'd come to help Toby."

Dazielle gave a single nod. "I've heard that strong succubi have regenerative magic. I've never heard it done on an individual before. Three powerful succubi working together might have the ability to return someone from the dead, with the right magic."

"So, it's possible," I said.

"Yes, but there's a problem."

"What problem?"

"The basement is empty," Dazielle said. "When we looked around, we found no stone table or magic objects."

"When was the last time you looked?"

"During our initial sweep of the building."

"Things have changed," I said. "We have to go back there."

She shook her head. "There is no we. You're staying locked up. I'll check out Toby's basement."

"Do you believe me?" I asked. "I didn't kill Toby."

Dazielle's lips pursed. "I'm still undecided."

"Undecided enough not to charge me and ship me out of the village?"

Dazielle leaned forward. "You're on a temporary reprieve while I'll double check Nolan's alibi and his power. I also need to check if he's on the register for siphons and if the Magic Council knows about him. If they do, why are they letting him walk around a free man?"

"I appreciate the reprieve, but all of that will take too much time," I said. "If somebody wants Toby brought back to life, they'll be working on him now."

"And you think the succubi have him?"

"It's either them or Nolan."

"Nolan I can handle, but without evidence, I'm accusing the succubi of nothing."

"Don't tell me you're scared of three hotter than Hades, powerful, ancient magical beings?"

"Cautious, not scared. If we make the wrong move, all that will happen is the killer will slip away and never be caught."

I sighed and slumped in my seat. There had to be a way I could get Dazielle on side. She needed to get all the suspects here before it was too late.

"You need another undercover visit," Wiggles said. "It worked the first time."

"It sort of worked," I said. "If Nolan hadn't used his ability on me, I might have learned more."

"Undercover? What do you mean?" Dazielle asked.

"My disguise as Marianne. Nolan was opening up and talking to me. He was letting his guard down."

"Do it again. You could find the answers you need," Wiggles said.

Dazielle's expression soured. "You're not going anywhere on your own. How do I know this isn't a bluff?"

"I want this cleared up as much as you do. More so, because it's my neck on the line if you charge me with killing Toby."

"If I let you leave the station, you'll slip through the magic barrier. I'll never find you."

"I'm not going anywhere. I'm invested in this place. I have family here. I won't abandon all of that."

"And you have me," Wiggles said.

"Of course. I go where my hellhound goes."

"Since you won't let Tempest leave on her own, why don't you go with her?" Wiggles said.

I shook my head. "That won't look at all suspicious. Me disguised as Marianne being escorted by an angel."

"Then Dazielle goes in disguise, too," Wiggles said.

"Disguise myself as what?" Dazielle asked.

"Actually, that's not a bad idea," I said. "There are three succubi. We disguise ourselves as two of them and question the remaining succubus. She won't hide anything from her succubi sisters."

Dazielle shook her head. "I'm not disguising myself as a succubus."

"It'll take strong magic," I said as I warmed to the idea. "But I reckon it can be done."

"It's not happening," Dazielle said.

I glowered at her. "So, what's your brilliant plan? Everyone has an alibi for Toby's murder. I'm innocent. What's your next move? Tell me how you're going to figure this out."

Dazielle opened her mouth then snapped it shut. "By following the evidence."

"Which leads you to me. The evidence is wrong. And now you have a body missing. We need to investigate this fast. You refuse to let me do this on my own, so come with me. You'll see then that I'm telling the truth, and we'll get to the bottom of this mystery."

Dazielle ran a hand down her face. "It's one option."

"We're running out of time. Toby's body has gone, and the succubi could slip away at any moment."

"What about Nolan?" Dazielle asked. "How will we get what we need out of him?"

"Let's see what the succubi know first," I said. "If Nolan's involved, I'll remain as Marianne and get answers out of him. He'd do anything to make her like him. Maybe even go as far as kill his brother."

Dazielle glanced at her white uniform. "Very well. I can handle transformation magic, but no funny business. You make one wrong move, and I'll knock you off your feet. You won't be able to get up for a week."

"Duly noted," I looked at Wiggles. "We need to call in reinforcements."

Chapter 20

"Who do you have in mind?" Dazielle's expression grew sharp.

"You know Suki?"

"The giant wood nymph who knocked out several of my angels not so long ago?"

"The very same. Suki's sweet when you don't try to arrest her."

"Hmmm. Anyone else?"

"Fallon. The forest guardian."

"I've heard terrible things about her."

"They're all true," Wiggles said. "She's a monster."

"She's not," I said. "Fallon's just very enthusiastic about her job. And she loves dangerous magic. And is a bit obsessed with killing. Other than that, she's perfect."

Dazielle frowned. "Anyone else?"

"Wiggles also helped when I was transformed. That will do."

"Very well." Dazielle clasped her hands together. "Let's get on with this."

I nodded at Wiggles. "You know where to find them."

Wiggles jumped up. "Permission to bite Fallon if she jumps on me?"

"Denied. Gentle nipping only."

Wiggles growled as he hurried away.

"This had better work, Tempest," Dazielle said.

"I promise nothing." I rolled my shoulders. "This is a last resort deal. If this doesn't work, I'm not sure what else to do."

"Charge you with the murder."

I smirked. "And let the killer go?"

"Who says you aren't the killer?"

"You do! Remember, I got a reprieve."

"It's temporary." Dazielle sighed. "But maybe this is more complicated than it first appeared to be."

"I'm here to clear my name and find Aurora."

Dazielle blew out a breath. "You don't think she could be involved?"

"Nope. Not for a second." I was not delving into that horrible possibility.

"I did wonder." Dazielle twirled her hair around her fingers. "I never could see the appeal of Toby Matlock."

"At least that's something we agree on."

"Do you think Toby has hurt Aurora? That's why she's missing?"

My gut clenched. "I don't know for certain, but she'd never vanish without letting someone know. Aurora hates anyone to worry about her."

The door crashed open. "We're here to save the day." Fallon strode through, Suki right behind her, a nervous expression on her face.

I jumped up. "That was fast!"

"My pony never lets me down," Fallon said.

Wiggles grumbled under his breath as he stomped into the room.

Suki shrugged. "We were on the edge of the forest, waiting for you."

"Great! We don't have much time," I said. "Has Wiggles told you the plan?"

"He has." Fallon rubbed her hands together. "Who are we transforming?"

Dazielle stood and moved next to me, her expression grim. "No funny business, wood nymph. I know about the magic you use in the forest. I plan to talk to you about it."

"Maybe now's not the time to reprimand the person who's about to transform you using magic," I muttered to her. "If you're not careful, she'll turn you into a one-eyed troll."

Dazielle scowled at me. "Very well. What do we need to do?"

Suki's expression grew panicked. "Tempest, are you sure this is a good idea?" She looked over her shoulder and jumped as two angels peered in the room.

"Right now, we have a truce with the angels," I said. "I doubt it'll last for long. I'll be disguised as Marianne again. Dazielle can be Olivia."

"An angel turned into a succubus." Fallon clicked her tongue against the roof of her mouth. "That's pushing the boundaries."

"You can't do it?" Dazielle asked.

"No such thing as can't." Fallon smiled. "Do I want to, though?"

"Fallon, no fooling around," I said.

"I'll work out my payment plan."

"No payment, Fallon." Suki pressed a hand on her shoulder. "These are our friends."

"Friends! I love the pony. Tempest is okay. The angel? I'm not convinced," Fallon said.

"Fallon." Menace laced Suki's tone.

"Fine. I'll do it. No charge." Fallon glanced up at Suki.

"A magic disguise can only do so much, though," Suki said. "Dazielle gives off a very angel-like vibe."

"We'll work on that," I said. "Wiggles knows what Olivia looks like, so he can lead on getting the disguise right. Then we can practise moving in our new forms. Dazielle, you need to be less angel."

"How do I do that?" Dazielle asked.

"Stop walking around like you own the place," Wiggles said.

"I don't..." She shook her head. "Forget it. Let's do this before I change my mind."

"Can an angel even be sexy?" Fallon asked. "Those wings are a right turn off."

"Not helping, Fallon," I muttered.

"You won't see my wings when I'm disguised," Dazielle said. "My wings are beautiful."

"If you call shedding sexy," Fallon said. "Right, who's first?"

"Do me first," I said. "We can show Dazielle how it's done." I still wore the black tank top and shorts I'd stripped down to before I'd been transformed the first time.

Wiggles, Suki, and Fallon stood around me. Wiggles stood up my leg while the others touched my bare arms.

I relaxed as the magic flooded over me. Hot, warm waves stroked my skin as I was slowly transformed. My nose itched, and I wriggled it to stop from sneezing.

"Wow!" Dazielle's eyes widened. "That's not bad."

I looked down to see I was draped in green silk, my hair shiny and darker than my usual color.

"We still need to work on the face," Fallon said. "I've brought the makeup." She turned to Dazielle and grinned.

Dazielle took a step back.

"There's no backing out now," I said. "It's time for your transformation."

Five minutes later, Dazielle, now transformed into Olivia, stood in front of me, a look of extreme discomfort on her face. Now and again, a stray feather floated through the air.

Wiggles sat on top of the table as he watched me and Dazielle walk around in our new magic disguises. "Dazielle, stop walking like someone's hobbled you."

Dazielle glared at him. "Angels are used to practical clothing."

"Sure, you are," I muttered. "That's why you wear white. It never shows the dirt." I stopped by the desk and watched Dazielle stomp backwards and forwards, trying to look sexy.

"Glide, don't stomp." Fallon leaned against a filing cabinet.

"If you want to change your mind, you can," I said. "I'm happy to do this on my own."

"You're not leaving my sight," Dazielle said.

"Then stop shedding feathers, and let's get out of here," I said. "Is everything set?" I looked over at Suki.

Suki nodded. "Tabitha passed on the message to Ava, asking her to meet at Toby's house in twenty minutes."

"What about the real Marianne and Olivia?" Dazielle asked.

"They've just taken a delivery of a sumptuous takeout feast courtesy of Mystic Mushroom," I said. "Rhett confirmed that they're in their rooms. He'll watch them and make sure they stay there."

"Which doesn't give us a lot of time," Dazielle said.

"Exactly. So, stop fiddling with your dress and let's move."

"I'm not sure I can move." Dazielle twisted the sheath dress she wore. "I can't fly in this."

"You can walk, though."

"Slowly and painfully." Dazielle finally stopped fussing with her hem. "Are you certain that Ava is the weakest link in the trio?"

"She seemed the angriest and least stable. It might be easier to get her to confess if she's holding onto a lot of bitterness. I'm going to reveal that Toby's body is missing and see how she reacts."

"Isn't that a risk?" Dazielle asked. "If they all know about Toby's body being taken, you'll blow our cover."

"We don't have the time to be subtle," I said. "I'll mention the body and see if she freaks out."

"Very well. I've got a troop of angels positioned near Toby's house," Dazielle said. "On my signal, they know to move in if anything happens."

"And I've got my own crew," I said.

"If you're talking about Rhett's gang, they need to stay out of this," Dazielle said.

"Not the gang. Wiggles, Suki, and Fallon are my backup."

"For a price of—" Fallon's words were cut off by Suki's large hand clamping over her mouth.

Suki nodded. "Of course. Whatever you need."

"I trust them more than I do your angels, especially after you all roughed me up," I said.

Dazielle shrugged, looking unapologetic. "I had to be sure you were telling the truth."

I scowled at her. This angel wasn't as angelic as she appeared to be. "Let's move."

Wiggles trotted beside me as we left the office and headed to Toby's house. The group radiated with anticipation and nerves. I wanted this over. I wanted my name cleared, Aurora found, and never to have to wear high heels again.

"This is where you leave us," I said to Wiggles. "We can't have Ava being suspicious that Marianne has inherited a hellhound."

"I'll be hiding behind a bush with the others," Wiggles said. "Ready to pounce at a moment's notice."

I nodded at him and hurried away with Dazielle.

There was no angel standing outside the door as I walked with her past the stone dragons and entered the house.

The air inside was still, as if no one had been living here for some time.

I walked into the study and shuddered. Although some of my memory had returned from that fateful night, I still wasn't completely sure what had happened. Waking up next to a body would give anyone a few nightmares.

"We should check out the basement," I said to Dazielle. "I can show you what I discovered."

"Are you in here, ladies?" Ava's voice sounded from the doorway.

"There's no time for that," Dazielle said.

"Stop looking so worried. Succubi never look worried. Remember, you're a sexy, confident woman."

"Let's just get on with this," Dazielle muttered. "I'll be competently attractive, but that's about it."

We walked back into the hallway to see Ava standing just inside the door.

"There you are! How did you finally get rid of the angels?" Ava hurried over. "I thought we'd never get the chance to poke around."

"They're winding down their interest in this case," Dazielle said. "It wasn't so hard."

Ava's eyes narrowed. "And you know that how? Have you been speaking to them without me? Don't try to cut me out of this deal. Toby owes me."

Dazielle glanced at me. "It's nothing like that. I saw an angel earlier today. She told me everything."

"Isn't that sweet of her." Ava reached forward and plucked a white feather from the air. It must have slid through Dazielle's disguise. "It looks like you got very close to this angel. Was she cute?"

"None of the angels are a patch on us," I said.

"Absolutely," Ava said. "Have you been looking around without me?"

"We just arrived," I said.

"You shouldn't have left me behind at the hotel."

"We knocked. You didn't answer," I said. "That's why we left the message with Tabitha for you to meet us here."

Ava shrugged. "I was in the bath. I must have missed you."

"We're all here now. Where shall we start looking?" Dazielle asked.

"I don't mind, but we need to be careful," Ava said. "Tempest Crypt is still on the loose."

"Which is a good thing. It will distract the angels from being interested in us," I said.

"I hated being questioned by those angels," Ava said. "Not that I think they're any threat. The longer they hold things up, the longer it'll take for us to get what we deserve."

"And what do you deserve?" I asked her.

Ava's full lips pursed. "Let's not discuss that again. We agreed on a three-way split. Although, I still think I should get more. I was Toby's favorite. He loved me the best."

I couldn't help but snort. "Toby Matlock loved himself more than anyone else."

"You never knew him like I did," Ava said. "He will always be in my heart."

"Do you miss him?" Dazielle asked.

"Of course." Ava tilted her head. "Although, I miss his gifts more. Come on. We're not going to get anything that's owed us if we keep gossiping. We have to find his will. Nolan said we're all in it."

"Are you even sure Toby wrote one?" I asked.

Ava squinted at me. "Why would Nolan lie about the contents of the will? He knows what his brother was like. Nolan understands that we deserve to be compensated for our loss."

"Why don't we just take back what's ours?" Dazielle asked.

"I would if I knew where he hid my magic," Ava said. "I doubt Toby would have been foolish enough to store it here."

"Maybe that's what he wanted us to think," I said. "Toby hid it in the house because he knew we wouldn't look here."

Ava's bottom lip jutted out. "He always was a sly one. We'll look around just to be safe. My Toby was always so clever."

"We were all involved with him," I said, deciding it was time to stir things up. "Maybe he loved me more than you."

"You keep believing that, sister. We all know you're the plain one. The one the guys turn to when both of us are occupied."

Dazielle snorted a laugh. "That's so true."

I spluttered in disbelief as I watched them high-five. "That's not what Toby told me."

Dazielle nudged me with her elbow. "Enough of your jealous words. Let's search together."

"It'll be quicker if we split up," Ava said. "This is a big house. We don't know when the angels will be coming back."

"They won't be back," Dazielle said. "They're too busy looking for Tempest."

"That's true." Ava pursed her lips. "But I want to keep an eye on you both. I don't want you getting your hands on the will and hiding what I'm entitled to. And, if you find my magic, give it back."

"As if we'd take anything from you," I said.

"I know what my two dear sisters are like," Ava said. "You'll stab me in the back because Toby loved me more than either of you."

"I hope you don't have anything unpleasant planned for his body." I glanced at Dazielle and raised my eyebrows.

"Of course not! We'll give Toby a good send off. He'd expect it."

My head tilted. It sounded like she didn't know about Toby's body going missing. "That will be tricky."

"Why so? I expect the angels will have finished with him soon. Nolan, of course, will have a say in what happens, but we knew him better than anyone else. I have some lovely ideas for my final farewell with Toby."

"Does that include taking his body?" I asked.

Ava's cheeks paled. "His body? What are you talking about?"

Her shock seemed genuine. Maybe she wasn't aware that he'd vanished. "I'm surprised you don't know. Toby's body has gone from the morgue. What do you know about that?"

"Why would I take his body?" Ava shook her head. "It's that evil witch. Tempest has him."

"No, she doesn't," I said. "What would she want with Toby's body?"

"She hated him. Maybe she wants to do something gross with his precious body. That family is twisted and dark. She took it because she knows how much it will upset me. I hope, when the angels catch her, they lock her away for life. She deserves nothing less. Actually, she deserves to be shoved in that demon prison her family runs. That'll teach her a lesson. The demons will make mincemeat of her."

"I'd like to see them try," I muttered.

"I don't think it was Tempest who took the body," Dazielle said.

"Maybe it was you." Ava jammed her hands on her hips and glared at Dazielle. "You were always jealous of Toby's fondness for me."

"Why would I want Toby's body?"

"You have a thing for those gross stuffed animals. Maybe you thought you could stuff Toby and mount him as an ornament."

"Mount Toby!" Dazielle looked as shocked as I felt. "I'd never do that. Maybe you took him!"

"Me! I had no clue his body was even missing until Marianne told me. This is your doing, both of you. You're shutting me out, like you always do. You're a pair of—" Ava's hand flew to her mouth. "Oh! If we had all of our magic, we really could do something with Toby's body. Something amazing. Why didn't I think of that until now?"

I grabbed her arm. My magic disguise shifted. It felt like it was about to split apart. I dropped my hold on her and backed away. "What are you thinking?"

Ava stepped away from me, and her eyes narrowed. "Is this a trick?"

My stomach clenched, and I glanced at my clothes. My magic felt like it was holding. I looked at Dazielle. Her disguise was in place. She still looked just like Olivia. "Why would we want to trick you?"

Ava snorted a laugh. "Yeah, right. Like it hasn't happened before."

"What were you going to say?" I asked. "It's got to do with Toby's body."

Her mouth twisted. "If we work together, instead of bickering about Toby, we can bring him back." Ava whispered her words as if she didn't believe them.

I tilted my head, my heart racing. "How?"

"It would be difficult, and the result wouldn't be perfect." Ava frowned. "The trouble is, we're missing my gems."

"Gems? What gems?" Dazielle asked. "What do you mean? I'm not a mind reader."

"You sometimes are." Ava's gaze ran over Dazielle. "You're being weird. What's up with you?"

"Ignore Olivia," I said. "Our sister is out of sorts. It's the grief. Focus on Toby. Can we bring him back?"

Ava continued to stare at Dazielle before shaking her head. "Not without the Gems of Starlaine. The gems Toby stole from my collection. If we can find them and locate Toby's body, we might have a chance to restore him."

My chin lifted as I processed this new detail. Toby had gems that would bring him back to life. He'd also enthralled three powerful magic users, who could combine their powers to return him to life. This couldn't be a coincidence.

My heart gave three swift thuds. Toby's murder was planned. He'd wooed the succubi so they'd do anything he asked. He'd also taken their magic items. Items that could restore life. He wanted people to think he'd been murdered and that I'd done it. He was behind this whole thing.

Dazielle nudged me. "Sister, are you feeling okay?"

I cleared my throat. "Toby wants to be immortal."

"Duh! Of course!" Ava said. "That's all he's talked about for months. Remember, how he kept on about everything he could achieve if he had limitless time?" She jutted out a hip and rested her hand on it. "What's up with you, too? You're both being strange."

"If Toby became immortal, he could rule over the demons." I wasn't talking to anyone when I said that.

"Marianne!" Dazielle's elbow jabbed me again.

Ava's gaze was full of suspicion as she glared at me. "Losing Toby has made you stupid. Although, you said something similar the other night." Her gaze was on Dazielle.

Dazielle's worried gaze went to me. "I did?"

"What's the matter with you both?" Ava asked. "After Tempest came to see us at the hotel, you said that she had an idea about the demons and what Toby wants with them. How can you forget that, Olivia? You ranted about it for ages."

I winced. I couldn't help Dazielle without giving away the game.

Dazielle fussed with her hem. "Of course, I hadn't forgotten. I'm just focused on finding our missing magic."

This plan was unraveling fast. "Which one of you lost your demon hammers?" I recalled the ceremonial paraphernalia we'd discovered in the basement. It included an ancient set of demon hammers. Hammers that controlled demons.

Ava glanced at Dazielle. "Those ugly hammers were hers. They vanished ages ago. Why do you care about them?"

"Oh! Sure! Me. I lost them." Dazielle shrugged discreetly.

I nodded. That meant Toby had magic to return to life, a way to become immortal, and the ability to control demons. He was tangled up in this. He'd set this whole thing up.

"Anyway, weirdos," Ava sucked in a breath, "we need to find that witch."

"You want to go after Tempest?" I asked.

"If neither of you have Toby's body, she must have it. If we can find the gems and get the body, we can get Toby back." She clapped her hands together. "Think how amazing that will be."

"What about the will?" Dazielle asked. "Isn't that all we care about?"

"Forget the will. If Toby's body is at risk, we must get it. To have him back in any form will be wonderful."

My nose wrinkled. "No, it won't. Bringing him back is a terrible idea."

"You only think it's a terrible idea because you didn't come up with it." Ava scowled at me. "If you'd suggested it and I'd disagreed, you'd have kept on nagging like you always do until I gave in and we did it."

"Not about this. We're not bringing Toby back."

Ava grabbed my arm and pinched. "Stop being mean. Once we get the body and find the gems, we can get him back."

Her succubus power rippled through my magic disguise again. I felt it shift. I gritted my teeth, trying to hold the focus and keep the magic together, but I could feel it slipping.

I tried to pull my arm from Ava's grip, but she held on tight.

Ava tilted her head. "You look odd. Is your face... melting?"

"I'm not feeling well." I yanked my arm out of her grip, but it was too late. The magic slid off me like a warm, sticky wave. It started at my head, slid down my shoulders, and right to my toes.

Ava sucked in a breath. Her eyes widened as she continued to stare at me. "Tempest!" Her gaze turned to Olivia. "What's going on?"

Dazielle backed away. "I have no idea."

"You, too?" Ava grabbed Dazielle.

Her disguise fizzled off her, leaving Dazielle standing in her pink underwear.

Ava gasped. "What have you done with my sisters?"

Chapter 21

I held my hands up. "Let me explain."

"You expect me to believe a word you say?" Ava snarled at me. "You disguised yourself as my succubus sister. What did you expect to learn? Do you think I killed Toby?"

"It's a possibility," I said. "You were Marianne and Olivia's alibi for the time of his death. I can't figure out why, though. You're all weirdly competitive over Toby and aren't very nice to each other. What would you do to have him all to yourself?"

"Anything! Nothing! I mean, I loved him. We all loved him," Ava said. "You won't get a confession out of me. I had nothing to do with his death." Her wild gaze flashed around the hallway. "And you can't think my sisters had anything to do with it."

"We're really not sure," Dazielle said.

Ava's eyes narrowed. "I wondered where the feathers were coming from. They kept drifting off you when you were disguised."

Dazielle shrugged. "It's the wings. They're hard to keep in place when I'm tense."

"Why are you working with Toby's killer?" Ava asked.

Dazielle glanced at me. "This case is more complicated than we believed. It's possible that Tempest was framed. The disappearance of Toby's body is a cause for concern. We believe other people are involved."

"Tempest took him." Ava jabbed a finger at me. "She wants to perform some twisted ritual on Toby's body. You should arrest her."

"That option is still on the table," Dazielle said.

I glared at her. So much for working together. "Tell us more about the stolen magic items. What exactly did Toby take from all of you?"

Ava crossed her arms over her chest. "Why should I help you?"

"Because if you don't have Toby's body, and I don't, your sisters probably do."

"Oh! No way! They're not having him and leaving me out." Ava's top lip curled. "He loved me more than them."

"What's so important about these items?" Dazielle asked, looking at me.

"The demon hammers that Marianne owned weaken demons and make them easier to control. Ava's gems can restore life. What did Olivia lose?"

Ava's brow furrowed. "The Blood of Zanthar."

"Holy angels!" Dazielle's wings fluttered. "That's a myth."

"No, it's very real," Ava said. "I've seen it."

"Clue me in," I said. "What's this blood supposed to do?"

"It's from the first vampire." Dazielle licked her lips. "His full name is Zantharius Cublick Tarin De'ath. Zanthar for short. He was the first immortal being to walk this earth. If his blood is used in a regeneration ritual, the person who receives it—"

"Becomes immortal," I said. "Combine that with the gems' restorative powers and hand Toby the demon hammers, and he can control whoever he likes, including a demon army."

Dazielle's gaze lasered in on Ava. "Are you sure you were with your sisters the night Toby died?"

Ava's bottom lip trembled. "I trust my succubus sisters."

My gut clenched. "You weren't. You lied for them."

Her chin lifted. "I saw no harm in saying we were together."

"They weren't with you," I said. "I bet they were in Willow Tree Falls."

"That's not true." Ava clasped her hands together. "I wasn't with them, but they promised me they were together. They were worried about me. I had no alibi for that night. I was on my own. They were concerned that I might be a suspect when we learned of his death."

"They weren't concerned about you," I said. "They were covering their backs."

"No! They can't be involved in this." She worried her bottom lip with her teeth. "Although, I loved Toby the most. Even when he lied to me and stole my magic items, I couldn't hate him."

"Did Marianne and Olivia hate Toby for what he did?"

Ava shook her head. "They cared for him, but they were jealous about my relationship with Toby. Toby loved me the most out of all of us."

"If that's correct, why didn't he stay just with you?" I asked.

"Toby had a lot of love to give. He was a generous man with a big heart."

"Or he was a cheating louse," I said. "He played you. And he played your succubus sisters. I doubt if he loved any of you. Toby used people to get what he wanted. He knew of your powerful magic and your collections of magic items. That's what he wanted."

"You're wrong. Like attracts like," Ava said. "I'm a strong magic user, and Toby was a powerful warlock. His mind manipulation ability was second to none."

"An ability he used on you," I said.

Ava's fingers stroked over the snake tattoo on her wrist. "Toby would never do that."

"You still love a man who cheated on you, lied to you, and stole from you. How is that normal? You should be cursing his name. You should be dancing on his grave. You should be happy that Toby's dead. Instead, you pine after him and tell us that you miss him."

Ava blinked slowly several times. "That's because I do. It's hard to explain. I understand that what you're saying is true, but the words fade from my thoughts as soon as I hear them. They have no meaning. I still love Toby. I want to be with him."

It looked like Toby still had his claws deep in Ava. "Did he give you gifts when you were together?" My gaze ran over her. She wore a beautiful garnet pendant, two bracelets, and several silver rings.

"Of course. Toby was generous with his gifts."

"Any jewelry?"

"Yes! This ring with the emerald. It's so beautiful." She smiled as she looked at the ring.

"You've worn that ring ever since Toby gave it to you?"

"That's right. I cherish it." Ava lowered her hand. "I only remove it to have it cleaned. Toby always used to take care of that for me. He was such a thoughtful man."

"You have to take the ring off," I said. "That's how Toby's manipulated you. I bet he's infused that gem with his magic. He did it to Aurora. I'm certain of it."

Ava stared at the ring. "I can't take it off."

"You must. It will make you think differently about Toby. Do Marianne and Olivia also wear rings he gave them?"

"They do," Ava said. "We cherish our gifts from Toby."

"They aren't gifts. Those rings are a problem."

Ava's hand went to her mouth. "Toby would never do anything so deceitful."

"He's done exactly that," I said. "Take off the ring and you'll see for yourself."

Ava shook her head. "It's a part of me. If I take it off, it will feel like I'm losing a finger."

I glanced at Dazielle. "We'll have to do this the hard way."

We pounced at the same time. Dazielle leaped behind Ava and wrapped her huge wings around her, covering her from head to toe in long white feathers.

A muffled scream of outrage came from out of the feathers.

"Don't let her go!" I yanked Ava's hand out.

"Hurry!" Dazielle said.

I wasn't sure which ring to remove, so I yanked them all off. I backed away and nodded at Dazielle. "She's free to go." I kept hold of the rings to stop Ava from being tempted into putting them back on.

Ava staggered away from Dazielle, coughing and spluttering, her eyes glowing with fury. "Give them back! They're my rings."

"Ava, calm down," I said. "Think about Toby. How do you feel about him?"

"I can't think about him, when all I want to do is kill you," she snarled at me. "In fact, I don't care about Toby. Wait! I don't... care about Toby Matlock?"

"That's it! Keep going. You don't love Toby."

Ava shook her head. "What's going on? I've always loved him."

"Not anymore," I said. "It was all a lie."

Ava's jaw dropped, and she rested a hand over her heart. "I feel strange. My feelings for Toby are mixed with a deep hatred. My mind feels weird. I love him, but I hate him. He cheated on me, but I still want to be with him."

"It could take time for the magic to leave your system," Dazielle said. "You've been under Toby's influence for a long time."

The sound of slow hand-clapping had me tensing. I turned to look in the direction of the noise.

Toby stood at the top of the stairs. He was very much alive and as smug as ever.

Chapter 22

Standing on either side of Toby were the real Marianne and Olivia. So much for our plan to distract them with tasty pizza. Toby's influence over them must beat amazing takeout food.

"Toby!" Ava took several steps toward him. "What have you done?"

He ignored her. "Congratulations, Tempest. I'm not sure how you did it, but you almost figured out what I've been planning."

"I've figured it all out," I said. "Tell me where my sister is, you deceitful, slimy piece of—"

"Sweet little Aurora. She was a charming gift. I enjoyed her company very much." Toby descended the stairs slowly, the succubi flanking him. His gaze flickered to Dazielle, and his smugness faded.

As he drew closer, I saw his skin had a gray tinge, and he limped when he put any weight on his right leg. The magic that had brought him back wasn't perfect.

"Tell me where Aurora is, and I might let you live." I moved closer.

Marianne and Olivia jumped in front of Toby, acting like a shield, their eyes flashing and their fingers curled.

"You're almost as determined as your sister to seek out the truth," Toby said.

I glared at him. "I knew it! Aurora figured out the truth about you."

"Perhaps."

"Where. Is. She." My fingers flexed as my desire to punch him grew.

"Your sister is no longer important. My ambition to become immortal has been achieved. It's time to move on to the next phase of my plan."

I growled at him. "I will destroy you."

Dazielle touched my arm. "Wait! We need to know the truth, or we may never find Aurora."

"You should listen to your angel friend," Toby said. "Besides, it's not possible to kill me."

"I'll give it a really good try." I stalked toward Toby.

Marianne and Olivia hissed at me.

"Stop hiding behind your women," I snapped, keeping a wary eye on the succubi.

"My women will always protect me. That is their job." Toby made no move toward me. He must still be weak after his near-death experience.

Ava staggered toward Toby, hatred contorting her face. "If Tempest doesn't kill you, I will. You tricked me. All this time, you fooled me into loving you."

Toby's gaze shifted to Ava's bare hand, and he winced. "That's such a shame. You always were my favorite."

Marianne and Olivia turned and looked at him. "I thought I was your favorite," they said at the same time.

He stroked their faces. "My lovelies, I adore you both equally."

"Toby's lying to you. He set this whole thing up," I said. "He conned Nolan into draining me of my power and framed me for his murder. Did you have Nolan kill you? Was he in on this the whole time?"

Toby shrugged. "You're half-right. My brother is a simpleton. He's easy to bend to my will."

"You manipulated Nolan," I said. "How did you make your death seems so convincing?"

"I might have the answer to that," Dazielle said. "Just before Toby's body was taken, Cassiel drew some fluids. The test results are back. It showed a magic preservative in Toby's system. It had the ability to stop a person's heart but preserve the body."

"Suspending Toby in limbo," I said.

He stroked his fingers down his goatee. "I was simply resting."

"Which is why your body never cooled," I said. "You faked your death and set me up using your brother."

"Toby's an honest man," Marianne said. "Everything you say is a lie."

"It isn't a lie," Ava said. "I'm no fan of Tempest's, but she figured it out. Toby's deceived us all."

"Don't waste your breath," I said. "While Marianne and Olivia wear those rings, Toby has them exactly where he wants them."

Toby gestured to the succubi. "My wonderful women have the ability to break the death magic that held me. Of course, I would keep them by my side."

"Why not me?" Ava stamped her foot.

I stared at her. "You want to be an accomplice in a murder? Well, I mean, a stooge in a fake murder? A fake murder that would have seen me behind bars."

"Or rather, an accomplice in creating an immortal being who wishes to rule the demons," Dazielle said.

I jabbed a finger at her. "Yes! That. That's the most important thing. Toby wants our demons."

Ava pouted. "Am I not good enough to keep around, Toby?"

I slapped a hand against my forehead. "Ava! You're the lucky one. You got free. Your sisters are stuck with that sicko."

"Marianne and Olivia acted willingly. They love me and wish to ensure my safety. When they realized you were a threat to me, we devised the plan between us," Toby said.

I didn't believe that, especially not with the silver rings I'd spotted on Marianne and Olivia's fingers. "Willingly my butt. You've played them and me. You used your brother to drain me of magic. Then you influenced me using the hair you stole months ago, setting me up to look like I killed you."

"I technically did die," Toby said. "Those injuries couldn't be faked."

"But I didn't kill you," I said. "Nolan helped."

"As I said, my brother is easy to influence. You made something of a mess before Nolan stepped in and laid things out so neatly."

"The rings!" Ava said. "Marianne and Olivia are also wearing Toby's gifts. They must be just like mine."

Toby's eyes narrowed. "And they will continue to wear them until I have no further use for their abilities."

"Huh?" Marianne looked confused.

Olivia's lips pursed, and her brow crinkled as if she was trying to solve a complicated equation.

"No, they won't." I lunged at the succubi.

Ava was right alongside me, snarling at her sisters as she tore at their hands. I wasn't certain what her motives were for helping me. She probably wasn't certain herself, having been manipulated for such a long time, but I was glad to have her fighting on my side.

Toby was quick to back away and remained hidden behind Marianne and Olivia. I snarled my disgust at him. There wasn't a shred of a hero about Toby. This man might now be immortal, but he was still a coward.

I yanked the rings from Olivia's fingers just as something hot, hard, and painfully magical slammed into my back. I kept hold of my handful of rings as I tumbled down the stairs and landed at Dazielle's feet.

She stared at me, not offering to help me up. "I can't decide if that was brave or foolish."

"Probably a bit of both." I kept hold of the rings as Ava tackled Marianne to the ground. They bounced down the stairs screeching at each other.

"I got them!" Ava rolled away and leaped to her feet, holding out Marianne's rings.

"Give it a few minutes," I said as I staggered upright. "They'll soon feel differently about Toby."

Marianne advanced on Ava. "Traitor!"

"You're the traitor. You should have involved me. I've always been a part of Toby's life."

I didn't know whether to roll my eyes or slap her. Ava was still jealous. After everything she knew about Toby, the thing that bothered her the most was that she'd been excluded from framing me and bringing a monster to life.

"None of you should have been involved," I yelled. "Toby betrayed you all. He won't want any of you now you've served your purpose."

Marianne shook her head and glanced at Olivia, who stood on the stairs, her confused gaze moving from me to Toby.

"You said you never loved Ava," Olivia said. "Toby, you said I was your true love, and you felt sorry for the others."

"And you are." Toby licked his lips. "Ava has never been important to me. She was always the weak link. Focus on my voice, ladies. Listen to everything I tell you."

"No, no, no! Hold on a pretty second." Olivia wheeled on Toby. "You said you loved me the best. Me! I'm your true love. Was that a lie?"

"I love both of you." Toby raised a hand and backed up a step. "You'll always assist me and want to help me, no matter what I ask you to do."

Marianne and Olivia moved to stand together. Their fingers flexed, and their expressions hardened as they looked first at each other and then back at Toby. His control over them was fading.

"I am feeling different now my ring has gone," Marianne said. "What's the meaning of this, Toby?"

Olivia jabbed a finger at him. "You claim to love us both equally, but that's not fair. You're lying to one of us."

"Me included," Ava muttered. She joined her sisters and took hold of their hands. "Toby always told me to keep quiet and never reveal this to you, but he never stopped seeing me. He claimed he couldn't let me go."

Marianne glowered at Toby. "You sneaky, lying little creep. You said exactly the same thing to me."

"And me," Olivia said. "You were seeing all of us at the same time and making us keep it a secret."

"He did it by using the rings. They controlled you," I said. A flicker of delight ran through me as I saw the worry cross Toby's face. "He stole your magic items and used you to help fake his death."

"It's coming back to me," Olivia said softly. "Toby insisted I break him out of the morgue. Before he died, he told me to visit him and he would be restored. I remember helping him through the doors at Angel Force. I saw you, Tempest."

Toby backed up several more steps. He might be immortal, but he could still sense when danger surrounded him. "Ladies, this has all been a big mistake. Don't trust Tempest. She hates me."

"She's not the only one," Ava growled.

"Where have you been hiding?" I asked him. "Once you left the morgue where did you go?"

"He's been in this house," Marianne said. "We've been covering for him, using our abilities to shield him."

"That's true," Olivia said. "Toby said he was waiting for things to blow over. Once you were charged with his murder, Tempest, your family would be devastated. Their focus would be on trying to prove your innocence."

I bared my teeth at Toby. "And while they were doing that, you'd get what you wanted. Access to the demons in the prison. Is that why the demons have been so restless? They knew you were coming. What did you promise them?"

"I have no idea what you're talking about." Toby's gaze flickered to Dazielle before he looked away.

"Liar!" Ava shouted. "You told me about the demons. That's why you gave me that blood to look after."

I stared at her. "What blood?"

"Your sister's blood," Ava said. "To begin with, I couldn't figure out why he was draining her of blood. Then Toby told me about the demon prison. He made me promise to keep quiet about it. I wasn't to tell anyone, not even Marianne and Olivia."

My stomach dropped as I stared at Toby. "Aurora revealed that Crypt witch blood is needed to access the prison, didn't she?"

"Aurora talked a lot of fluffy nonsense. I remember nothing about demons. She was mostly interested in planning our wedding." Toby continued to inch away.

"You've been draining Aurora's blood all this time?" My hands clenched into fists, enraged that he'd harmed her. "I'll find a way around your new immortality. If it takes me the rest of my life, you're going to end up in the ground."

"Calm yourself, Tempest," Toby said. "It was only a little blood."

"There were pints of the stuff," Ava said. "Your sister's fortunate to be alive."

"Maybe she's not." My teeth ground. It was only Dazielle's restraining hand that stopped me from leaping up the stairs and slamming my fist into Toby's face.

"You can't take him on," she muttered. "He's immortal and powerful. You're barely a witch. Cool your heels."

Some of my anger gave way to terror. "Tell me one thing, and I might let you leave this place."

Toby smirked. "You may ask."

"Is Aurora still alive?"

He chuckled. "In a manner of speaking. You'll never find her."

"I swear on all the goddesses that I won't stop hounding you until I do. I'll make your immortal life a misery."

"I have all the time in the world. Yours is limited. I won't reveal my secret, and you will die a broken witch. You will never find your sister. You have failed her."

I was too angry to get upset. I hated to admit that Toby could be right. He'd gotten what he wanted and had discarded Aurora just like all the other women he'd used over the years.

Ava reached over, and her hand wrapped around mine. "I sense your pain. Sisters stick together. We've all been wronged by Toby."

I nodded, not able to speak as my throat tightened, my thoughts on Aurora. Wherever she was, she must be so scared and confused.

"We'll see that justice is done," Marianne said. "With your permission, we'll exact revenge on your behalf."

"Revenge." Olivia's eyes sparkled. "We owe ourselves that."

"Hold on a moment, ladies." Toby's panicked gaze shot around the succubi. "We're a team. We work together. Put your rings back on, and this will all make sense."

"Not anymore." Olivia took a step toward him, taking us all with her. "You cheated us. You lied to us, and you used us. And now you've taken Tempest's sister. Her true blood family. Shame on you."

"It was for the greater good," Toby said. "Stay by my side, all of you. I'll rule the demons, and you can be my princesses. You can have as much power as me. Think about it, with all those demons under our command, we can rule anywhere we like. We can control any magic community or even go into the human world and dominate. Whatever we desire, it will be ours."

Marianne's eyes met mine. A question lingered in her gaze. I smiled. She hadn't been swayed by Toby's silken words. These powerful women were finally free, and they were mad as hell.

As much as I wanted to take Toby down myself, I couldn't in my weakened condition. The succubi had been twisted by Toby all these years. They deserved their own payback. Their sisterhood, for all its sniping and bitchiness, had stood the test of Toby's deviance. They stood with each other, fury simmering off them as they waited for my permission to strike.

I nodded at Marianne and dropped Ava's hand. "Make him pay."

"Tempest," Dazielle hissed, "I cannot allow that."

I watched as they stalked up the stairs toward Toby. "Give them five minutes. If what Toby said is true, he cannot die, but he needs to pay. You can have him when they're finished. He's taken Aurora. Maybe a beating from the succubi will loosen his tongue and we can find out where she is."

"Angel, you cannot permit this." Toby was already surrounded by the succubi, his anxious gaze on Dazielle. Magic sparkled around him like jagged crystals.

My gaze turned pleading as I stared up at Dazielle. "Five minutes. For Aurora."

She looked away. "I guess I do like Aurora."

I let out a sigh. "Succubi, get to work." I didn't wince once at the sounds of them tearing into Toby.

Dazielle grimaced and turned her back on the scene. "I'm not involved with this."

"If it makes you feel any better, you couldn't have stopped them. One angel against three succubi, you had no choice but to agree to this."

"Maybe not," Dazielle muttered. "But after this, Toby comes with me."

"Agreed," I said. "Although, what are you planning on charging him with?"

"The illegal use of mind manipulation. Theft. Trying to destroy the world and become a demon master." She glanced at me. "I could go on."

"Kidnapping," I whispered. "Aurora's still missing. Maybe you'll even have to charge him with murder."

Dazielle patted my arm. "Let's hope it doesn't come to that. You're free to go, Tempest. From what I've heard here, you had no active part in this crime. Toby is alive, which means you can't have murdered him."

I swallowed my sadness. "I always told you I was innocent."

Dazielle shrugged. "I follow the clues. They led me to you."

I watched with a certain amount of twisted satisfaction as Toby vanished beneath the wrath of the succubi. This victory felt like a hollow one. A part of me felt like it was missing. Aurora. Toby was out of her life for good, but that gave me no comfort until I found her.

I looked around the hallway for a second, my heart twisting with grief. Where was she? I had to find her. Until I did, this mystery wasn't solved.

Chapter 23

I stood outside Toby's house with my family, including my cousins Raine and Azura. They'd stuck around after helping settle the demon prison. I was glad to have them by my side.

It had been two days since the succubi had tried to beat the truth out of Toby about what he'd done to Aurora. He hadn't said anything.

Dazielle had given them their five minutes then summoned her angels, and they'd escorted Toby and the succubi to the station to tidy up this mess.

Nolan had also been rounded up. Technically, he had killed his brother; although, when he'd been questioned, he said I'd inflicted some damage on Toby to ensure there was evidence to frame me. Questioning was still ongoing as the angels figured out exactly what to charge everyone with.

Rhett was also with me. He wrapped an arm around my shoulders. "How are you feeling?"

I felt better, but I didn't feel complete. "I'm on the mend."

"It will take time," Granny Dottie said. "With your magic so drained by the siphon, you won't be back to full strength for months. No demon hunting for you until then."

"I still want to help," I said. "I can cover some shifts at the cemetery. Just until Aurora... well, until she gets back."

Everyone was quiet. No one wanted to admit that Aurora might be gone for good.

"You need to rest," Mom said. "I don't want you exerting yourself if the demons try to get out. You focus on Cloven Hoof."

"Not that they've bothered to escape anymore," Grandpa Lucius said. "It looks like word has gotten out that their new lord and master has been arrested. They won't get a free pass from prison anytime soon."

I nodded grimly. Toby Matlock would never see the outside of a cell again. His everlasting life would be a miserable one. He deserved every second of it.

"We just need Aurora back." I stared at the house. Every time I was here, I expected to see her. It seemed like being here made me closer to her.

"The angels can't torture the answer out of Toby?" Raine tugged on the end of her magenta tipped black ponytail.

"They aren't into torture," I said.

"They should let us at him," Azura said. She was a petite version of Raine, with close cut black hair and long limbs. Both were equally deadly, despite their elven looks. "We know a few tricks to make him talk. He might not be so smug when he's missing a few limbs."

"We'd all like to torture Toby Matlock," Auntie Queenie said. "Whilst he knows where Aurora is, he has power over us. He'll hold on to any shred of influence he can."

"Aurora's here," I said. "I know she is."

"The angels have searched the house several times," Mom said. "Nothing was found."

"Don't you feel it?" I turned to her. "I expect to see her wander out the front door and past those dragons. She's here."

Mom stroked my hair off my face. "Perhaps it's just because she spent so long in this place. There's nothing inside to suggest she's in hiding."

Someone cleared their throat. I turned to see Dazielle looking awkward as she stood away from the group. "Mind if I have a minute of your time, Tempest?"

"Sure." I ducked under Rhett's arm and walked over to her. "I thought you'd still be busy questioning everyone."

"We're almost done," Dazielle said. "I'll also need your statement."

"Sure, whatever you need to make sure Toby never gets out."

"He's going nowhere," Dazielle said.

I tilted my head. "Has Toby told you something about Aurora?"

"Nothing. Every time I mention her name, he just looks smug and refuses to talk."

My stomach sank. "I'd expect nothing less of him."

"However, I have been talking to his brother, Nolan. He's embarrassed about his involvement. He feels humiliated that his brother manipulated him into setting the fake murder scene." Dazielle raised an eyebrow. "We've done a deal of sorts."

"What kind of deal?"

"In exchange for Nolan returning your power, he's getting a reduced sentence."

My eyes widened. "Wow! You did that for me?"

Dazielle shook her head as she extracted a dark purple vial from beneath her wings. "Not for you, for your sister. Everyone misses her. It's wrong what Toby did."

I went to grab the vial, but she held it up. "Come on. I need those powers."

"Hear me out before you take them," Dazielle said. "There's no guarantee that getting your powers back will help you find Aurora."

"It can't do any harm."

"I guess not. You have a close bond with your sister. Maybe when you're operating on full strength, you'll figure out what Toby did."

I gritted my teeth. "Has he told you that he hurt her? Is that why you're doing this? I'm going to find her body when my powers kick in, aren't I?"

"No! Toby has said she's alive, but he's hiding something."

I blew out a breath. "I can live with that for now. Give me my powers."

"One more thing. There's a problem."

"Which is?"

Dazielle stared at the vial. "Something went wrong when Nolan took your power. Or rather, not wrong as such, but he took more than he meant to. When he siphoned your witch ability, he also removed Frank."

I closed my eyes for a second as the realization struck me like a giant, spiked club. "If I take my power back, Frank comes too?"

"I believe so."

I dropped my chin to my chest. "I stay weak and never regain my ability, which means I'll never find Aurora, or I get back my power and my demon." That sucked. I was getting used to not having inappropriate, murderous thoughts about Aurora. Once I had him inside me again, all that stress would return.

"That's about the size of it," Dazielle said. "I know you struggle with Frank. We all struggle with Frank. I understand you've been looking to remove him for some time. Now, he's gone."

"If I accept that, I might as well have killed Aurora myself. Or rather, let Frank loose to do what he always wanted."

"That's the choice. You stay weak and free of Frank, or you get back everything."

My gut twisted. There was no perfect solution. But Dazielle was right; my tie to Aurora was solid and so was Frank's. He could sense her wherever she was. Would having my demon back be such a bad thing? If she was alive, he'd know it. He'd go hunting for her.

If I took Frank back, Aurora would always be vulnerable around me. We could never be normal sisters, just hanging out and enjoying life. But who wanted normal? I wanted my sister back, no matter the cost.

"What's it going to be, Tempest?" Dazielle asked.

I held out my hand. "Give me the vial."

Dazielle handed me the vial. "Be careful. Frank could be spitting mad over what happened." She held out a brown bag that she had tucked under her arm.

"What's in that?"

"I figured you'd choose the vial. There are half a dozen muffins in that bag. You might need them to control Frank."

I chuckled as I took the bag. "For an angel, you're not so terrible, Dazielle."

"And for a witch with an attitude and a demon about to be living inside her again, you're not so terrible either."

I nodded before downing the vial. My breath shot out of me, and my stomach clenched. Sparks flooded my vision, and my body shook as power flooded through me. Although the feelings were intense, I recognized them. I'd missed them. I'd missed my magic.

Dazielle backed away. "I'll leave you to it. Enjoy the return of your power. Good luck finding your sister."

I nodded, not wanting to speak in case I bit off my own tongue. Heat flooded from my feet and up through my body as my magic reassembled itself.

"Tempest, is everything okay?" Granny Dottie reached my side. "What did that angel want?"

"Give me a minute," I said through gritted teeth.

The rest of the family joined Granny Dottie as I stood there shaking. Rhett reached out a hand, but I shook my head. I couldn't risk anyone touching me, not until my magic was fully formed and I could get a handle on just how mad Frank was.

More energy flooded through me, heating my veins and making me feel alive for the first time in days. I hadn't realized how weak I'd been. The world seemed brighter, and my lungs filled with air as if I'd just taken my first full breath in a long time.

The vial I held dropped to the ground and shattered. With one more violent shake, I was back. My head snapped up, and I stared around the group.

Granny Dottie grinned at me. "Would you look at that? Tempest Crypt has her magic back. How did that happen?"

I glanced at the retreating form of Dazielle. "The angels have their uses. She convinced Nolan to give me back what he'd taken." I breathed in a deep breath, and my nose wrinkled. Everything smelled so pungent. I didn't even need to look for Wiggles. I could smell his sulfur stink.

"Does that include Frank?" Mom asked.

I reached inside my head. There he was. He felt asleep, not mad. Maybe being siphoned had drained him. I could only hope so. "Frank's back."

"Well, you're back to your old self," Mom said. "That's the most important thing. How do you feel?"

"Alive." I also felt a little unstable on my feet. My magic was settling into place, and energy buzzed through me like I'd had a dozen shots of espresso.

"This is something to celebrate." Granny Dottie wrapped me in a big hug.

As I hugged her back, my gaze drifted to the house. It settled on the stone dragons outside the entrance.

I pulled away from Granny Dottie's embrace and stepped closer to the stone dragons. Something was odd about one of them.

"Is everything okay?" Granny Dottie joined me.

I blinked several times. "Is that dragon crying?" I walked closer with Granny Dottie. The rest of the family followed.

"It does look like it's crying," Granny Dottie said. "How is that possible? It's made of stone."

"This dragon is a new addition to Toby's collection," I said. "I've been here several times, and there were only ever two dragons outside until recently." The liquid leaking out of the dragon's eyes intensified.

I rested a hand on its stone flank and gasped. There was a lot more to this dragon than met my eye. My magic still felt hazy and unfocused, but it was strong and ready to be used.

The dragon vibrated under my touch. Something was hiding inside the stone. My heart pounded as I watched the dragon's tears drip to the ground. It wasn't a thing; it was a person.

"Everyone, gather around this dragon," I said. "Someone's inside it."

"There's a person in there?" Mom touched the stone, and her eyes widened. "What is this?"

Hope surged through me. "Everyone touch the dragon."

Auntie Queenie leaned in close. "Could it be Aurora?"

I glanced at her and nodded. I hadn't dared say it out loud in case I was wrong. "We have to break this spell."

"Is it safe?" Mom asked.

I looked at Auntie Queenie and she nodded, encouraging me. "The safest. I think this is where Aurora's been hiding." My gaze went around the group to see a mix of hope, fear, and joy. "Are we all ready?"

Everyone nodded.

I closed my eyes and focused my messy feeling magic on breaking the spell.

"It's working!" Mom cried. "Everybody keep going."

My eyes snapped open. I saw the dragon's form melting in front of us. A whoop of joy flew from my lips as Aurora appeared, her eyes wide and red-rimmed.

A sob fell from her mouth as she dropped from the stone platform the dragon had been resting on.

Rhett caught her in his arms before she hit the ground. Everyone crowded around Aurora, all talking at once and touching her, not able to believe she was there.

"My baby girl! You're alive!" Mom kissed Aurora's face repeatedly, laughing and crying as she did so.

Aurora blinked, confusion on her face. "I could see you all. And hear you. I couldn't tell you where I was. Everything was so muddled."

"You're safe now." Granny Dottie clasped her hand. "We've got you."

"It was so scary," Aurora whispered. "I thought I'd never get free. I screamed until my voice vanished, but no one knew I was here."

I grabbed hold of her other hand. "Do you remember what happened?"

She nodded. "It was Toby. He tricked me all this time. It was horrible. I knew something was wrong, but I couldn't break free from him. It wasn't until I took off my pendant to have a bath one night that something jogged my thoughts. I kept the pendant off all night. That was when I figured out he'd been using me."

"Forget about him," I said.

"I saw the angels take Toby," Aurora said. "Do they know what he did?"

"They're figuring it out," I said. "Can you stand?"

Aurora glanced up at Rhett, who still held her. "I think so. Thanks for catching me, Rhett."

"Anytime." Rhett gently lowered her to the ground.

I caught hold of her and hugged her tightly. "You're back with us. Toby can't do anything to you ever again."

She clung to me, her mouth pressed against my ear. "I'm so embarrassed. Can you forgive me?"

"There's nothing to forgive. You're my sister, and I love you. I was never going to stop fighting to get you free from him."

"I'm so glad you didn't."

I stepped back, tears in my eyes as I watched everyone else hug Aurora and fuss around her.

Rhett caught hold of my hand and squeezed. "You did a great job, Tempest. We might never have figured out where Toby had hidden Aurora if it wasn't for you."

"When I saw the dragon's tears, I just knew. It had to be her. Only Aurora could be sweet enough to make a stone dragon sad."

He kissed my cheek. "You're an amazing witch."

I rested my head on his shoulder as I listened to Aurora laugh. It was a sound I'd missed. Everyone was back where they belonged. Toby would go to prison, and the mystery had been solved.

"Are you glad to have me back, as well?" Frank whispered in my head.

Despite not being thrilled to have my demon return, it felt like I was whole again.

"You'd have never found Aurora if it wasn't for me," Frank continued. "I showed you the dragon's tears. I'm bonded with your sister as strongly as you are to me. You should be thanking me."

I didn't and simply shoved him back down. I'd deal with Frank another day. Maybe he did deserve a treat if he really had shown me those tears, though. Right now, I wanted to be surrounded by my family and the people I loved.

We were back together. Willow Tree Falls was safe, Aurora wasn't marrying a nightmare of a man, justice had been served, and I'd never have to wear a lemon-yellow bridesmaid's dress again.

About Author

K.E. O'Connor (Karen) is a cozy mystery author living in the beautiful British countryside. She loves all things mystery, animals, and cake. When she's not writing about mysteries, murder, and treats, she volunteers at a local animal sanctuary, reads a ton of books, binge watches mystery series, and dreams about living somewhere warmer.

To stay in touch with the fun mysteries:

Newsletter:
www.subscribepage.com/cozymysteries

Website:
www.keoconnor.com/writing

Facebook:
www.facebook.com/keoconnorauthor

Also By

Luck of the Witch
Hell of a Witch
Revenge of the Witch
Curse of the Witch
Son of a Witch
Framing of the Witch
Trickery of the Witch
Wishes of the Witch
Harmony of the Witch
Remedy of the Witch
Gift of the Witch
Toil of the Witch
Jinxing of the Witch
Craving of the Witch
Union of the Witch
Chaos of the Witch
Sleighing of the Witch

If you enjoyed

Framing of the Witch

turn the page to read an extract from the next Crypt
Witch Mystery

TRICKERY OF THE WITCH

Chapter 1

"Move over a bit, Tempest. I've got no room." My cousin, Azura nudged me with her elbow.

I shifted over, but there was barely any space around the crowded table in Mom's kitchen. Everyone was there, including my cousins, Azura and Raine, who'd arranged a last-minute visit and were staying for the weekend.

"Ouch! You're squashing my foot." Aurora sat on my other side, smooshed between Uncle Kenny and me.

"It's not my fault we don't have a bigger table." I grabbed for the bread as it passed by, taking two white slices so I wouldn't be left with the healthy wholemeal.

"It's great to have you all here." Auntie Queenie bustled in and kissed Raine and Azura's cheeks in turn. "My girls so rarely visit. This is a perfect surprise." She shoved her way into a seat next to Uncle Kenny and helped herself to a mountain of creamed potato.

"It was Raine's idea," Azura said, a mirror of her sister with pale skin and black hair. "She announced a couple of days ago that we were coming to Willow Tree Falls."

Raine shrugged. "What can I say? I missed you all."

"Of course you did, darling," Auntie Queenie said.

"We're always happy to have you." Mom hurried around the table, checking that everyone had enough to eat.

"You'll have to come to Cloven Hoof one night," I said.

"Definitely," Azura said. "I love it there. Have you got those mushrooms that make you feel all floaty and giggly?"

"Always."

Raine nodded, her mouth full of food. "We'll be there."

Wiggles' paws settled on my knees, and he pressed down hard to get my attention.

I peered at him. "What are you doing?"

"Avoiding being crushed to death by so many feet. Get me out of here. I've already had my tail trodden on twice."

I shoved my seat back and pulled him onto my lap.

He grabbed a potato from my plate and swallowed it whole.

"If you do that again, I'm putting you back under the table to face trial by sweaty feet."

"It's the only way I can get food," he said. "It's like a pack of vultures around this table."

"It's grab it and growl around here when we're all together," Granny Dottie said with a chuckle. She tossed Wiggles a piece of bread, which he caught in mid-air.

It was rare my entire family got together. Someone always needed to keep an eye on the demon prison. Not today. We had spells in place to alert us of any trouble, and the demons were on their best behavior ever since the extra protection spells were put in place. It was a precautionary measure following a near miss when the demons revolted and tried to escape.

The new spells stung them like a mass of angry hornets and helped to remind them that no one broke out of a prison guarded by the Crypt witches.

I looked around the crowded table and smiled. When the family converged in one place, it was always like this. Everyone talked over each other, excited to share their news and find out what everyone else was doing.

It felt good to be surrounded by this kind of chaos. It had been a tricky couple of months since we'd almost lost Aurora to her unscrupulous fiancé, but finally, things were getting back to normal.

I nudged Aurora with my elbow. "How's the food?"

She pushed her potato salad around with a fork. "Good."

"Did you see the apple pie Mom made?"

"I think I'll skip dessert," she said.

My eyebrows rose. Aurora never skipped dessert. She'd been down ever since discovering her fiancé was a lying, deceitful swine. Her usually bubbly personality had been squashed by him, and she was struggling to get back to her old self. I worried she might never get over what Toby did to her.

"You know what you need." I leaned closer to Aurora, even though only inches separated us. "To go out on a few dates. Find somebody to make you laugh again."

She shook her head, her gaze downcast. "Not a chance."

"You're not interested in getting a new boyfriend?"

"Absolutely not. What's the point? You can't trust any of them."

That definitely wasn't Aurora talking. She was usually the cheery one. I could be, well, a little grumpy at times. We balanced each other out.

"Some of them aren't so bad. Rhett's decent," I said.

"Rhett's also a fallen angel, who heads up a biker gang," Aurora said. "Hardly a glowing character reference."

I didn't miss the sharpness in her tone. I let it slide. She was having a rough time. "I'm not saying you need to find someone to marry, but someone who'll show you a good time wouldn't be a bad thing."

"You don't want to stay out of the saddle too long," Granny Dottie said way too loudly, obviously listening in to the conversation. "You don't want your skills to get rusty."

I shook my head at Granny Dottie. Now wasn't the time for her to dish out her pearls of wisdom when it came to romance.

She continued, ignoring my signal to put a sock in it. "How about that charming Tate from Mystic

Mushroom? I'm always trying to get him married off."

Aurora lowered her fork. "Tate's nice. I'm just not interested in a relationship. I've decided to stick to work and not think about love. I intend to expand Heaven's Door. I let things slide when I was with Toby, and I've lost customers."

"They'll be back," I said. "No one can resist your store for long." Heaven's Door always smelled of brownies, vanilla, and hope. Aurora always had a smile and a solution for every customer.

She sighed. "I hope so. Still, that will be my focus for now. Maybe forever."

Wiggles rested his head on her knees, his back end splayed across my thighs. "I'll be your furry boyfriend if you ask nicely."

She petted his head. "That's sweet of you. Where shall we go on our first date?"

He flipped on his back and exposed his belly. "Give me a rub while I think about it. Do you like muddy holes and sticks?"

Aurora obliged with a belly rub. "Not so much."

"Then we might have a problem," Wiggles said.

"How about you get a pet, like Wiggles?" I said.

Aurora lifted her gaze to mine. A little sparkle of happiness appeared in her blue eyes. "That's not a bad idea. I don't have a familiar."

My mouth twisted to the side. "I hadn't thought about you getting a familiar, but why not?" Familiars were magic users' companions. They healed and enhanced magic and came in all different forms, from cute dogs to enormous owls.

Wiggles was definitely not a familiar and marched firmly to the beat of his own stubby paws while stealing food and talking back. But he was my best buddy, and although he could be a huge pain in my behind, I wouldn't change him.

"That's a great idea," Mom said. "A familiar will be excellent company, Aurora. They can help you in the store while you get everything back together."

"Cats. That's what you should stick to," Auntie Queenie said. "You never see our three giving you problems."

I arched a brow. That was debatable. Mom, Granny Dottie, and Auntie Queenie had three black cats as their familiars. They were spiky, difficult, and rude to everybody apart from them.

"Let's finish here and go to Fur Baby Emporium," I said. "Abigail always has plenty of familiars for sale."

Wiggles grunted. "Do I have to come? Abigail might try to sell me because of my unique skill set."

"Your skill set is stealing from the trash and breaking wind," I said. "Who would find that desirable?"

"You do."

I rubbed his head. I sort of did.

"You absolutely must come with us," Aurora said. "You can give me advice on suitable familiars."

"So long as there are doughnuts involved afterwards, I'm in," he said.

Aurora touched my arm, and she smiled. "Thanks, Tempest. It's a great idea. I would like some company. I get lonely on my own now that, well, now things are different."

I grimaced. I was glad she didn't say Toby's name in front of everyone. It always riled people up when they were reminded of what happened.

She'd been living with Toby before his lies had been exposed, and it would take her a while to get used to her own company again. But if she got a familiar, she'd have nothing to worry about. Problem solved.

We raced through the rest of lunch, and I grabbed three slices of apple pie to go from Mom before hurrying out the front door.

As much as I loved my family, they were chaotic and noisy. I was more into the chilled, relaxed vibe at my club, Cloven Hoof. Short periods of exposure to my family I could handle. Anything else and I got stressed and started to snap.

We walked side-by-side, taking bites of our pie as Wiggles romped ahead. It had been a stressful few months. I'd come so close to losing my sister. My blood chilled every time I thought about how we almost lost her.

The same went for Frank, my incumbent demon. I'd had a blissful few days when he hadn't been living inside me, but he was also back, and amazingly, he was on his best behavior. He'd also had a shock at the thought of never being able to get his demon claws into my sister. For now, he seemed content to be in her presence. It wouldn't last; it never did.

Right now, everything was good. I had my sister back, her sleazy ex-fiancé was never getting out of prison, and Willow Tree Falls basked in a fabulous spell of sunshine.

Plus, everything was good at Cloven Hoof. The clientele was rarely a problem, the staff were happy, and my relationship with Rhett was great. My life had never felt so stable.

"Hey, look! It's Axel," Aurora said. "And isn't that one of his sisters?"

I nodded as Axel Shadowsoul strolled toward us.

He lifted a hand. "The Crypt sisters. Great to see you. You know my sister, Foxglove." He gestured to the darkly gorgeous woman next to him dressed in a fitted black cat suit and a leather jacket.

"Sure. Nice to see you again," I said.

She nodded. "I'm checking up on my brother and making sure he's not getting in too much trouble." Foxglove had a melodious tone to her voice. Just like Axel, she was a half-demon.

"Axel has his moments," I said. "Although, recently, he's been behaving himself."

"Keep quiet about that," he said. "I have a reputation to keep intact."

"It's Merrie's good influence," I said. Axel had been dating my bar manager, Merrie Noble, for months. It was the longest relationship he'd been in, and she was certainly doing him good. Although he still came with a dark edge, it was tinged with happiness. Being in a stable relationship suited Axel.

"Oh, yes. We're going to meet her later," Foxglove said. "I'm looking forward to meeting the woman who's finally tamed my brother."

He shrugged, and his cheeks flushed. "I'm not tamed."

"You shouldn't protest. Being tamed suits you," I said. "So long as you're treating Merrie right, I fully endorse the relationship."

Axel tugged at the neck of his shirt. "Everyone's making out like it's such a big deal. I have dated women before."

His pink cheeks and shifty glances showed he also thought it was a big deal. I grinned at him. "Introducing Merrie to one of your sisters must mean things are serious."

"Tempest, quit it," he muttered.

Aurora's smile faded. "It's nice to see someone's relationship is working."

I tucked my hand through her elbow, sensing a dip in her fragile happiness. "We need to get on. Nice to see you, Foxglove."

She nodded. "You too. I'll drop by the club one evening, and we can catch up. You can tell me all about Axel's sickeningly good behavior."

"It's a date. See you there." I walked away with Wiggles and Aurora.

She sighed and dragged her feet.

"Hey, things will get better. It's only been a couple of months since the whole Toby incident," I said.

"We're not saying his name, remember," she said. "Every time I think about him, I want to die of shame."

"I'm not denying that you have lousy taste in guys," I said. "But now that you know what you definitely don't want, you can focus on what you do."

"I don't want a boyfriend," Aurora said. "I'm sticking to work. And maybe a familiar, as long as we find the right one."

"Then focus on that. Let's go have some fur-filled fun and find you a true love who won't turn you into a stone dragon."

Trickery of the Witch is available in e-book and paperback.